PURRFECT BOOKSHOP

THE MYSTERIES OF MAX 73

NIC SAINT

PURRFECT BOOKSHOP

The Mysteries of Max 73

Copyright © 2023 by Nic Saint

All rights reserved. No part of this book may be reproduced in any form by any electronic or mechanical means including photocopying, recording, or information storage and retrieval without permission in writing from the author.

This is a work of fiction. Names, characters, places, brands, media, and incidents are either the product of the author's imagination or are used fictitiously. The author acknowledges the trademarked status and trademark owners of various products referenced in this work of fiction, which have been used without permission. The publication/use of these trademarks is not authorized, associated with, or sponsored by the trademark owners.

Edited by Chereese Graves

www.nicsaint.com

Give feedback on the book at: info@nicsaint.com

facebook.com/nicsaintauthor
@nicsaintauthor

First Edition

Printed in the U.S.A

PURRFECT BOOKSHOP

Read in Order to Die
A wedding between Chief of Police Alec Lip and Mayor Charlene Butterwick has been announced and will soon be taking place in the cozy little hamlet of Hampton Cove. Unfortunately the groom seems less than overjoyed at the prospect of plighting his troth, and even the bride has second thoughts.

And then of course there is the murder of Vernon Langridge, member of a local writers' group found dead in The Mighty Pen, a bookstore known for hosting frequent author signings and high-profile events. It doesn't take long for Detective Chase Kingsley to make an arrest when a valuable first-edition book is discovered in the possession of an ex-convict. But when a series of poison-pen letters starts arriving that point to the other members of the writers' group, revealing their dark secrets, it soon transpires that a lot of people had good reason to want Vernon dead.

Now it's up to Max, that formidable feline sleuth, to figure out what's going on. Will the blorange detective be able to save an innocent man from being convicted for a crime he didn't commit? Will the society wedding of the decade go off without a hitch? And will Harriet write her autobiography and become the star she knows in her heart she truly is? Find out in *Purrfect Bookshop*, the cleverly plotted new installment in the popular *Mysteries of Max* series.

CHAPTER 1

Odelia Kingsley had been looking forward to the day the new Chanel Birdsey book would finally be available. Blair Beacock only wrote one book a year about her plucky private detective, and since the bestselling author was also a resident of Hampton Cove, the honor of receiving one of the first copies hot off the press was usually reserved for her fellow Hampton Covians. Last year, Blair had selected their local library, where Odelia's mom Marge worked, as the place for her first reading from the new book. But this year, the honor had been bestowed on The Mighty Pen, that pleasant local bookstore that prided itself on being the heart of the mystery readers' universe, a haven of everything to do with crime fiction and detective stories.

Which is why Odelia now sat next to her mom in eager anticipation for Mrs. Beacock to put in an appearance. The small room at the back of the store was abuzz with excitement. Many of Blair's fans practically vibrating with joy at this unique opportunity to meet the woman responsible for so many hours of reading pleasure over the years. The occasion was even more significant than usual due to the fact that it was exactly thirty years ago when Chanel Birdsey had first burst upon the scene, taking up her rightful place next to other fictional heroines like Kay Scarpetta, Kinsey Millhone, and Stephanie Plum. It was a milestone that made this year's entry into the series extra special.

"I just wish she had given us advance copies," said Odelia's mom. "Having to wait this long is like agony, don't you think?"

The year before, when Blair had picked the library as the venue for her reading, her publisher had been so kind as to offer advance copies to all those organizing the event. After Mom had finished reading the book, she had passed it on to Odelia, who had then passed it on to her grandmother, and so on and so forth until every family member and then some had read the book. This year they hadn't been so lucky and had to wait along with the rest of Blair's million-reader-strong global audience for a first glimpse of the book on the day it actually went on sale.

"It's going to be another great one," Odelia knew. "It's bound to be, especially since it's the thirtieth book in the series. It's nothing short of a milestone, isn't it?"

"Oh, of course," said Mom, who popped a peppermint into her mouth and crunched down on it. She had a sort of ecstatic look in her eyes, as if she was on the verge of meeting a celebrity, which in a sense she was since Blair had long since transcended the kind of life mere mortals lived and had become one of the world's most beloved authors. The fact that she was a Hampton Cove girl born and bred only augmented her stature in the eyes of her loyal local fans.

"Who's that guy?" asked Odelia, referring to the little man with the bald pate and the funny-looking mustache rearranging things on the table where presumably Blair would soon take place.

"Vernon Langridge," said Mom. "He owns The Mighty

Pen. He's an author in his own right, though as far as I know, he hasn't published a book yet."

Mom knew all about the local literary scene. Having been in charge of the library for many years now, she had met pretty much every writer or wannabe writer living in Hampton Cove and was a veritable who's who of authordom. "And that guy sitting in the front row is Kenton Clarey," she said, referring to a tall and distinguished-looking older man. "He's a thriller writer. Pretty good, actually. Rumor has it that he's been tapped by his publishers to write one the next Patterson books."

Odelia's eyes scanned the audience and settled on a tall man with gray hair swept back in a ponytail. She knew from last year's reading that this was Blair's husband, Teddy, who always accompanied his wife on her book tours. Next to him sat their son Dylan and daughter Carey, also fixtures at these events.

"So nice of Blair's family to support her career," she said.

"Oh, absolutely. Blair has never made a secret of the fact that she wouldn't be where she is today if it wasn't for her family."

"I just wish they would finally turn the Chanel Birdsey books into a television series," said Odelia. "Now there's something I'd watch."

But her mom didn't respond. Her eyes were fixed on the door leading into the room, where Blair had now appeared. Even though the author was probably older than Mom herself, she looked absolutely smashing for her age. Her hair was a bright and vivid red, her pantsuit aquamarine blue and her face didn't show a single wrinkle. She wore the same engaging smile that she always seemed to have and carried herself with grace and poise as she strode into the room, to the applause of the entire audience and not a few whoops and hollers, which she took in stride with a laugh.

Moments later, she had taken her place on the small makeshift stage, put on her reading glasses, and gave her audience what they had all come for: a few brief words of introduction to the new book, a word of thanks to her loyal readership, but also to her family for their enduring support. Then she launched into the first chapter of the new book.

All around, Odelia saw happy faces and big smiles as their favorite author read from the latest installment in their favorite series. And when Blair recounted how Chanel Birdsey stumbled upon a dead body in typically whimsical fashion within the first three pages, laughter filled the room.

"Looks like it's another superhit!" Odelia whispered in her mother's ear.

Mom nodded. "Can't wait to get my hands on it and dig in!"

The reading didn't last all that long, and then it was time for a Q&A, first with Vernon Langridge on stage asking Blair some of the more obligatory questions about her inspiration for the new book and a few snippets about the plot and what they could expect. And then it was time to turn it over to the audience. Just in time, remembering she wasn't merely there as a fan but also as a reporter, Odelia got up and asked, "How would you explain Chanel's enduring appeal, Mrs. Beacock? Even after thirty books still going as strong as ever?"

Blair smiled. "To be honest? I have absolutely no idea. When I wrote the first Birdsey novel, of course I hoped Chanel would find a readership, but I had never expected her to be this popular, and that I would still be writing her after thirty years. I guess Chanel must have touched a chord, and people really like her. I have to say I like her, and not only because she has changed my life."

"Are you Chanel Birdsey, Mrs. Beacock?"

"Well, partly I am, of course. Though I don't think I'd have the courage to go chasing the bad guys the way Chanel does." She laughed. "If someone pointed a gun at me, I'd run for cover!" She turned serious. "I have to say I still work very hard at the books and don't take their success for granted. I still get up at five o'clock every morning, plant my butt in my chair, and work all the hours that God gives me to bring you the best book I possibly can—seven days a week, twelve months a year. And then in the evenings Teddy mixes me a drink and we spend time relaxing in our Jacuzzi." She spread her arms. "Hey, it's a tough job, but somebody's gotta do it!"

This got a big laugh since they all knew that success had bought the Beacocks a very nice beachfront property and all the perks that went with being a bestselling author. It was rumored that Blair had bought Dylan and Carey their own adjacent properties and that the Beacock clan now pretty much owned the entire street. Still, nobody begrudged Blair her success, exactly since she worked so hard to achieve it. Plus, according to Odelia's mom, she was considered something of a patron saint of the local writers' scene since she could always be relied upon to give her fellow scribes the benefit of her extensive knowledge or put in a good word for them with her agent or publisher. 'A rising tide lifts all boats' was one of her favorite quotes, something she liked to put into practice.

Once the Q&A was over, it was time to get those copies signed. A long line formed in front of Blair's table, and before long, both Odelia and her mom had finally laid their hands on the latest shiny copy of 'Get Ready!' the thirtieth installment in the Chanel Birdsey series. It had that new book smell that Odelia loved so much, and when they reached Blair's table, the author was so kind to tell the reporter that she and her family were all avid readers of the *Gazette*, and especially Odelia's articles.

"You should try your hand at a book," Blair said. "I think you'd be great at it."

"Oh, I don't know," said Odelia modestly. "There's a big difference between writing an article and a book, Mrs. Beacock."

"Blair, please." She scribbled, 'To Odelia—the real-life Chanel Birdsey,' which gave the reporter no end of pleasure. "Just think about it," she said as she closed the book. "And if you want advice, you know where I live, Odelia. My door is always open to aspiring talent like you."

"Thanks, Mrs. B... Blair," Odelia murmured, suddenly feeling bashful.

Blair signed Mom's book, 'To the best librarian on the East Coast,' and then it was time to move along, both women clutching their treasures to their chests and walking out in something of a daze after having briefly rubbed shoulders with greatness. Exiting the store, for a moment they were at a loss where to go next. But then Mom suggested they get a cup of coffee at a nearby coffee shop.

As they took a seat in a window booth, the conversation soon turned to a topic that was perhaps a little more mundane but no less important or close to their hearts: the upcoming wedding of Odelia's uncle—Mom's brother Alec—and Charlene Butterwick, mayor of Hampton Cove. For both the bride and groom it was their second marriage, and they wanted to keep things small: family and friends.

"I'm glad Alec is finally tying the knot," said Mom as she sipped from her cappuccino. "He's such a great guy, and Charlene is a real sweetheart."

"They're so lucky that they found each other," Odelia agreed.

After Uncle Alec had lost his first wife a couple of years ago, the police chief had been in a real funk for a while. He had dated sporadically, most recently a woman who created commercials for a well-known brand of liquor, but with the peripatetic life Tracy Sting led, their romance had soon come to an end. So it was like a bolt from the blue when Alec and Charlene had somehow hit it off, much to the relief of the man's family, who thought it couldn't have happened to a better person.

Odelia, who had ordered herbal tea since she felt she drank too much coffee as it was, thought about the upcoming wedding and felt a little guilty for not having written her speech yet. Being a professional writer by trade, the family had naturally turned to her to give the speech at the wedding ceremony, representing Uncle Alec's loved ones. She had started several times but felt it quite hard to hit the right notes. Then again, she still had time and hoped inspiration would strike at the eleventh hour. The last thing she wanted was to have to improvise, though, so very soon now she would have to sit down and hammer something out—something meaningful, heartfelt, and poignant.

No pressure!

CHAPTER 2

Vernon Langridge was happy with the way the reading had gone. He had sold a fair few copies of Blair's new book, but most importantly, the presence of the bestselling author in his store had put The Mighty Pen on the map as the place to be for the book-loving audience. In this day and age of online bookstores and the digital revolution, it wasn't always a given that readers would purchase their favorite reading material from their local bookshop, so the fact that they had shown up en masse for this reading gave him hope that next time they were thinking about getting some new reading material, they would patronize his store first.

The last stragglers were chatting with Blair, who was giving them as much of her time and attention as she could, and in the most gracious way possible, showing what a true professional she really was. Vernon had been on hand to pass her the books and make sure they didn't run out, and as the famous author put the final couple of signatures in the final books for the day, he approached her with a smile. "Pretty great stuff, Blair. Thanks so much."

"Don't mention it, Vernon, dear," said Blair as she massaged her painful right wrist. "Though it has to be said that one of those automatic pens is starting to sound really good right now."

"It's not the same and you know it, honey," said Blair's husband Teddy, who had been keeping track of the number of books sold just as much as Vernon had. Blair's son and daughter now also joined them. The Beacocks were a tight-knit family and functioned as a well-oiled unit running the Blair Beacock brand. Dylan was in charge of contacts with publishers and agents and went over everything from movie rights to merchandising and translations. Teddy took care of the logistics of the book tours the publisher organized around the time a new Chanel Birdsey came out, and also the financial aspects of the business, and Carey handled her mother's social media, website, and general marketing. All in all, the family functioned like a small business, though small was perhaps not the right term for the multimillion-dollar empire they had built around Blair's phenomenal talent.

"So I wanted to ask you," said Vernon now as he took a seat at the table. "We've got our monthly writers' group tonight, and I was wondering if you would like to join us. I'm sure we'd all be honored," he added for good measure.

"And I'm honored you would think of me," Blair said. "But I couldn't possibly come, Vernon. After a reading, all I want is to relax and soak in a hot tub for a couple of hours."

"And a massage," Teddy added. "How about a nice massage?"

"It's almost as if you read my mind," said Blair as she directed a grateful look at her husband.

"Another time, maybe," said Vernon. He had known it was a long shot but felt he had to ask anyway. To have a writer of Blair's stature at their meeting would have been a major coup, and the other members had talked about nothing else since he had revealed the news that Blair had selected The Mighty Pen as the venue for her book launch this year.

Blair signed the remainder of the books to be sold in the store, and then the Beacocks said their goodbyes, with Blair giving Vernon a quick hug before impressing upon him to, "Keep up the good work."

He watched as they walked out of the store and was about to close for the day when a motorcycle roared up and pulled to a stop in front of the store. Immediately, his general feeling of benevolence was replaced by a sudden rage—the same rage that always assailed him whenever Jerald Exton entered his life. As he watched, the good-for-nothing punk helped Vernon's daughter off his bike. She took off her helmet and shook out her honey-colored hair. It was like a dagger to her dad's heart when he watched the two exchange a brief hug before Jerald got back on his bike and roared off again.

Gwen stood staring after the kid for a moment before approaching the store. When she caught sight of her dad staring daggers at her from behind the shop window, she paused, then seemed to steel herself and crossed the few yards to the entrance of the apartment they shared, located above the bookshop.

With long strides, Vernon walked to the back of the store and yanked open the door that led to the corridor in the private area.

"Didn't I tell you not to see that boy again?" he demanded heatedly.

Gwen, who had just put her foot on the first step, shrugged. "He came to pick me up. What was I going to tell him?"

"You should have told him no!" said Vernon as he joined his daughter. "Just like your mother and I have arranged."

Gwen lifted her chin defiantly, and Vernon recognized

the gesture. She was so much like her mother it was uncanny. "You can't tell me what to do, Dad. If you haven't noticed, I'm not a child anymore."

"You're seventeen!"

"So?"

"So, you *are* still a child! And as your parents, your mother and I are telling you to stop seeing that boy!"

"That boy has a name, Dad. And by the way, Jerald's mom and dad have specifically told me how happy they are that Jerald has finally met a nice girl for a change. At least they're not being all hysterical about our relationship."

"Relationship!" he cried, and had to resist a sudden urge to grab his hair and pull. As it was, it wouldn't do him a lot of good, since he didn't have any hair anymore to speak of—and consequently to pull at. "You're a child and he's a man! I should go to the police and report him!"

She gave him a look of concern. "You wouldn't do that, would you, Daddy? You wouldn't want to stand in the way of true love?"

"This isn't true love," he said, stabbing an angry finger in her direction. "This is… this is… this is child molestation!"

She giggled. "God, you're such a drama queen. Even Mom is starting to come around to our way of thinking. She can see how happy Jerald is making me." She started mounting the stairs. "By the way, he wants to meet you and Mom. Jerald? With my eighteenth birthday coming up, he says it's time that we make things official, and meeting my parents is part of that."

At this point, steam was practically pouring from Vernon's ears. "Well, I don't *want* to meet him. And you can forget about things becoming serious between you and this… this… this *hooligan*! From now on, you're grounded, young lady."

Gwen giggled again. "Of course I am." And with these

words, she tripped up the stairs and into the living room upstairs.

Vernon stood glaring after his one and only daughter, slightly panting and wondering how he had failed as a father. And then he thought that maybe he should make good on his threat. After all, when a nineteen-year-old kid dates a seventeen-year-old girl, there were probably laws against that kind of thing, right? Shaking his head, he returned to the store, then walked into his office located at the back and took out his phone. Moments later, he was in communication with his ex-wife Diana.

"Now what?" Diana asked, sounding harried, as she often did when he called.

"Gwen just came home," he announced. "On the back of Jerald's motorbike. They're in a relationship now, Diana. A relationship! And she says Jerald wants to meet us. Make things 'official.'"

"Look, I really don't have time for this," said Diana, and Vernon could hear the clanging of pots and pans. Either she was washing the dishes or cooking. Since she and her new conquest had moved in together, she seemed to spend all of her time in the kitchen. Cesar had political aspirations, and felt that it was important that he entertained the kind of people who were potentially instrumental in furthering his ambitions. Hence the endless string of dinner parties he and Diana liked to throw.

"I told her she's grounded. But I got the impression she's not taking me seriously."

"I think we're just going to have to accept that she's at a stage right now where she insists on dating this young man," said Diana, quite infuriatingly relaxed about the whole business.

"But she's a child!"

"She's turning eighteen next month, Vernon. So not exactly a child, I would say."

"I was thinking about reporting Jerald to the police," he said. "After all, what he's doing is probably illegal, right? He could go to jail for this."

"Please don't go to the police," said Diana with a sigh. "It will only make matters worse. Best-case scenario, she will get bored with this kid in a couple of weeks, and he'll be out of her life."

"And the worst-case scenario?"

"We'll be stuck with Jerald Exton as a son-in-law for the rest of our lives. In which case, it's probably a bad idea to report him to the police. So just relax, Vernon. It's not the end of the world."

It sure felt like it. His little girl, a child still, being involved with this grown man! "You know he's got a criminal record, don't you?"

"He was picked up for dealing," said Diana, continuing to be infuriatingly unconcerned and frankly flippant about the whole Jerald thing. "That doesn't exactly make him a hardened criminal."

"It makes him a drug dealer. Aren't you concerned that our daughter is involved with a drug dealer?"

"He's not a drug dealer, Vernon! And now I have to go. I'm organizing a garden party. My guests will arrive any minute, and the caterer just announced he'll be half an hour late."

"But what about Gwen?"

"Gwen is fine. Everything is fine. Just chill already, will you? Stop making such a fuss."

And with these words, she simply hung up on him!

CHAPTER 3

Vernon was actually glad that the monthly writers' group meeting coincided with Blair's book launch. The excitement that Blair's customary energetic reading elicited would hopefully carry over into the meeting, since all of the writers' group members had also been present at the big event. He'd exchanged a few brief words with Kenton at the reading but hadn't had an opportunity to talk to the other two members of the group, Marina and Tarsha, though he had seen them taking their seats at the back of the room, as eager as the rest of them to enjoy 'The Blair Show,' as Tarsha liked to call it.

There was a certain measure of jealousy hidden behind these words, but then that was only to be expected, as Tarsha's own books didn't exactly garner the level of interest Blair's did.

"I thought Blair was amazing, as usual," Marina gushed. The young writer—the latest addition to their group—was a self-proclaimed fan of Blair and never stinted when heaping praise on their bestselling colleague. "She's just so amazingly witty, you know. Not only a truly gifted writer, but also great at these public events." She sighed deeply. "I just wish I had the gift of the gab. I only have to think about a reporter peppering me with questions, and already I start feeling flustered!"

"It's important to hone that part of our craft as well," Kenton professed. The thriller writer spoke in his usual slightly pompous style, but then they were used to that by now. Of the four of them, Kenton was easily the most successful at what he did, and he had the book sales to prove it. He was the only one with an actual book deal in place, and so far, six of his Marvin Amis thrillers had been published to great acclaim. Kenton now assumed the position he often took when about to pontificate on one of his favorite subjects. But this time he wouldn't get the satisfaction of waxing philosophically on the requirements put upon the successful scribe, because Marina interrupted the man's harangue.

"I think in this day and age, it's probably more important to hone your Zoom skills," she said. "Or your online marketing skills. At least that's how I manage to sell my books to my audience—to the tune of thousands of them."

A silence followed these words, then Tarsha practically squeaked, "Thousands? You mean..."

"Yes, I did!" Marina triumphantly exclaimed. "The Dark Princeling launch was a resounding success! The most I've ever sold of any single book!"

Cheers rang out, heartily and earnestly expressed by Tarsha, a little less exuberantly by Vernon, and tepidly by Kenton.

They were in the same back room of the bookstore where that afternoon Blair had held forth about her new book. Gwen was upstairs, hopefully doing her homework, and since night had fallen, all was quiet except for the excitement expressed by Marina about the recent windfall she had experienced.

Vernon had to say nobody deserved it more than Marina, who worked tirelessly at honing both her craft and her marketing skills to turn her books into a resounding success. As a writer of steamy romance, the young woman had recently moved away from trying to secure a book deal and had tried her hand at self-publishing instead, following in the footsteps of many other romance writers. And it had to be said that so far, the signs were very promising indeed. So much so she was actually thinking about ditching her day job as a waitress and becoming a full-time writer.

It was certainly something Tarsha couldn't hope to accomplish any time soon. Even though she was nearing retirement, the septuagenarian had yet to make a splash. Like Marina, she had opted to self-publish her cozy mystery books, but not successfully. If she sold a handful of copies it was a lot.

Her protagonist wasn't into high-speed chases or thwarting global conspiracies like Kenton's but was more the Miss Marple type of amateur sleuth, forever snooping around other people's private lives and mining them for possible clues and secrets from their checkered pasts.

"I'm being faced with a different problem right now," Tarsha admitted. She patted her tiny white curls and wrinkled up her face. "I'm supposed to be writing my next Katrina Ford book, but I'm having trouble thinking up a plot."

"But I thought you had already started writing?" said Marina.

"Well, I had, but then I decided that the plot wasn't good enough, so I've decided to scrap the whole thing and start over. Only now inspiration seems to be in short supply, for I have absolutely no idea what new mystery Katrina should tackle next." She shrugged her bony shoulders. "As far as I can tell, everything has been done already, and the last thing I want is to repeat myself. So I'm stuck!"

"Writer's block only exists in the mind," Kenton professed severely.

"Well, be that as it may," said Tarsha, "but I'm still dealing with it."

"Maybe we could organize one of our brainstorming sessions," Marina suggested. Even though both women wrote in vastly diverging genres, they had been known to brainstorm together and come up with some good ideas for their respective works in progress that way.

"Oh, could we?" said Tarsha gratefully. "I don't know why, but every time we sit down together, my brain simply seems to open up like a flower, and the most amazing things start emerging."

"Same here," said Marina. "Every time I get stuck, I only have to talk to a colleague, and before I know it, the old noggin is buzzing again like a busy little bee, spewing ideas like nobody's business."

"A real writer writes alone," Kenton said with an air of dismissiveness. He was a tall man with an almost-military bearing, which wasn't surprising since he had been a colonel in the army at one time. Now he devoted his life to expounding on the wild and crazy adventures of his indomitable and daredevil hero Marvin Amis. The fact that Kenton was ex-military was part of his books' appeal, as he promised a sense of verisimilitude to his fans, which he seemed to deliver to some extent. Though as far as his publisher was concerned—not nearly enough.

"So what's going on with your contract?" Vernon asked, for there had been rumblings of trouble.

Kenton shrugged. Clearly, the subject wasn't one he liked

to elaborate on. After having established himself as the pre-eminent example of the successful working writer, it was quite the comedown to be having problems with his publisher like this. "My agent is still in talks with them. The latest seems to be that they feel that readers are tired of Marvin Amis and want a different character. Younger and more dynamic. So either I ditch Marvin and launch a new series, or I'll have to try different avenues."

"A different publisher, you mean?" asked Tarsha, who wasn't unfamiliar with the fractious relationship that often existed between a writer and their publisher. At one time she had signed a book deal with a small publisher who had promptly gone belly up, locking up her rights for years.

"That's what my agent is trying to determine now—if there is any interest with other publishers in taking over Marvin Amis. If not, I guess I'll have to say goodbye to the man."

"You could always try self-publishing," Marina suggested. As an avid proponent of publishing her books herself, she couldn't understand that there were still writers out there who insisted on chasing a contract with a publisher.

"I very much don't want to go that route," said Kenton, repeating a point he'd made at several of their meetings. "I need an advance, Marina. Without my advance, what am I going to live on while I write the actual book?"

"You could get the rights to your old titles back," Marina suggested. "Publish those, generate sales, and live on that while you write the next book in your series."

But Kenton shook his head. "I don't know."

"I've already told you that I can teach you all you need to know."

At their last meeting, she had regaled them with the skills you had to develop in order to be a successful self-published author, and frankly speaking, it was daunting. It wasn't enough to simply write the book and then hand it over to the publisher. You had to write the book, format the book, get a cover designed or design one yourself, then publish the book, and most importantly, work out a detailed and what sounded like a very elaborate marketing plan to sell the book! Just thinking about it made Vernon feel very tired indeed. And since Kenton had a few years on him, he could imagine the man wasn't chomping at the bit to go down that particular road this late in his career.

"I'll wait for the agent to get back to me," said Kenton. "I'm sure my publisher will see reason and decide to give it another go. Things can turn on the drop of a hat in this business, and who knows, maybe something will happen to make Marvin hit the big time—just like Blair's Birdsey has done."

It certainly had been a minor miracle and a major accomplishment for Blair to have become so successful. The Birdsey books weren't bad, but they weren't all that great either, and frankly speaking, Vernon was hard-pressed to point out why they were so popular. But then, wasn't that often the case? As a famous Hollywood screenwriter had once pointed out: nobody knows why one thing bombs and another thing becomes a hit. So maybe Kenton was right. Maybe things would turn around for him, and his books would suddenly start selling like hotcakes, like apparently Marina's now did.

"So what about you, Vernon?" asked Tarsha, leaning forward and studying the bookseller with interest. "What news on the book front?"

"Not much news, I'm afraid," said Vernon. Last month he had been able to deliver quite a coup himself, not unlike Marina now, when he had been able to announce, with a distinct sense of pride, that he was in the process of setting up his very first actual book deal at a genuine big-five publisher. "These things take a lot longer than I anticipated."

"So no white smoke yet?" asked Kenton.

"Not yet," he said with a smile. "They're still squabbling over some minor details in the contract. Auxiliary rights and ancillary rights and foreign rights and all of that jazz. It all sounds very technical to me, but my agent assures me it's crucial to get everything nailed down tight before I sign."

"You're effectively signing over your rights," Marina pointed out. "In perpetuity, Vernon. So if I were you, I'd think twice before I sign that contract."

They'd had this exact conversation many times before, with Marina arguing in favor of Vernon publishing his book himself, just like she had. But since Vernon's dream had always been to become a big-name writer, just like Blair Beacock, he simply couldn't see himself turning down a lucrative offer from a publisher. Not after all the work he had put into securing such a major deal.

"Let's just see how it all plays out," he said. He realized that as long as the contract wasn't signed, everything was up in the air. But he was essentially a glass-half-full kind of person and hoped his agent would be able to pull off a hat-trick and push the deal through the way they both envisioned.

"Any other news we need to be aware of?" asked Tarsha, and so the conversation swiftly moved on to more general subjects, like the rising price of printing costs and paper and the shifts in reader taste, which was something Vernon was a privileged observer of since he was a bookseller himself.

Before long, he was regaling his audience with a remarkable change he had observed, away from the supernatural romance trend and back to the billionaire romance trend that had dominated the market in years past. Kenton wasn't all that interested and seemed to revert to a brooding stance, presumably still thinking about his book deal. But Marina, especially, hung on his every word since she was a great proponent of 'writing to market' and liked to closely follow the trends as they came and went.

It certainly pleased him to no end that he could be instrumental in the success of at least one of his fellow writers.

* * *

THE MEETING ENDED at ten o'clock as usual, and after everyone had left, Vernon retreated into his office to work on his accounts for a while. As a small business owner, it was important that he didn't get behind on getting all those numbers to add up. Otherwise, both his accountant and the tax man wouldn't be happy! And he had just been poring over some bills that he couldn't make head nor tail of when he heard a noise coming from the bookstore. Frowning, he wondered if it could possibly be Gwen, sneaking out to meet her no-good boyfriend again.

"Gwen? Is that you?" he called out. When no response came, he got up from behind his desk and figured he might have forgotten to lock up again after the writing group contingent left. Wandering into his store, it took a moment for his eyes to adjust to the darkness, but then he saw it: a shadow stood next to the display case where he kept some of his most prized possessions, including a first edition of Mark Twain's *The Adventures of Huckleberry Finn* and a few books from less famous authors that were nevertheless worth a pretty penny.

He was about to retreat back into the safety of his office when the dark figure sprang forward and lunged at him. A shot rang out in the darkness, and Vernon clutched at his chest where a sudden pain had bloomed. His legs refused to function, and moments later, he was lying helpless on the floor.

The last thing he saw was that same dark figure hovering over him. Then a second shot, and Vernon Langridge knew no more.

CHAPTER 4

It had been a long day, and I was fully ready to enjoy a long night and an even longer nap. Somehow, I had missed out on an outing that Odelia and her mother had engaged in when they decided to pay a visit to a bookshop, of all places, to listen to a writer talking about her latest book. Even though Odelia had suggested we tag along, we had procrastinated to such an extent that by the time the event had finally taken place, Dooley and I were on the other side of town, investigating an urgent clue—the disappearance of a perfectly fine piece of cheese from our fridge overnight. Okay, so I guess I should probably make a full confession now: I had eaten that piece of cheese. But since I know that Odelia doesn't think cheese is all that great as a source of nourishment for her cats, I had refrained from admitting to this capital offense. As a consequence, Odelia had insisted we find out who had taken the cheese and where they had taken it, which is why Dooley and I had conveniently been in a situation where we could forgo having to listen to yet another author drone on and on about their perfectly boring book.

When one of your humans is a librarian, you can probably imagine that books and writers are quite prevalent and present in our daily lives, even though I still have to discover their purpose in the grand scheme of things. I mean, don't get me wrong, it's probably a good thing that writers exist, but in this day and age, what's the point? Where is their usefulness? We have television now, after all, and TikTok and YouTube. So who is interested in books, except of course librarians like Marge or writers themselves, who are still hoping to sell those books? Little do they know that the reading audience is dwindling year by year, and pretty soon, nobody will be reading anymore. And that's a good thing, too. Bad for one's eyesight, I'd say. And also bad for one's imagination if everything you put into your head has been conjured up by another person. Better to make up your own stories, am I right?

Our search for the missing piece of cheese led us to our local park, where we had spent a pleasant afternoon lounging in the shade of a tall tree and generally having a wonderful book-free time. When we figured the danger of being forced to attend the book thingy had passed, we returned home.

At the dinner table, Odelia regaled her husband with anecdotes from the reading and even read him snippets from the latest book of a woman answering to the unlikely name of Blair Beacock. It was all perfectly foul, I have to say. As we waited in vain for a piece of pork to fall from the table and land in front of us, or a slice of sausage, I finally decided to give up. Clearly, Odelia had forgotten all about the responsibility she shared with the rest of her family to take care of the well-being of her feline household—for better or for worse, for richer or for poorer, in sickness and in health, to love and to cherish, till death us do part. She was too entranced by her latest book-reading experience.

Dooley and I left the house through the pet flap and decided to head next door to see if we had better luck over there. Oftentimes, the whole family will share dinner together, and those are more often than not the best of times. Especially Uncle Alec doesn't stint on sharing the culinary wealth located on his plate with the rest of us and slips us some tasty morsels under the table, even though his sister Marge often tells him he shouldn't. The most stingy ones were actually Odelia, her mother, and grandmother. They have a firm policy in place that cats shouldn't be beggars, and they hate it when we circle the table, rub against their legs, or generally make a spectacle of ourselves.

They seem to think that it shows them in an unfavorable light, as if they're not feeding us well enough, and on more than one occasion they have told me to behave and to stop scrounging. But can I help it that our humans are such excellent cooks? And that the scent of their cooking is enough to cause our tummies to rumble with increased appetite for all the goodies they're cooking up?

The best persons to approach were the menfolk: Uncle Alec, Chase, and Tex. They are the ones who take pity on us and then feed us from their hands, when the womenfolk aren't watching, of course.

"So what happened to that cheese, Max?" asked Dooley as we traipsed across the backyard in the direction of Odelia's neighbors, who just happen to be her mom and dad and grandmother.

"I ate that cheese, Dooley," I pointed out. "I told you, remember?"

He frowned. "But... if you ate that cheese, then why did we have to go look for it in the park?"

"Because I can't admit to Odelia that I was the one who stole her cheese. She'd only get mad, and the last thing you want is for your humans to get mad at you." They might decide to put you on a diet, as Odelia has been known to do on more than one occasion, and always without reason.

Dooley laughed. "Odelia won't get mad at you for eating that cheese, Max. Odelia loves you! She would never get mad at you for exercising your right as a resident feline to eat a piece of cheese."

"It wasn't just 'a' piece of cheese," I said. "It was 'the' piece of cheese. The cheese that Odelia had earmarked for her own." Not all that long ago, a new cheese shop had opened its doors in town. It boasted its own cheese dairy where it created delicious cheeses entirely from its own cows. I'd passed by the store on more than one occasion, and I had never seen a single cow present in the store, so I had a hunch this was simply hearsay. But it was true that the cheese they produced was delicious beyond compare. In fact, it wasn't too much to say that it was probably the best cheese I had ever tasted—bar none. Unfortunately, it was also the most expensive cheese Odelia had ever bought—perhaps on account of the fact they had to provide those precious cows of theirs with room and board. So when Odelia arrived home a couple of days ago with the cheese she had bought, she had told her husband that this was her cheese and the precious piece was out of bounds for anyone. She had also told her grandmother, her mom, and her dad, and even had gone to the trouble of telling me! As if I would ever touch a piece of property that did not strictly belong to me.

And I would have kept my promise if she hadn't made one big mistake: last night she had decided to cut herself a piece of her precious cheese, and in the process of doing so, had dropped a sliver to the floor. Unbeknownst to her, I had licked up that sliver, and it had tasted so moreish that I had been unable to think of anything else from that moment onward. I guess I had fallen victim to a state that doctors like to describe as the addictive state. So last night, when the house was quiet and all were fast asleep in their beds, instead of venturing out to join my friends at cat choir, I had managed to pry open the fridge, locate the cheese, and take a nibble. One nibble led to a second, and when all was said and done, all that was left was the wrapping paper, which I had carefully replaced in the fridge.

That morning, when Odelia opened the fridge in search of her precious and outrageously expensive delicacy, she had kicked up quite a fuss when all she found was the paper, devoid of its contents. In turn, she had accused her husband, her grandmother, her mom, and dad of absconding with her beloved cheese, and when they all claimed not to have touched the stuff, she had finally turned to me and had beseeched me to put my best paw forward and find her cheese for her!

I was on the verge of pointing to my tummy, where the cheese had found a second home away from home, but seeing the look on her face, I decided against it. Like I told Dooley, it's always best not to antagonize one's human—a simple matter of common sense and instinct of survival.

"Please don't tell Odelia," I now beseeched my friend.

"Oh, of course," said Dooley vaguely, as he didn't meet my eyes for some reason.

"You've already told her, haven't you!" I cried, much dismayed.

"Oh, no, of course not," said Dooley. "But I have told Harriet, and she has told Brutus, and they probably have told about a dozen other cats, and so…" He swallowed uneasily.

I hung my head. It's all well and good that your humans can understand you, but it's not so good when you have a secret to hide. "They'll probably tell Odelia," I said resignedly.

"Unless you tell all of them not to tell her," Dooley said hopefully. But even he seemed to realize how unfeasible this suggestion was. Tell a cat not to pass on a secret, and the first thing they'll do is pass on the secret! That's what cats are like, after all, and why they're such great spies.

"She's going to be so mad," I said, as I placed my head on my paws. "So very mad."

Dooley gave this some thought, then finally seemed to have hit upon the solution. "You'll just have to get her another piece of cheese," he said. "Bigger and better than the cheese you ate." He then gave me a look of slight reproach. "By the way, why didn't you share that cheese with me, Max? If it was as good as you say it was, why didn't I get a piece? I'm your best friend, after all."

I gave him a shamefaced look. "I wanted to, I really did, but I simply couldn't stop myself from eating all of it, you know."

"That good, huh?"

"That good," I confirmed with a sigh.

My friend's eyes suddenly went wide. "Max! Oh no!"

I looked up in alarm. "What's wrong?"

"You're a cheeseaholic!"

CHAPTER 5

While Max and Dooley were dealing with the large blorange cat's fall from grace and into a pernicious cheese addiction, Harriet and Brutus had decided to go on an adventure of their own. Since Gran and Scarlett had returned the Neighborhood Watch Committee to its former glory, they had invited both cats to 'ride with them' and be their eyes and ears as they stopped at nothing to rid their fair town of Hampton Cove of the criminal element. And so it was that both cats now sat in the backseat of Gran's little red Peugeot while the two old ladies patrolled the streets in search of any representatives of the criminal classes creating havoc and generally making a nuisance of themselves.

"We should have asked Max and Dooley to tag along," Brutus now told his lady love. "They would have known where to find this so-called Pancake Burglar."

"Nonsense," said Harriet. The white Persian wasn't all too keen on the notion that Max was this master detective and the only one who could be instrumental in catching any crook. "Whatever Max can do, we can do better, sparky star."

"I'm not so sure," said Brutus. After all, they had been patrolling these streets for what felt like hours now, and still no sign of the miscreant who kept creeping into people's private homes, ridding them of their valuables, and in the process making himself a couple of pancakes and consuming them on the scene. The media called him the Pancake Burglar on account of this quirk, and since the police seemed incapable of stopping the man's reign of terror—and his penchant for thin, flat cakes of batter, fried up to a golden brown and tasty as can be—the watch had taken it upon itself to nab the reprobate.

"He must be around here somewhere," said Scarlett, not for the first time since they had set out on their patrol. "According to your son, his last couple of burglaries were all in this same neighborhood, so chances are he's from around here."

"He could be a local," Gran agreed.

"Or it could simply be a person who really loves pancakes but for some reason isn't allowed them at home."

But Gran shook her white, curly head. "It's not that. It's just a gimmick he chose to gain notoriety. Like the Boston Strangler or Jack the Ripper."

Scarlett shivered. "I hope he won't hurt anyone. Can you imagine he's in the middle of whipping up his next batch and suddenly he's interrupted?"

"What is he going to do? Throw a pancake at the person? No, I think we're simply dealing with a person who craves the attention his illegal activities bring, not a violent criminal by any means."

"Yeah, I guess a person who loves pancakes can't be evil through and through," Scarlett agreed. "After all, everybody loves a good pancake."

Gran and Scarlett hadn't actually admitted it, but the fact that they might be about to lay their hands on some very fine pancakes was a major part of their decision to go after this Pancake Burglar. To Brutus, pancakes held a lot less appeal. Frankly, he couldn't quite see why they were all that popular. They didn't even taste all that nice. But then he was a loyal kitty, and so when Gran had asked them to tag along on this nocturnal vigil, even though he wasn't exactly excited at the prospect, he couldn't very well say no, now could he?

"Let's hope he makes a meat pancake next," Harriet suggested.

"Is that even a thing?" asked Brutus.

"Oh, you can make any type of pancake," said Harriet, who seemed to know a lot about the stuff. "You can put pieces of chicken in your batter, or bacon, or slices of sausage. It's a lot more hearty that way and might even be digestible for us, sugar britches."

Somehow Brutus didn't think any pancake of any description would ever appeal to him the way they seemed to appeal to the two older ladies sitting in the car with them. But then what did he know? He wasn't exactly a gourmet. Not like Harriet was. She liked her kibble just so and actually preferred freshly cooked food to the store brands most cat owners like to get for their feline brood. Only last week she had demanded and received a piece of actual chateaubriand and had tucked in with visible and audible relish. When Brutus had sampled a bite, he had to admit it was pretty tasty indeed, but then Marge had immediately made it clear that her household budget didn't stretch to adding fresh meats to their menu on a daily basis. From time to time it was a nice addition, but they shouldn't expect this to become a regular thing.

The street the car was parked on didn't look all that appealing from a criminal point of view. Then again, he wasn't a criminal himself. And according to Gran, this was the street where the Pancake Burglar was most likely to strike next. It boasted a lot of very nice family homes. Not exactly the type your local billionaire or even millionaire would favor, but then their homes were more like Fort Knox and thus inaccessible to a common burglar who didn't want to be chased by Rottweilers, caught on HD-CCTV, and tackled by burly security types the moment he broke through the perimeter fence.

"Are you looking forward to the wedding?" asked Scarlett now, returning to a favorite topic of hers.

"Absolutely," said Gran. "It isn't every day that your kid gets married, even though in Alec's case it's the second time, of course."

"I liked Ginny," said Scarlett. "Though I have to say I think Charlene is a better fit for Alec. Ginny was a sweetheart, but she was a little too sweet, if you know what I mean. Charlene will really take Alec in hand. And if there's anything a man needs, it's a wife who takes him in hand, you know."

"I know what you mean," said Gran. "And it's true that Alec really let himself go these last couple of years. With the eating and the smoking and the drinking."

Scarlett looked shocked. "Alec drinks? Well, I never."

"Not a lot, but after Ginny died, he was in such a funk that it was sad to see him like that. Good thing he had us to put him back on the right track, and now with Charlene in his life, he's really on the right path again." She made a face. "Though I still think he should have done a better job at losing those extra pounds for the wedding. Charlene looks so beautiful, and Alec should have followed her example and put in an effort, but of course he wouldn't listen, and now it's too late."

Ever since the wedding had been announced, Gran had been on her son's case about slimming down so he would at least fit into the suit he'd worn at his first wedding. But since that was thirty years ago and probably twice as many pounds, that was never going to happen.

"I think he looks fine," said Scarlett. "A chief of police needs a little heft. Can you imagine Alec as a skinny little runt trying to put the fear of God into a suspect? It just wouldn't work, Vesta."

"At least he'd be able to chase after a suspect without having a heart attack," said Gran stubbornly. "Though you're probably right that he was never going to fit into his wedding suit again. That was too much to hope for." She looked thoroughly unhappy though, for not only had she hoped that her son would slim down to his former weight, but also that he would do something about his general appearance, and most notably about his hair. "He should have gone to the clinic when I suggested," she continued. "Then he would have gone into his second marriage with a full head of hair again."

"It's painful, though, both on the skull and the wallet," said Scarlett, who was something of an expert in beauty treatments of every kind. "They have to make tiny incisions in your scalp, then plant the grafts they harvested from another part of your scalp in those holes one by one, and it remains to be seen if the treatment will take, so you might have to go through this process more than once."

"But the result is worth it, wouldn't you say? Imagine Alec standing at the altar with a full head of wavy dark hair. Now wouldn't that be something?"

"I'm sure Charlene likes him just the way he is."

"She would like him a whole lot more with hair." She sighed. "I'm putting it all in my autobiography, you know. Whatever Alec says, I'm pulling no punches this time."

Scarlett smiled. "I can't wait to read all about it. You have led such an interesting life, Vesta. I'm sure your autobiography will be a major bestseller."

"Of course it will be," said Gran, who never stinted on self-esteem.

Brutus turned to his partner. "Is Gran writing her autobiography?"

"This is the first I'm hearing of it," said Harriet. "Though I have to say it's a wonderful idea."

They both turned to address their human. "What's all this about an autobiography, Gran?" asked Brutus.

Gran smiled. "Oh, you heard that, did you? Well, I found this site where all you have to do is answer a couple of questions about yourself, and then the computer automatically turns it into an autobiography. Isn't that the most amazing thing? And then after you're all done, it even sends it to the printer and gets the copies delivered to your doorstep!"

"It's amazing the things they can do with technology nowadays," said Scarlett.

"It absolutely is," said Gran. "I'm hoping to get it done before the wedding. My autobiography will be the best present Alec will receive." She grinned. "He'll be so pleased to read all about his beloved mother's exploits!"

Somehow, Brutus wasn't all that convinced that an autobiography presented the perfect wedding gift, but then what did he know? He was just a cat, and even though Harriet and he had been dating for a while now, they had no plans to get married any time soon. As far as he could tell, that wasn't the done thing for cats. And maybe a good thing, too. When he saw how much went into organizing even a simple wedding like Alec and Charlene's, he would hate to be involved in one himself. Very stressful, he would think.

"Oh, look," said Scarlett suddenly as she pointed to a man dressed in a hoodie sneaking along the deserted street. It was nearing one o'clock, and since this guy wasn't walking a dog and looking kind of furtively at the houses he passed, he immediately stood out like a sore thumb with the four members of the neighborhood watch, two humans, and two felines.

"That just might be our guy," said Gran. "Though I don't see any paraphernalia for making pancakes on his person."

"He probably doesn't bring them along but instead uses the stuff people have in their kitchens," said Scarlett.

"Let's follow him and find out," Gran suggested.

And so all of them got out of the car and snuck along the sidewalk, keeping tabs on their mystery quarry. After a moment, the man halted in front of a house, looked left and right, then resolutely set foot for the place, fiddling with the front door for a few moments, and then he was in.

"Maybe he lives there?" Scarlett suggested.

"It's possible," Gran agreed. "But then why is he behaving so suspiciously?"

It was true that he had behaved quite suspiciously indeed, by sneaking along the street like that. Most people didn't go for a walk at one o'clock at night unless it was to walk their dogs. Honest citizens were in bed at this time of night, fast asleep. So what was this man doing up and about at this hour?

"Let's go around the back and see what he is up to," Gran suggested.

And so they took the small paved path that led between this house and the adjacent one and soon found themselves in the backyard of the house under consideration. Ducking down so they wouldn't be seen, they approached the window to take a look inside and see what the man was up to in there. As luck would have it, the window they had selected was the kitchen window, and as they slowly raised their heads to take a peek inside, much to their rising excitement, they saw that the man was taking ingredients out of the fridge and the kitchen cupboards.

"Milk, flour, sugar, butter, eggs, vanilla powder," Gran

said as she subjected the man's movements to her eagle-eyed scrutiny. She smiled. "He's making pancakes!"

"You think?" said Scarlett, sounding a little breathless all of a sudden. For if what Gran was saying was true, this man was their man: the notorious Pancake Burglar!

As they watched on, they saw that the man was mixing the ingredients in a big bowl, while a pan was on the stove. "I think Gran is right," said Harriet. "I think he's about to make pancakes!"

"He must be hungry," Brutus said. He could sympathize, for he was pretty hungry himself. It's one thing to be instrumental in the safety and security of their local community, but it wouldn't have been out of place for Gran to suggest bringing along a snack of some kind. After all, how could they be expected to be vigilant on an empty stomach? Cops had donuts, Gran and Scarlett had those little sesame tahini cookies that Scarlett had baked for the occasion, but what did they have? Nothing!

"Okay, I think it's time to call the cops," Scarlett said as she took out her phone.

"No way!" said Gran. "First we catch him, *then* we call the cops."

"You mean..."

"We're going in," said Gran determinedly.

Scarlett swallowed a lump of uneasiness. "But..."

"We're going in!" Gran insisted. "We're the watch, honey. If we don't do it, who will?"

"Well, the police, obviously," Scarlett suggested.

But Gran wouldn't hear of it, and it became clear that she craved the credit of having nabbed the infamous Pancake Burglar all on her own—or with the assistance of her friend and two cats.

"Maybe it's the homeowner," Scarlett said, suffering from a clear case of cold feet. "Maybe he likes to make pancakes in the middle of the night. Stranger things have happened."

"And I think it's the burglar. Though you're probably right. We should wait until he actually starts stealing stuff."

And so they waited. It didn't take long. After the guy had mixed all the ingredients, he placed the batter on the kitchen table, draped a towel over it, and let it rest, as Gran explained was the done thing. Half an hour, she reckoned, before the batter was ready. Then he took a large bag from the recesses of his costume and started going around the place, shoving sundry items of value into the bag. When he was done, he returned to the kitchen, checked on the batter, and turned on the stove.

The thieving was done, now it was time for his reward!

They watched as the fellow ladled the batter into the pan and allowed the pancake to turn a nice golden brown. He sure knew what he was doing.

"When are we going to nab him?" Scarlett whispered.

"Once he's got a couple of pancakes done," Gran whispered back.

Brutus could see where she was coming from. Why go in before those pancakes were good and ready? Preferably a nice tall stack of the stuff.

She waited until he'd done about a dozen pancakes, then quickly rose from her awkward position and gave the window a vigorous rap with her knuckles, pressing her face against the pane in a forbidding fashion. The effect was immediate. Confronted with the vision of a little old lady staring back at him from the other side of the window, and looking none too pleased, the thief seemed startled to a great degree. So he dropped what he was doing and made a run for it.

"Scarlett! Front door!" Gran yelled.

They probably should have thought this through a little

more, because by the time Scarlett reached the front door, along with Harriet and Brutus, the bird had flown the coop. They could see him running off at a high rate of speed. And since Brutus hadn't eaten, and neither had Harriet, they didn't really feel like going in pursuit of the man.

At least they'd taken a good look at his face.

And at least the pancakes were still there.

When they entered the house and set paw in the kitchen, they saw that Gran was already seated at the kitchen table, tucking in for dear life. "They're pretty darn good!" she announced happily.

So Scarlett also took a seat, and they both enjoyed the fruits of their vigilance, with Brutus and Harriet watching with a certain sense of dismay.

"I'm hungry," Harriet announced.

"Me too," Brutus said miserably.

Finally, Gran took pity on them and started rooting around in the fridge, looking for something to eat. She found some cold chicken and placed it on a plate. Brutus and Harriet happily dug in. Cold chicken had never tasted this good! And they would have enjoyed more of it if not for the sudden blue flashing lights announcing that the constabulary had arrived.

"Did you call the cops?" asked Gran.

"No, I didn't," said Scarlett.

Before long, the officers of the law walked in and arrested both Scarlett and Gran on the spot, much against their protestations. Apparently, one of the neighbors had heard or seen something untoward and had called it in. And even though Gran and Scarlett tried to convince the long arm of the law that they were the good guys and that they had actually prevented the house from being burgled, they were still hauled off to the pokey.

When you're discovered by a pair of officers of the law

sitting in a kitchen that's not your own, eating pancakes made from ingredients that are not yours, with a big bag full of stolen loot at your feet, it's probably not a long stretch to assume that you are actually the culprit under consideration.

The worst part was that the cops took that delicious cold chicken and put it back in the fridge.

All in all, perhaps not the most successful entry in the annals of the neighborhood watch.

But what an exciting chapter for Gran's autobiography!

CHAPTER 6

When I woke up the next morning, lounging at the foot of the bed as usual, the first thought that entered my head was the matter of the Cheese Transgression. I knew I'd have to face the music at some point, and so I decided then and there to come clean right away, rather than having to go through the agony of waiting for Odelia to hear it from some third party, possibly embellished to a large degree.

Grace, who sleeps in her own cot next to the big bed of her parents, was already up and about and playing with the curtain, pulling it this way and that. The sun, always a stealthy bandit eager for any opportunity to throw its rays around, momentarily blinded me with its radiance and reminded me of a large ball of cheese.

So I snuck up to Odelia and started kneading her forearm in preparation for my confession, and she had just opened her eyes and I had opened my mouth to speak when Chase's phone blared out its annoying tune—a song from a well-known rap artist, apparently—and he groaned in irritation as he picked up the device from the nightstand. "Kingsley," he barked into the phone. He listened for a moment then said, "I'll be there in ten."

"Where are you going to be in ten, babe?" asked Odelia as she stretched her arms and yawned.

"There's been a murder," said Chase. "Vernon Langridge?"

"Vernon!" said Odelia, immediately wide awake. "But I saw him only yesterday. He hosted Blair Beacock's book launch at The Mighty Pen."

"And now he's dead," said Chase, displaying a stunning lack of sensitivity. Then again, humans are often that way when you wake them up from a deep sleep in the early hours of the morning. It annoys them and then they take it out on their fellow man. "I'm sorry," he said as he saw how shaken Odelia really was. "Did you know him well?"

"I wouldn't say that. I interviewed him last year when he celebrated the fifteenth anniversary of The Mighty Pen. He seemed like a nice guy. A writer in his own right, who was about to sign a contract to publish a book. After the reading yesterday, we stood chatting with him for a while, me and Mom, and he told us all about it. Said it was the proudest moment of his life to be able to sell his own book in his own store."

"I can imagine," said Chase dryly. Like myself, the cop isn't all that much into literature. Unlike Odelia, who simply loves to read, and also Odelia's mom.

"Poor man," said Dooley. "Now he will never be able to sell his own book in his own store."

"No, I guess that must sting," I said for lack of anything else to say. I could have told him that being murdered is probably a lot worse than not seeing one's own book in print, but then I wasn't in a terribly good mood myself, owing to the Cheese Transgression. Something told me that now wasn't a good time to come clean, so I wisely kept my tongue.

Odelia and Chase rose from their respective sides of the bed, with Odelia picking an eager Grace from her cot, and moments later, mother and daughter were downstairs in the kitchen making preparations for breakfast while Chase jumped into the shower.

"Do you think he was murdered because of his book, Max?" asked Dooley as we traipsed down the stairs.

"Mh?" I said, still thinking about the cheese thing.

"The guy who was murdered. Maybe someone didn't like the book he had written and decided it shouldn't be published. It's often that way, you know. Writers like to reveal secrets in their books, but they're not always so good at asking permission to reveal those secrets."

"I have absolutely no idea, Dooley," I said, perhaps a little more forceful than I should have, owing to my peculiar state of mind.

"Oh," said Dooley, then eyed me with distinct interest. "You're not still brooding about that cheese, are you?"

"As a matter of fact, I am," I admitted. "When Odelia finds out I ate her favorite and quite expensive piece of cheese, she will be very upset, and I hate it when she's angry with me, so I'm worried. Can you blame me?"

"You shouldn't be worried, Max. Odelia loves you very much. And she probably loves you more than she loves cheese."

"I wouldn't be too sure about that," I murmured.

Humans are strange and fickle creatures, and sometimes they will love a material object far more than an actual living, breathing being—whether human or feline.

"I think what we need to address right now," said Dooley, as we hopped up onto the couch and assumed our respective positions, "is not whether Odelia will be cross with you or not. It's your addiction, Max. We need to fight it. Maybe even put you in one of those programs?"

"What programs?" I asked, eyeing Odelia closely and wondering if she knew.

"Well, one of those programs for addicts, of course. Put you up in one of those addiction clinics. That way, you might be able to kick the habit, Max."

"I'm not actually addicted to cheese, buddy," I said. "I like it, that's true, even though I probably shouldn't because cheese isn't all that good for me, but I can leave it if I wanted to."

"Can you, though?" he asked seriously. "Can you really?"

"Of course. I haven't eaten cheese since... yesterday. And I'm fine."

"But the cravings, Max. Don't you experience any cravings?"

"As a matter of fact, I don't." Though it was true that I had been thinking about cheese almost constantly, it wasn't any cravings for the stuff I had been struggling with but more the consequences of the midnight binge I had been dreading, which was an entirely different thing altogether.

"Or we could try hypnosis," said Dooley.

I turned to him with just a touch of irritation. "What?"

"Hypnosis," he said, nodding. "It's rumored to have a great effect on addicts."

"But I'm not an addict!"

"Only an addict would say that," said my friend with perfectly imperfect logic.

Suddenly, the sliding glass door in the living room opened, and Marge strode in. She looked a little anxious, I thought. "Odelia, have you heard?"

"I have," Odelia assured her mother. "Such a terrible thing, isn't it?"

"I know! We have to go over there right now and get her out."

"Get who out?"

"Why, your grandmother, of course! And Scarlett."

Odelia frowned. "Why, what's happened?"

"They've been arrested! The police think they're the Pancake Burglars!"

"But they're not," Odelia said.

"I know that, and you know that, but apparently the police don't."

"But isn't Uncle Alec..."

"He's not in his office right now. He's home, getting ready to go fit his suit. With me, I might add!" She waved her hands. "Don't worry, he's already been told, and he's trying to get them sprung from prison. But the evidence is staggering, honey. They were caught, red-handed, a big bag full of loot at their feet, eating pancakes in the victim's kitchen!"

"Oh, dear."

"I know."

Both women thought for a moment how to proceed, but then Chase joined them, and the conversation naturally turned to the death of Vernon Langridge, which somehow seemed a lot more important than the fact that Gran and Scarlett had been arrested and thrown in jail.

Harriet and Brutus now strode in through the pet flap. They looked a little dejected, I thought.

"Gran and Scarlett were arrested last night," Brutus announced without preamble.

"You were there?" I asked.

Brutus nodded. "We were trying to catch the Pancake Burglar, but unfortunately, he got away. And since Gran and Scarlett didn't want to let those nice pancakes go to waste, they decided to eat them. Which they probably shouldn't have done. So when the police arrived, they were promptly arrested."

"Uncle Alec should have gotten them out by now," said Harriet. "And I don't understand why he won't."

Marge knew the answer to that one. "Because it would look bad for my brother if every time his mom got into trouble he was there to bail her out. Pretty soon people would accuse him of favoritism, or nepotism, or something. Anyway, it wouldn't be long before Alec would be out of a job, and we can't have that."

"It wouldn't do for the groom to be jobless on the eve of his wedding," Harriet agreed.

"So you're sure that Gran and Scarlett had nothing to do with this burglary business?" asked Odelia.

"Of course!" said Harriet. "We tried to grab him, but he was too quick. We got a good look at his face, though." She closed her eyes. "Young, good-looking, sort of thin face, skinny, and a good runner. And he makes great pancakes, at least if Gran and Scarlett are to be believed."

"And the police," said Marge. "Apparently, after they arrested my mother and Scarlett, they decided to finish those pancakes themselves."

"They destroyed evidence?" asked Odelia, sounding aghast.

"They figured they didn't need it anymore, since they had their culprits."

"God. Let's go and spring them from prison now—although..." She directed a glance at Chase, who had entered the kitchen and was helping himself to a cup of coffee. "Could you do the honors, Mom? I probably should join Chase on this murder business."

"Of course," Marge assured her. "I'll go down to the police station and try to convince them that your grandmother and Scarlett had nothing to do with this burglary. Though they did eat the pancakes, so that's probably incriminating behavior all in itself."

"Yum, pancakes," said Grace, who was sitting at the kitchen counter, eagerly waiting to be fed. "I love pancakes, don't you?"

"Not really," Brutus said.

"Me neither," Harriet said.

"Same here," I grunted.

"Max is addicted to cheese," Dooley announced. "In fact, he loves cheese so much he can think of nothing else. Which isn't good, since he has to get that big brain of his ready for yet another murder case."

"Dooley," I hissed, "enough with the cheese references!"

"But it's a problem, Max," said my 'friend.' "A problem that should be addressed."

"What's all this about cheese?" asked Odelia.

"Nothing," I hastened to say.

"Max says that cheese you got was really good," said Harriet. "I would have loved to have a taste, but he ate it all by himself, leaving not a single crumb for the rest of us."

Odelia's jaw dropped a little. "You ate my cheese?"

I hung my head in abject shame. "I did," I said quietly.

"Max! How could you!"

"I couldn't help it," I murmured.

"Did Max eat your cheese?" asked Marge.

"He did!" Odelia had planted her hands on her hips, and I knew what that meant. She was upset. Very upset.

"He's going to get you another piece of cheese," said Dooley, continuing to be very unhelpfully helpful. "And he's going to enter an addiction clinic to get rid of his cheeseaholism."

Odelia ignored him. "Eating that much cheese is bad for you, Max," she said, and actually looked concerned when she said it. She sat down next to me and put her hand on my tummy. "How is your stomach?"

"Fine," I said. "A little heaviness and some bloat, but otherwise I'm all right."

"Any diarrhea?"

"No diarrhea."

"Hmm. When did you eat that cheese?"

"Well, two nights ago," I said. "You had dropped a sliver on the floor, and so I licked it up. And it tasted so good I couldn't stop thinking about it, and so once you had gone to bed I went back for more. And before I knew it, it was gone."

She smiled. "I know the feeling. It's pretty tasty, isn't it?"

I returned her smile with a tentative smile of my own. "Incredible."

"I probably shouldn't buy any more. It's too expensive and too delicious. If I'm not careful, I'll eat a whole pound, and before you know it, I'll be the one who has to go on a diet before the wedding."

There had been a lot of talk about dieting, apparently in connection with Uncle Alec's upcoming wedding, though I failed to see the reason. As far as I can tell, there's no legal requirement to go on a diet before you can get married, but still, it was all anyone could talk about, and then especially in reference to Uncle Alec, the general consensus being that he was too heavy to get married.

Odelia rubbed my head. "Next time, don't touch my cheese, Max."

"I won't," I said ruefully.

"Though I can only blame myself. What was I thinking? First giving you a taste and then not expecting you to want more?"

"It wasn't your fault. It was mine entirely."

"It's fine. You probably did me a favor."

She got up, and Dooley actually gave me two thumbs up

—though since cats don't have thumbs, he gave me two paws up instead.

And since Odelia had no cheese to accompany her piece of toast, she decided to revert to her usual breakfast of cereal instead, which was probably a better choice anyway. Cheese is delicious, but it is a little heavy on the tummy when you eat too much of it.

CHAPTER 7

The bookstore where Vernon Langridge had lost his life was buzzing with life of a different kind as police officers and crime scene people descended on the shop. The man had died in the bookstore he had operated for over fifteen years and had been found dead that morning by his daughter Gwen when she came downstairs looking for her dad after she couldn't find him upstairs in the apartment where they lived.

The front-door lock of the bookstore was broken, indicating that whoever had shot Mr. Langridge had gained access by force. The man had been shot twice, according to the forensic people, once in the chest and once in the head, with a rather large-caliber type of gun, possibly nine millimeter. Death must have been instantaneous, since apparently the human body doesn't enjoy being assaulted by bullets in vital places like the heart or the head. Time of death, according to Abe Cornwall, our county coroner who sat examining the body, must have been around eleven o'clock last night.

The body had been found lying next to a broken display

case, and the odd thing was that a piece of paper had been thrust into the man's mouth. Upon closer inspection, it was a piece of a printed page containing a single paragraph.

The display case itself was empty. According to Gwen Langridge, it used to contain an original manuscript as penned by Mark Twain and was the pride of her father's collection, for sale for no less than twenty-five thousand dollars.

The gun that had taken the man's life wasn't present at the scene, and apart from the valuable tome, the cash register was emptied out, the safe in his office was burgled, and his laptop and phone had been stolen. All in all, a nice haul. Which automatically led Odelia and Chase to assume that whoever had murdered the bookstore owner had been after the money, Vernon had come across them as they were carrying out their raid and they had shot him.

"An open-and-shut case," said Chase as he studied one of the other display cases located in the store.

"I wouldn't be so sure," said Odelia. She pointed to those very same display cases. "These are also worth a lot of money, so why didn't the killer steal them also?"

"Because... he was caught by Vernon?" Chase suggested.

"It's possible," said Odelia. She didn't look convinced, though, and neither was I. She glanced in the direction of the body of the bookseller, still being examined by Abe Cornwall. "Poor guy. He looked so happy yesterday, what with pulling off such a coup."

"Coup?" asked her husband as he picked up a book, studied it as if it was a strange specimen, then put it down again.

"The Blair Beacock book reading. For Blair to pick The Mighty Pen to host the event was quite the coup for Vernon. Lots of free publicity for his store."

A police officer beckoned us over, and we followed the

man upstairs, where Gwen Langridge was seated on a sofa, accompanied by another police officer and also by a woman who bore a slight resemblance to the girl. Gwen couldn't have been more than sixteen or seventeen, I thought, and looked very pale and very stricken, as was to be expected. The woman was holding the girl's hand, and it soon transpired that she was Diana Ludick, Vernon's ex-wife and Gwen's mother. "Will this take long?" asked Diana.

"Just a few questions," Chase assured her. Diana shared the same fine-boned features with her daughter and also the same fine blond hair. "Can you tell us if you heard anything out of the ordinary last night, Gwen?"

The girl shook her head. "I like to listen to music as I fall asleep. Dad is always pottering about downstairs, and I have to get up early to go to school, so I've gotten into the habit of listening to music to drown out the noise."

Chase nodded. "Is there anyone you can think of who would have meant your father harm, Miss Langridge? A disgruntled customer, perhaps? Someone he got into an argument with recently?"

"Nothing like that," said Gwen as she rubbed her nose. "Dad got along with everybody. He was easygoing and very friendly to people." She sniffed. "I will miss him terribly."

Her mom pressed her hand between hers. "Of course you will, sweetie."

Gwen raised a pair of frightened eyes to her mother. "Will I have to go and live with you and Cesar now, Mom?"

"Yes," her mother confirmed curtly.

The girl didn't seem overly pleased by this prospect but didn't say anything.

"Officer Flunk asked you to take a look around the apartment," said Chase. "Did you notice anything missing, Gwen?"

Gwen shook her head. "Nothing. Everything is still there."

"What was stolen downstairs, detective?" asked her mom.

"Um... a Mark Twain first edition," said Chase, "the contents of the cash register, the safe, and your ex-husband's computer and phone."

"Both computers?" asked Gwen.

"Your father had two computers?"

"He did. One laptop for his store business and one he used for writing. The store laptop was an old one, but the writing laptop was state-of-the-art." She made a face. "He wouldn't let me touch that one. Said it was off-limits."

"Well, we found no laptops in his office, so it's safe to say they were both stolen by whoever it was that attacked your dad last night."

"You and Mr. Langridge were divorced, Mrs. Ludick?" asked Odelia.

"Separated," Diana Ludick specified. "My lawyer had sent Vernon the divorce papers, but he hadn't signed them yet."

"You're probably glad now that he's dead," Gwen muttered.

Diana looked up sharply at this. "What's that supposed to mean?"

"Well, you know how Dad hated the separation," said the girl with a shrug. "And how he was hoping that you would get back together again."

Diana's expression softened. "I know he did, sweetie. But our marriage was over, and the sooner Vernon realized that, the better."

"So you can go and marry your politician?"

Diana winced slightly. "Cesar and I would very much like to get married, that's true." She raised her head to Chase. "But we had time. I wasn't going to pressure my ex-husband into signing the divorce papers as long as he wasn't ready. I could see how badly he felt about the separation, but then sometimes couples do drift apart."

"Or fall in love with another man," Gwen said with a touch of viciousness.

"That's quite enough of that, young lady," said Diana crisply and got up. "Will that be all, detective?"

"One more question, Mrs. Ludick," said Chase and produced the piece of paper that had been found in the victim's mouth. It had been straightened and placed inside a clear plastic bag. "Do you recognize this, Gwen?"

Gwen took the item and studied it with a frown. "It's from Dad's book. At least I think it is. He never let me read it, but I know Mark Barker was his main character. An antique dealer who solves mysteries." She handed it back to the detective, who exchanged a look of significance with Odelia.

"Thank you very much, Gwen," said Odelia. "That's all for now."

We watched mother and daughter leave, and I had the impression that once they were out of earshot a lot more would be said about this divorce business. Clearly, it didn't sit well with Gwen that her mother had made plans to marry another man. Which was understandable, of course.

But did it also have a bearing on the case?

Two officers joined us to report to Chase about the neighborhood canvass they had engaged in. Apparently, it wasn't unusual for Vernon Langridge to be working late. Oftentimes, neighbors could see light on in the store until well past midnight, and last night hadn't been different. One of the neighbors had passed by the store around ten-thirty and had seen Vernon moving around in there. Unfortunately, nobody had seen the killer enter or leave, though according to the bookseller's neighbors, whoever had killed him couldn't have done so because they held a grudge against the man. In line with what Gwen had already told us, Mr. Langridge was universally described as a friendly and extremely kind man who was beloved by all who knew him.

All in all, the consensus seemed to favor Chase's determination that the murder must have been the consequence of a botched robbery.

I wasn't convinced, though. Like Odelia had already pointed out: Why had only the single valuable book been stolen, with the rest being left untouched? And more importantly, why had a page of the man's own manuscript been stuffed into his mouth? It seemed quite out of character for any burglar to do such a thing.

CHAPTER 8

We were at the police station where Uncle Alec looked understandably flustered, what with his impending wedding and now this murder case being thrown into his lap. If he had thought that he was going to have a relaxed couple of days before tying the knot, he was sadly mistaken. Lucky for him, Chase was on the case, and so was Odelia. And to a lesser extent, Dooley and myself, of course.

The Chief should have been out shopping with his sister —fitting a nice tux for the wedding, but with his mother and Scarlett being arrested last night, and now this murder business, he had decided to come into the office.

When we arrived at the police station, Chase made a beeline for his boss's office, so when we found it devoid of police chiefs of any description, it wasn't too much to say the detective was momentarily at a loss. He possibly experienced the same sensation when you hurry down the stairs, fully expecting one final step and discovering there isn't any. Disconcerting, if you know what I mean. But Chase wouldn't be the detective that he is if he hadn't immediately set about casting a net for the Chief in an effort to find the missing man.

We finally found him in interview room number two, where he was talking to his mother and Scarlett Canyon. I would have thought that these family meetings were better conducted in the pleasant confines of a kitchen or a cozily decorated living room, but apparently Uncle Alec liked to talk to his mother in the stark confines of a police station interview room.

"For the umpteenth time," said Gran, "we are not the Pancake Burglars!"

"I don't even know how to make a pancake," Scarlett revealed as she tapped an impatient finger on the table. "It's tricky, you know. Once I tried to make them and it was a complete disaster. My great-nephew Kevin had come over, you see, and he loves pancakes, so I figured I'd make him some as a treat. But even he said they were horrible. So that was the first and last time I ever made pancakes. I do make a mean waffle, though."

The Chief looked a little harried, I had to say. From behind the safety of the one-way mirror, and looking at the spectacle, I thought he didn't look like the happy groom he should have been. More like the put-upon son of the Pancake Burglar.

"Okay, I'm going to let you both off the hook," he now announced. "But if my officers catch you again, that's it. I'm officially washing my hands of you."

Dooley took a closer look at the Chief's hands and frowned. "Why would Uncle Alec be washing his hands with Gran, Max? She's not a bar of soap."

"It's just an expression, Dooley. It means he won't be able to spring her from jail if she pulls another stunt like this."

"Eat pancakes, you mean? I didn't know eating pancakes was illegal now."

"It's not. But breaking into other people's homes and stealing their stuff is."

He laughed. "Gran would never do such a thing. She's got too much stuff as it is without having to go out and steal other people's things. Tell them, Max."

As it turned out, I didn't need to tell anyone since Gran was quite capable of voicing this exact opinion herself, and very loudly too!

"And I'm telling *you* that if *you* pull another stunt like this," said the old lady as she wagged a finger in her son's face, "I'm going to put a stop to the wedding!"

The Chief grimaced. "Ma, please."

"No, I mean it. If you can't even put a little faith in your own mother, you don't deserve your future happiness. And here I was preparing you a wonderful and most original gift. Well, you can kiss your gift goodbye, sonny boy!"

And with these words, she got up and swept from the room. Scarlett, who had been intently studying her fingernails, now looked up. "Are we done? Can we go now?"

"You can go," said the Chief, sounding tired.

"Oh, goodie. I hope you catch the real Pancake Burglar, Alec. He looked like a real piece of work. Young, too." She sighed in a wistful sort of way. "Too bad he didn't stick around. I would have loved to get his recipe. Those pancakes were to die for. Oh, well. Maybe next time."

The Chief didn't seem to agree. "Better let there be no next time," he warned.

"Of course there will be a next time. These burglars don't stop, Alec. Unless someone makes them."

Uncle Alec gave her a look of incredulity. "You're not going to try and catch him again, are you?"

"And why not? As Hampton Cove's neighborhood watch, it is our duty to catch this man. So as long as he's out there, we will be out there as well." She patted the Chief's cheek. "But don't you worry, sweetheart. Next time we'll save some pancakes for you. Well, toodle-ooh."

And then she was off, after giving the Chief a pinkie wave.

He closed his eyes and shook his weary head.

And we hadn't even discussed the murder yet!

* * *

"I don't understand why anyone would steal pancakes, Max," said Dooley. "It's not exactly a luxury item, is it? Why doesn't he steal televisions and computers and jewelry like regular burglars?"

"He doesn't actually steal pancakes, Dooley," I said.

"Then why do they call him the Pancake Burglar?"

"Because every time he breaks into a person's home, he bakes himself pancakes and eats them. It's his calling card, so to speak. Like the Scarlet Pimpernel?"

"Who's the Scarlet Pimpernel? Does he like pancakes, too?"

"I'm not sure, but I doubt it," I said. After all, the burglarious element of society is something of a mystery to us regular folks who abide by the law and wouldn't want to be seen dead breaking into other people's homes to abscond with their personal stuff. I guess criminals are wired differently in that sense.

Once again, we were in Uncle Alec's office, and this time the Chief was actually present. "Okay, so lay it all out for me, will you?" he said, still looking rattled after his run-in with his mother and Scarlett. "Vernon Langridge, a bookseller by trade, found dead this morning by his daughter Gwen?"

"That's right," said Chase as he consulted his notes. "Time of death was around eleven o'clock last night, according to Abe's preliminary conclusions, and he was found by his daughter when she woke up this morning at seven and couldn't locate her dad. He was killed with a shot to the chest and one to the head, possibly nine-millimeter and possibly using a silencer since nobody seems to have heard the shots, and whoever killed him stuffed a piece of paper into the dead man's mouth."

"What piece of paper?" asked the Chief with a frown.

"According to his daughter, a page from a manuscript for a book he was working on."

"So he was a writer?"

"An aspiring writer. Gwen wasn't sure if he had actually sold the book or not, but he definitely had plans in that direction."

"Several items were missing from the shop," Odelia continued the report from the front line. "Two laptops, his phone, the contents of the safe, the contents of the cash register, and also a valuable first edition of a Mark Twain book."

"It's probably too early for the results from the crime scene people," said the Chief as he nervously checked his watch.

"Going places, Chief?" asked Chase.

"Shopping for a suit with my sister," Uncle Alec grumbled. "Talk about torture. Is there anything worse than shopping for a suit? And knowing Marge, she'll want to drag me from store to store until we hit on the 'perfect' suit, if such a thing even exists. She even wants me to get a haircut, can you believe it? Even though I've got practically no hair left to speak of."

Chase and Odelia shared a look of amusement at the Chief's gripes.

"Shouldn't you have gone shopping for your suit weeks ago, Chief?" asked Chase.

"I should have, but Charlene thought it better to wait." He gave them a slight look of embarrassment. "My weight... it seems to be in a state of flux, so... Oh, well, I guess I'll just have to grin and bear it," he grumbled. He got up from behind his desk. "So if there's nothing else..."

"Vernon was a member of a writers' group," said Odelia as she and Chase also got up. "Apparently, last night they had a meeting. It could very well be that they were the last people to see Vernon alive."

"So talk to them," Uncle Alec grunted. "See what they have to say. Though as far as I can tell, this is simply a case of a burglary gone wrong. It might even be that Pancake fella your grandmother keeps harping on about. Only this time he didn't have time to whip himself up a batch, seeing as how he killed a man."

Having received our marching orders, we filed out of the office, followed by the big man himself, who was sweating bullets, I now saw. I'd never realized this before, but apparently, humans are more afraid of getting married than they are of anything else, if Uncle Alec's behavior was anything to go by.

Dooley had noticed the same strange phenomenon. "I thought a person's wedding day was supposed to be the most beautiful day of their lives, Max?"

"I thought so, too," I agreed. "But clearly Uncle Alec doesn't feel that way."

"He looks scared to death. On the verge of suffering a nervous breakdown."

"Maybe he doesn't really want to get married, and he's being coerced into it by his future wife?"

Dooley stared at me in dismay. "But that means we have

to save him, Max! We have to stop that wedding before it's too late!"

I hated to admit it, but I felt that Dooley just might have a point.

But how do you stop a wedding?

Now that was a tricky proposition.

CHAPTER 9

We found Kenton Clarey in the small apartment where he lived with his wife and dog. According to the information Chase had gathered, there used to be a son and a daughter as well, but they had flown the coop and now lived in different parts of the country. Mr. Clarey was a man in his mid-fifties with a military bearing and a sort of neckless head. This is a type of person where the head seems directly attached to the shoulders without the benefit of a neck. It gave him a funny aspect, I thought, though Dooley revealed that he found the man scary-looking. Either way, he greeted us in quite an amiable way in the living room that was absent of Mrs. Clarey but contained the dog in question.

The canine belonged to the pug breed and breathed a little stertorously when he caught sight of us. At first, I thought he was either scared or excited to make our acquaintance, but soon enough it transpired that this was simply the way he was. Pugs, you see, often suffer from some malady of the airways that makes them sound as if they've got a permanent cold, and Mickey, as the dog had been christened by Mr. Clarey, was no exception.

"Cats," he said in a sort of astonished undertone, as if the mere presence of a pair of cats in his home came as a great shock to him, as well it might have, of course.

Dooley and I introduced ourselves, indicating that we might be cats, but that didn't mean we weren't also pets of the world and knew our manners.

He nodded curtly. "Mickey," he said. "Though I should probably say Mickey 5 since that's my official name."

"What happened to Mickeys one through four?" I asked.

"Dead," he said in a sort of mournful undertone. Then he perked up. "Not that I care too much. I never met these Mickeys, you see, only heard about them—and seen their pictures, of course."

"Were they also pugs?" I asked politely.

"Absolutely. Once a pug lover, always a pug lover. Kenton and Mikaela are big on pugs. They're members of the World Wide Pug Club, the WWPC, and go to all the different pug gatherings."

"I didn't know there were pug gatherings," I admitted.

"Oh, absolutely. Pug people are a close-knit and devoted community. They've got their own club magazine, calendars, all sorts of paraphernalia, and of course, the annual pug show."

"So only pugs are allowed at this show?" I asked.

"That's correct, sir," said Mickey 5, head held high. "Us pugs are a very proud breed. In fact, it's not too much to say that we aren't actually dogs. And we're not cats, either, of course. We're pugs."

"I see," I said, even though I really didn't.

"So what can you tell us about Vernon Langridge, Mr. Clarey?" asked Odelia, launching into her interview. I had a feeling not much would be said about pugs and a whole lot about the dead man.

"It's a tragedy, isn't it?" said Mr. Clarey as he shook his head. Even neckless people can shake their heads. I don't know how they do it, and I can imagine the mechanics are quite complex, but there you have it. "I only saw him last night, you see, at the monthly meeting of our writers' group."

"What time did you leave, Mr. Clarey?" asked Chase.

"Must have been around ten o'clock," said the man. "Our meetings usually ran from eight to ten, though sometimes they ran a little late. But yesterday had been a long day for all of us, with the Blair Beacock event in the afternoon, and then we all had dinner together and then our meeting. So by the time the clock hit ten, we all decided to call it a night and left the store."

"The meetings always took place at The Mighty Pen?"

"Yes, they did. In the same room where Blair Beacock did her book reading."

"How did Mr. Langridge seem to you?" asked Odelia.

"Tired, I must say," said Mr. Clarey. "But then we were all a little fatigued. Though Vernon more than the rest of us, obviously, because the organization of the book presentation fell squarely on his shoulders, though I can imagine the Beacocks also chipped in. Usually, they do."

"Can you think of anything out of the ordinary that took place last night, sir?" asked Chase. "Anything that was said, maybe?"

The writer frowned. "I don't understand. I thought Vernon was killed by a burglar who stole some of his priceless first editions?"

"We like to keep our options open in these early stages of the investigation," Chase clarified.

Mr. Clarey thought for a moment. "Well, like I said, Vernon was feeling tired, but apart from that... I would say he was rather upbeat, actually. He was on the verge of signing a contract with one of the major publishers, so he was pretty excited about that."

"He sold his book?"

"Yes, he did. A crime thriller. He'd been working on it for years, and he read us snippets of his work in progress during that time. I must say I read the whole thing, and it's pretty darn good. No wonder a publisher snapped it up."

"You are also a published author, aren't you, Mr. Clarey?" asked Odelia.

The man's face cleared. "That's right. I write the Marvin Amis thrillers. Six books have been published so far, with a seventh on the way. Though it's not finished yet, so there's not a lot I can tell you about it. Are you a reader, Mrs. Kingsley?"

"Oh, yes," said Odelia with a smile. "We were there at the reading yesterday, me and my mother. That's Marge Poole. She's the librarian at our local library."

"Marge Poole, of course! Why, your mother and I go way back. Every time a new Marvin Amis novel is published, she's been so kind to organize a reading at the library."

"I know my mother is a big fan," said Odelia. "And so am I," she hastened to add.

"That's very gratifying to hear," he said with a pleased nod of the head.

"Can you think of any enemies Vernon may have had?" asked Chase, trying to keep the conversation focused on the matter at hand. "Any arguments he had with people?"

"Look, I won't conceal from you the fact that I'm astonished at your particular line of questioning, detective," said the writer. "If there was a break-in, with several expensive manuscripts stolen, then it stands to reason that the killer's motive was financial gain, correct? Or am I missing something?"

"Like I said, in these early stages of the investigation we like to cast a wide net," said Chase. He then arched an inquisitive eyebrow. "Please answer the question, Mr. Clarey."

"Well, I have to admit I can't think of anyone who might have been harboring some kind of grudge against Vernon. The man was a sweetheart, pure and simple. And a very talented writer. Of course, there was this business of the separation from his wife, but as far as I know, that all happened in an entirely amicable manner. Both Vernon and Diana agreed that they should keep the acrimony to a minimum for Gwen's sake. And so they did. The whole thing was handled in a most civilized way."

"No big fights?"

"No big fights."

"And you and Vernon got along well?"

"Oh, absolutely. Vernon and I were great friends. We'd known each other for so many years. He started his writers' group fifteen years ago, if you please. And we had known each other for at least twenty-five years. So we had been friends for a long time. Celebrated each other's successes, mourned our failures."

"So you weren't jealous of Vernon's book sale?" asked Odelia.

The man looked astonished. "My dear lady—absolutely not! It couldn't have happened to a better man, and I was exceedingly happy for him. And besides, why would I be jealous of Vernon's success? I'm a very successful author in my own right and, over the years, have been instrumental in the success of others. Pay it forward and all that, you know. So I'm afraid you're barking up the wrong tree here—entirely so, in fact."

"After you left the meeting yesterday," said Chase, "where did you go?"

"Home," said the man immediately. "My wife can verify

that." But then he wavered. "What time did you say Vernon died?"

"Eleven."

"I think I may have stepped out of the house around that time to take Mickey for a walk. I'd say ask him, but of course, that would be impossible." He barked a pleasant laugh at this little joke, but confronted with a stony-faced response from both detectives, the smile quickly slipped off his face. "You could ask my neighbors," he suggested. "There's always some busybody looking out of their windows to see what's going on. So if you insist I need an alibi—even though I can assure you I would never hurt my good friend Vernon—you can ask them. I'm sure they'll confirm I never came anywhere close to The Mighty Pen." He seemed a little peeved that he would be suspected of committing such a heinous crime, even though as a thriller writer, he should have known that in a police investigation everybody is a suspect until further notice.

Dooley and I turned to Mickey, who stared back innocently. "What?" he finally asked.

"Can you confirm that Kenton took you for a walk last night around eleven o'clock and that he never came anywhere near The Mighty Pen?"

"Well, he definitely took me for a walk," said Mickey. "But if you want to know what time it was, I'm afraid I can't tell you. I don't wear a watch, you see. All I know is that it was dark out and that he was in a lousy mood."

"A lousy mood? Do you know why?"

The dog shrugged. "Do humans ever need a reason to be in a foul mood? Seems to me it simply hits them out of the blue, for no reason at all."

He was right, of course. Sometimes people simply feel bad for no objective reason at all. And apparently Kenton Clarey was just such a person.

"But while you were out on your walk, did you pass by The Mighty Pen?"

"No, we didn't," the dog confirmed. "Does that answer your question?"

"It does," I said with satisfaction. "It does indeed, Mickey. Thank you."

* * *

STANDING WELL AWAY from the window so they wouldn't see him, Kenton stared at the two detectives. They were talking amongst themselves, probably discussing the recent interview. He didn't understand why they had been so insistent that he talk about Vernon's enemies, but it did give him the idea that there was probably more to this murder business than a simple break-in gone wrong. So who could possibly have targeted Vernon, of all people? The man was such a pussycat, even though lately he had developed a certain arrogance, but that probably came with the territory.

When Kenton had signed his first book deal with a major publisher, Mikaela had told him to watch out about getting too cocky for his own good, and she was right. It was so easy to be swept up in a celebration of one's own brilliance once you saw your own name in print and a large blown-up photograph of your likeness adorning the window of your local bookstore. Now, all these many years later, there wasn't a whole lot left of that initial cockiness—quite the contrary.

He just hoped the detectives wouldn't be back. He hated getting involved in other people's mess. If Vernon was murdered, as they seemed to believe he was, then he had brought it upon himself, and it was all Kenton could do to distance himself from the dead man as much as possible. He suddenly realized that he shouldn't have said all that stuff about Vernon being a close friend of his. He should have stressed they were merely acquaintances, thrown together through their mutual love of writing.

"Dammit," he muttered. Mickey looked up from his basket where he had laid down after the visit from the constabulary. Kenton crouched down next to the precious mutt and tickled his ears. "Were they mean to you, those cats?" he asked. "They sure looked mean." Especially that big orange bruiser. He had heard stories about Odelia Kingsley never going anywhere without her cats in tow but had ascribed them to gossip. But now he knew it was all too true. He wondered what was up with that.

"Kenton!" a weak voice sounded from the back of the apartment.

"I'm coming, sweetheart!" he called back.

At least he hadn't mentioned Mikaela's condition. If only they knew the truth of what he'd had to endure these past couple of years, they might have hauled him off to prison without delay.

He hurried to the bedroom he and Mikaela shared and was shocked to find his wife looking even paler than usual.

"Who were those people?" she asked as he sat down next to her.

"Just some people from the writers' group," he said.

"What did they want?"

"Some tips about their writing," he said.

She gave him a weak smile. "Tips from the master."

"That's exactly right," he said as he touched her cheek. "How are you feeling today?"

"Rotten." She coughed. He helped her drink from the bottle he had placed on the nightstand. It competed for space with a plethora of medicine boxes and syrups to ease the strain on Mikaela's lungs. It was a vicious disease, and no mistake, but he had every confidence she would beat it—if only they could afford the treatment.

It wasn't fair, he felt. Mikaela had never smoked a cigarette in her life and had always been a proponent of clean living, even more than Kenton himself. And still, she had developed this debilitating lung disease. According to the doctors, it was perfectly feasible that she would pull through, but it would take time, and time was exactly what they didn't have. Not with bills piling up.

He now cursed himself for revealing to the other members of the writers' group that the publisher was having second thoughts about the future of the Marvin Amis series. If they told those cops…

But then that couldn't be helped.

Mikaela must have noticed his concern, for she asked, "What's wrong?"

"Nothing's wrong, darling," he assured her. But he must be a pretty lousy liar because instead of relaxing, she doubled down and wouldn't rest until he had told her the truth.

He never could hide anything from her.

CHAPTER 10

We met Marina Steele at No Spring Chicks, where she worked as a waitress. Miss Steele was a young woman with spiky pink hair and a nose piercing that was quite prominent. I have to admit I couldn't stop staring at it and wondered if it hurt to have such a big thing piercing one's septum. I didn't think I would enjoy finding out.

"Why does she have that thing in her nose, Max?" asked Dooley.

"I'm not sure, Dooley. I guess she likes it."

"Maybe it's a fashion statement?"

"I'm sure it is."

"I wouldn't like to have something like that in my nose, Max. Or anywhere else, for that matter."

It is true that cats only very rarely ask for their noses to be pierced, or their eyebrows or their ears. And as far as I can tell, the same goes for dogs. I still have yet to meet the first dog with a nose piercing. Or even a tattoo. So it very much looks as if humans are the only species of the animal kingdom who voluntarily allow their bodies to be mutilated in this way—for reasons of fashion.

"What is fashion, Max?" asked Dooley, becoming philosophical all of a sudden. "And why do people follow it so slavishly?"

"I guess… fashion is the individual expression of one's… individuality?" I suggested. I guess I'm not exactly a philosopher at heart.

"But if fashion is a way to express one's individuality, then why do all people follow it so slavishly? Copying other people? Doesn't that negate the whole concept of individuality?"

"I guess it kinda does?" I said. Like I said, I'm not big on philosophy.

"I mean, if everyone else is getting a nose piercing, maybe the purest expression of one's individuality would be not to get a nose piercing also?" He was warming to the topic and really developing the theme now, even though we should have been monitoring Odelia and Chase's conversation with Marina Steele. But there's no stopping Dooley when he's caught in the heat of his argument.

Lucky for us, Miss Steele didn't have much to say about Vernon Langridge apart from the fact that the man had been a great friend of hers, an excellent writer, and she had no idea who would have wanted to murder him since he was loved by one and all. And so, after exchanging a few more words about the dearly departed, we took our leave. I noticed that no pets were in evidence, so we couldn't ask them to confirm Miss Steele's alibi, which mainly consisted of her being home alone with her dog on her lap, watching Netflix.

When asked where this dog was at that moment, she said that Meena stayed with a friend who worked from home during the day, since she hated being alone in the apartment.

I could very much sympathize. I wouldn't enjoy being locked up in an apartment while my human went out to earn her daily bread all day either.

Now if only we could have a little chat with Meena, then we could safely cross Marina Steele off our tentative list of suspects in one fell swoop.

But Odelia and Chase seemed satisfied that she couldn't have done it, and so we went on our way.

"I wonder how she blows her nose, Max," said Dooley, who still couldn't be induced to drop the subject of the nose piercing. "It must get very icky up there. Mucus does have a tendency to coalesce."

"Nose piercings can be removed," I said. "Like earrings. So I guess when she has to blow her nose, she simply removes it and then puts it back in."

"It all seems unnecessarily complicated, Max. And life being complicated enough as it is, it adds a lot of superfluous stress where it's not needed."

I smiled at my friend. "That's a big word, Dooley."

He beamed at me. "It was in this Discovery Channel documentary Gran and I watched the other night. It was about superfluous species and their impending extinction."

"Oh? And what species are those?"

"I'm not sure. They never actually got around to naming them. Gran said it was bankers, lawyers and politicians, but that could be her own opinion, of course."

Marina excused herself to Aissa Spring, who owned the restaurant and therefore was her boss, and repaired to the storage room at the back, which doubled as a dressing room for the waitstaff. She sank down on a bench and burst into tears. She could hardly believe it. Vernon, dead? It wasn't possible. She buried her face in her hands and soon was reduced to great desperate sobs. She had been able to stay strong during the interview, even though she was on the verge of going to pieces. Mercifully, the cops hadn't pressured her, and she had been able to answer in a composed manner.

No, she had no idea who could hold a grudge against Vernon. No, Vernon was not a friend of hers but merely an esteemed colleague. No, she hardly knew the man, so she couldn't possibly comment on his private life or what had caused his death. But now that she was alone, she couldn't contain her shock any longer and freely gave herself up to the terrible grief and heartache she was feeling. Her phone placed next to her, she idly thumbed through the hundreds of pictures of Vernon she had on her phone—some taken herself, others downloaded from his social media. One picture, in particular, stood out. It was a selfie she had taken with the man on the occasion of the publication of her first book. Vernon had insisted they go out and celebrate, and so they had.

Even though he was by no means a wealthy man, he had taken her to one of the fanciest restaurants in town, and they had enjoyed a wonderful dinner. It had only cemented the notion in her heart that Vernon was the most wonderful man in her life. And now he was dead. It wasn't possible. It simply couldn't be. And yet it was.

Studying the picture they had taken that night, with Marina placing her head on Vernon's shoulder, the two of them smiling at the camera, both a little tipsy after their date that wasn't a date, it had been the best night of her life. At the time, she had hoped it would lead to more—she desperately wanted it to lead to more. And when it hadn't, it had left her feeling frustrated and sad.

But at least they had been close friends. At least they had that.

CHAPTER 11

The final member of Vernon's little writers' group we met was a woman named Tarsha Kettles. We met her in her pleasant home, which was decorated with plenty of plants and knickknacks that covered every available surface. Plants dangled from the ceiling, plants sat poised on the furniture, flower pots adorned the windowsill. In fact, it wasn't too much to say Mrs. Kettles's home reminded me of a greenhouse, and I have to say I found her dedication to plant life refreshing in the extreme!

I like plants, you see. I like to sniff at them, I like to chew on them, and I like to lie on top of them—especially in the summer months. There's nothing more refreshing than lying on top of a nice flowerbed. Almost as if they seem to be placed there especially for our needs. Odelia doesn't seem to feel the same way, though, for every time I grace one of her flowerbeds with my presence, she erupts into a stream of mild vituperative designed to discourage this behavior.

But since Odelia was busy interviewing Mrs. Kettles, Dooley and I decided to use this opportunity to go on a tour of the place. We soon discovered that the woman had installed a large planter box in the center of her living room. It measured at least six feet by six and housed several plants that looked extremely appetizing indeed, along with a riot of colorful little flowers that simply seemed to beckon us over to have a lie-down. And since we were both feeling a little tired at this point, we decided not to resist this urgent call and draped ourselves across this expanse of pure loveliness and coolness.

"This is the life, isn't it, buddy?" I said with a sigh of relish.

"This is absolutely the life," Dooley agreed.

And we had been lying there for about five minutes when all of a sudden a furry face peered over the edge of the indoor planter box. It belonged to a cat whose acquaintance we hadn't yet made.

"Guys, I wouldn't do that if I were you," the cat admonished us.

"Oh, are we lying in your spot?" I asked.

"I wish. Every time I lie down where you're lying, she chases me away. Last time she even gave my tush a flick with her finger. And I have to say, it hurt!"

"Flicks of the finger do hurt," I agreed. "But maybe you misunderstood? Maybe she simply wanted to remove a piece of fluff from your butt?"

"Oh, she knew what she was doing," the cat assured us. "You see, the flick was accompanied by words to the same effect. I don't know why, but for some reason she doesn't like it when I lie on top of her flowers."

"Odelia is much the same way," I lamented.

"It's the only habit of hers we disagree with," Dooley added.

"I know, right? Flowers were made to lie on. Otherwise, what's their purpose?"

"I agree with you one hundred percent, Mrs..."

"Miss. Minoes," said the cat. "But you can call me Min. All my friends do."

"You're not a member of cat choir, are you?" I asked.

"No, I'm not. I've been meaning to go, but Tarsha doesn't like it when I leave the house. She pretty much keeps me under lock and key. And when I do manage to escape her vigilance, she screams down the neighborhood, starts putting up flyers all along the street, and generally makes a big stink."

"Some humans are like that," I said commiseratively.

"She's afraid I'll get run over or knocked down or kidnapped."

"Isn't that often the way?" I sighed as I stretched out luxuriously.

"Seriously, though. If she sees you like this, she'll be all over you."

I don't know why, but Min's words were starting to detract slightly from my enjoyment of the pleasant experience Dooley and I were having.

"So, are your humans friends of my human?" asked Min.

"Not friends, no," I said. "They're here because a man was murdered, so now they're talking to all the people who knew him, hoping to find out more about the man and eventually establish a motive for his murder."

"Murder!" said Min. "No, really?" She seemed a little too happy about the fact that one of her human's friends had been murdered, in my personal opinion. Then again, if she was never allowed out of the house, she had to get her kicks somewhere, of course. "So who was it?"

"Vernon Langridge," I said. "Owner of The Mighty Pen."

"Ooh, I knew him," said Min, practically clapping her paws with unadulterated glee. "How was he killed? Shot, stabbed, poisoned... *strangled*?!"

"Shot," I clarified.

"Shot twice," Dooley added. "Once in the chest and once in the head."

"That should do the trick," Min breathed ecstatically. "Was there a lot of brain matter smeared all across the floor, big chunks of the stuff covering the wall?"

I stared at her with a touch of unease. "Um..."

"And tell me about the blood. Was there a lot of blood? Buckets of the stuff?"

"There was a sufficient amount of blood," I agreed.

"Ooh, isn't this simply wonderful? You see, Tarsha writes cozy mysteries, so she's forever investigating ways of murdering a person. Different types of exotic poisons, strange and obscure murder methods, serrated knives of all types, so I'm sure she'll have a field day with this murder."

"I wouldn't be too sure about that," I said. "After all, if Vernon was a close friend of hers..."

"Oh, but he wasn't. He was simply a member of the same writers' group. As far as I could tell, they weren't especially close or anything. For one thing, the man has never set foot inside this house, and if he really were a friend of Tarsha, he would have done so at some point, right? Come over for dinner, maybe? Dropped by to pay us a visit? But nothing. Ever."

"So they were merely colleagues, is that what you're saying?"

"That's exactly right. They were colleagues, but not friends. And besides, I'm not even sure Tarsha liked him all that much."

"What makes you say that?"

"Well, I remember she complained about Vernon once. He had sent her a copy of his manuscript. A big book that he wanted her to read. And she complained that it was practically unreadable. Said it appeared to have been written by a child. And a very untalented child at that."

"But I thought Vernon had sold his book to a publisher?"

Min shrugged. "If you've been around the block a few times, like we have, Max, you know as well as I do that there's no accounting for taste. It may very well be that this horrible book that Tarsha found perfectly unreadable would go on to sell millions of copies. Often these big bestsellers are terrible, their authors untalented hacks, so Vernon may have been on to something."

All of a sudden, another face appeared right next to Min's. It belonged to Tarsha herself, and she looked exactly as Min had described her: mad as a wet hen.

"Uh-oh," said Dooley. "I can see a butt flick in our near future, Max."

I could, too, and it was only through Odelia's intervention that we were spared such an ordeal. We were forced to shift ourselves from our perfect spot to the carpet below, and after a lot of wailing and gnashing of teeth as Tarsha examined her precious flowers, now a good deal flatter and a lot less perky after our passage, the interview finally recommenced.

"If you really want to know who killed Vernon, look no further than Jerald Exton," Tarsha was saying. She darted frequent angry glances in our direction, and judging from the twitch she had developed in her index finger, visibly itching to deliver that dreaded flick, I had the impression we had already outstayed our welcome. Then again, if a human is going to keep their cat under lock and key at all times, it was probably to be expected that they should also try to limit their exposure to the more unruly element: me and Dooley. She probably thought we were a bad influence. Funnily enough, she said as much, though not in reference to us but to this Jerald Exton person.

"Who is Jerald Exton?" asked Chase.

"Gwen Langridge's boyfriend. It's a disgrace, really, and caused Vernon no end of grief. I mean, the girl is only seventeen, for crying out loud. She should be at home playing with her dolls, not being seduced by the likes of Jerald Exton."

"How old is this kid?"

"Nineteen, if you please. And a convicted criminal to boot!"

"He's been in jail?"

"Absolutely! He deals drugs. And that's the kind of person poor Vernon's little girl was hanging out with. He tried to stop the whole sordid business, of course. Nip it in the bud. But Gwen said she was in love and said that if Vernon forbade her from seeing Jerald she was going to live with her mother from now on. Can you believe it? Dreadful business —absolutely dreadful."

"Did her mother approve?" asked Odelia.

"I don't think she cared. Diana is too busy with that hotshot boyfriend of hers to bother with her own daughter. If only those two could have presented a united front, they might have stood a chance of breaking up that extremely unsuitable relationship. But what with the upcoming divorce and everything, clearly Gwen was completely adrift. And can you blame her? She's only a child, after all." The woman shook her head. Somehow she reminded me of Gran, with her little white curls and her slight physique. Contrary to Gran, she seemed a little less crotchety, though her recent behavior with us would have indicated the contrary.

"Are girls of seventeen children, Max?" asked Dooley. "Do they still play with their dolls?"

"I'm not sure, Dooley," I admitted. Humans age differently than cats. One moment they're kids playing with their dolls and the next they're getting married and having kids themselves. Whether seventeen was the appropriate age to play with Ken dolls or to date actual nineteen-year-old Kens was entirely beyond me. Though something told me that Tarsha Kettles might be exaggerating.

"Thank you so much, Mrs. Kettles," said Chase, after exchanging a look with his wife. Clearly, he seemed to feel that they had their first real suspect in young Mr. Jerald Exton. "That's very helpful."

"Odd that none of the others have told you," said the woman. "But then I guess they didn't think it as important as I do. Did you talk to Diana?"

"We did, but she didn't mention Jerald Exton."

"Well, she wouldn't, would she? After all, she's mostly to blame for what happened. If only she had been more strict with the girl, Gwen would never have drifted into this delinquent's ken and been subjected to his pernicious influence." She sighed deeply. "And we all know what these drug addicts are like. Always looking for their next fix and in search of money to fund their habit. So is it any surprise that Jerald wanted to lay his hands on Vernon's valuable first editions? He's probably hawking them as we speak so he can buy himself more drugs."

"Only one of Vernon's first editions was stolen," Odelia said. "The Mark Twain?"

"Probably didn't have time to grab the other ones. When Vernon interrupted him, the young scoundrel must have gotten the fright of his life. So he shot the poor man and got out of there as quick as he could. If I were you, I'd put a police officer in front of that store. You know what they say about crooks: they always return to the scene of the crime. Wouldn't surprise me if Jerald came back tonight to steal the rest of those first editions. Finish the job he started!"

* * *

THE MOMENT that detective and his wife had left, Tarsha checked on her poor African violets and her kalanchoes. Of all the places those cats could have picked, they had to go and lie on top of her precious flowers! She should have known. Her own Min was exactly the same way. She had named the gray tabby after a Dutch kids' movie she had once seen. It was called 'Miss Minoes' and was about a cat who turns into a young woman and makes the acquaintance of a reporter. It was a wonderfully imaginative movie, and her own Minoes looked exactly like the cat in the movie.

She repaired as much of the damage as she could, then responded to Min's call attracting her attention to the empty bowl in the kitchen.

"You poor thing," she murmured as she filled up the bowl again. Presumably, these unwanted feline visitors hadn't merely tried to destroy those flowers but had also eaten Min's food. She sincerely hoped they wouldn't darken her doorstep again—neither the cats nor the detective and the reporter. She had said all she had to say on the subject of Vernon's murder and hoped they would leave her alone from now on.

It was a sad affair, of course, especially for her. Vernon had more or less promised her that once the sale of his book was a done deal, he would put Tarsha in contact with his agent and his publisher and see if they couldn't make her dream come true as well. Even though she had tried Marina's approach and had published her cozy mystery all by herself, sales were dismal and the whole experience disappointing to the extreme. So when Vernon announced he had finally sold his book, she had pinned all of her hopes on him and his contacts. Now that he was dead, nothing would come of that.

She sighed deeply as she removed a dead leaf from a flowering maple and rolled it into a ball before depositing it into the appropriate recycling bin.

Looked like she'd have to start again from scratch.

CHAPTER 12

On our way back to the police station, Chase received a phone call from his colleague Sarah Flunk. She informed him that a search of the store had revealed a lighter found underneath one of the bookcases. The fingerprints on the lighter were a match for Jerald Exton, indicating that the man had been at the store at some point, though it wasn't possible to determine when this could have been.

"We'll pay him a visit," said Chase with the kind of grim-faced determination he often gets when he's picked up the scent of a suspect. Sarah gave him the address where we could find Mr. Exton, and before long, we were on our way over there.

Jerald still lived with his parents, more precisely in a van located in the backyard of the young man's parental home. When we arrived there, nobody appeared to be home: not Jerald but also not his parents. But since Chase is both very nosy and also dogged in his determination, not to mention of the gung-ho variety, he decided not to let that stop him from having a look-see around the place.

Technically he wasn't allowed to search the property

since he didn't have a search warrant, but he quickly solved this by tasking Dooley and me with the assignment of breaking and entering into that van to look for anything that might incriminate Gwen's boyfriend—anything at all.

"The gun would be good," he told us. "Or that book he took."

"What does it look like, this book?" I asked.

Odelia, who acted as an intermediary, explained that it was a very old book, and the moment we laid eyes on it, we would know what it was. She was probably right. Kids like Jerald Exton probably don't keep ancient books lying around their van. Mostly they like to play video games and such.

So while Chase and Odelia sat in their car parked in front of the house, Dooley and I snuck around the back and soon found ourselves entering the backyard. When humans do this it's called trespassing, but when we do it's called going for a walk. It didn't take us long to locate the van, and after a moment dedicated to an inspection of the exterior, we discovered that one of the windows was ajar. Unfortunately, it wasn't all the way open, and the crack was far too narrow for me to slip through. I'm one of the heftier specimens of the species, you see. Built for comfort, not speed. But Dooley might be able to do the trick. He's a lot smaller than me and also very light on his paws.

"So look for a very old book," I instructed him. "You'll probably be able to smell it. Old books have a funny smell, like rotting leaves."

"Gotcha," said my friend. He looked a little nervous because all of a sudden, this whole mission rested squarely on his narrow shoulders. But as far as I could see, nothing could possibly go wrong. He would be in and out in a matter of minutes, and even if Jerald unexpectedly arrived home, Dooley could hide under the bed and then sneak out unseen the moment the kid's back was turned.

"And if you find the gun, even better. Guns also have a distinctive smell."

"I know. They smell like death, right?"

"Well, not exactly. More a pungent sort of smell."

"Pungent. Gotcha." He took a deep breath and sort of braced himself. "Wish me luck, Max."

"Good luck, buddy. And if there's anything wrong, just shout, all right? Then I'll go and get Odelia, and she can bust you out."

"Bust me out. Gotcha!" And with these words, he took the jump to that window. He got it the first time and gracefully disappeared from view.

I have to say I don't much like having to wait around while my friend puts himself in harm's way. For I suddenly realized that even though the Extons hadn't responded to Chase's knock on the door, that didn't mean that Jerald wasn't home and spending time in his van. For all I knew, he was in there, thinking about the heinous crime he committed. Or maybe he was doing whatever it was that drug addicts did: tripping, as the vernacular goes. So when suddenly a cat landed squarely on his chest, he might not enjoy the experience. Then again, maybe he was so out of it he wouldn't even notice.

At any rate, for the next ten minutes or so, I was feeling quite nervous. Before long, I was eyeing that window, wondering if I couldn't possibly slip through. And after fifteen minutes, I was so worked up that I softly started yelling, "Dooley, is everything all right in there? Dooley!"

When no response came, I started thinking the worst. Maybe Jerald had captured Dooley and was smoking him now in his crack pipe, for wasn't that what druggies did? Take anything and smoke it?

"Oh, God," I groaned, in agony at this point.

Which is why I decided to brave it all and make the big

leap. It took me three tries, but finally, I made it to that window. Unfortunately, instead of gracefully slipping inside, I found myself truly and thoroughly stuck, suspended in midair.

Ugh!

The disadvantage was that I couldn't move, with the lower part of my anatomy dangling on the outside of the van. The upshot was that the upper portion of my physique was inside the van, and so I had a good overview of the goings-on in there. And much to my relief, I could actually see my friend—and he was still alive!

"Dooley!" I said, in a strangled sort of voice.

"Oh, hey, Max," said my friend, pleased to see me. Then he frowned. "Why are you hanging there?"

"I'm stuck," I explained, slightly wheezing. "I thought something happened to you, so I made the jump. Unfortunately, as we thought, I'm too big-boned for this window."

"I think I found your book, Max," said Dooley. "It's big and it's old, and it smells really funny. It's located at the back of that there cabinet. So do you think that's enough for Chase to arrest this man and lock him away for good?"

"Probably," I managed with some effort. "If it's the right book. So what took you so long?"

"I tried smelling out the book, just as you said: try and locate anything that smells funny. But I have to say there are a lot of very funny smells in here, Max. For instance, there's a lot of very smelly clothes in the bathroom, and also a lot of funny-smelling stuff on that table over there. And the bed smells extremely funny. As if something died there."

He was right. Even from my awkward position hovering about six feet above the floor, I could smell that the entire van smelled like sweaty socks, unwashed armpits, and bad breath. In other words, it smelled exactly like the bedroom of a teenager. I could also smell weed—a lot of it.

I wrinkled my nose, then sneezed, which wasn't a good idea since my diaphragm was already contracted and jammed between the wall and the window. "You have to get me out of here, buddy," I told my friend.

"The problem is that you're blocking the only route of escape, Max," he pointed out.

He was right, of course. Which meant that we were both stuck, and would have to wait until either Jerald arrived on the scene, which probably wasn't ideal. Or Odelia got so worried that she came to our rescue. Which was probably illegal.

In other words, we were in quite the pickle.

On the bright side, we had caught the killer.

Now if only the killer didn't catch us!

CHAPTER 13

Jerald Exton came home after a morning spent at the bus depot where he worked part-time as a mechanic to find a cat stuck in the window of his van. For a moment he stood staring at the creature, wondering what it hoped to accomplish. Then when he opened the door, he found another cat, seated on top of his bed, looking at him in a defiant sort of way, as only cats can. As if he was the one at fault here.

The cat stuck in the window meowed in a piteous way, and he approached the creature carefully. He had heard stories about what cats that are cornered can do and didn't want to be turned into the creature's personal scratching post. So, after he had grabbed a blanket from the bed and worked out a strategy, he said, "I'm going to get you out of there, cat. But please don't scratch my eyes out, all right? If you do, I'm just going to leave you there. Do we have an understanding?"

Oddly enough, the cat seemed to nod, which was impossible, of course. Then again, rumor had it that cats were intelligent creatures. Not as intelligent as dogs, obviously, but still. So maybe this wouldn't end badly after all?

He stepped closer, quickly wrapped the cat in the blanket, lifted it from its precarious position, and deposited it on the floor of his van.

"There. That's better, isn't it?"

The cat stared up at him and actually seemed to smile. It then uttered a single sound, which could only be interpreted as a sign of gratitude. But before he could respond, both cats skedaddled through the open door of his van.

Shaking his head, he threw himself down on his bed and checked his phone. This whole business with Gwen's dad had thrown him. He didn't like the guy, but that didn't mean he wanted him dead. But he was. Dead as a dodo if Gwen was to be believed. He hadn't seen anything online yet, but Gwen wouldn't lie about something like that, would she? Though it was entirely possible. He liked her, he really did, but she was incredibly immature. Which probably was to be expected at her age. She was, after all, eighteen months his junior. Plus, all girls were immature. That was just a fact of life.

He placed his hands behind his head and stared up at the ceiling, giving himself up to thought about the girl. His parents didn't like that they were an item, and neither did Gwen's folks. Even though he'd told them they weren't actually *together* together. Gwen wanted to, but he preferred to wait until she turned eighteen. Which wasn't until next month. So they had plenty of time before—

He looked up when suddenly a knock sounded at the door and a big burly fella burst in.

He quickly rose from the bed. "Hey, what do you think—"

"Chase Kingsley, Hampton Cove PD," the big guy grunted in an implacable way. He produced a badge to support his claim, then continued, "Jerald Exton, you're under arrest on suspicion of the murder of Vernon Langridge."

And as the cop rattled off Jerald's rights, a woman now joined the cop, donning plastic gloves for some reason, and started rifling through his stuff. Much to his surprise, she suddenly extracted an old book from the bottom of his clothes cabinet and held it up in a triumphant sort of way.

"You stole this from Mr. Langridge last night, didn't you, Jerald?" she asked. It seemed to be a rhetorical question, for she didn't bother waiting for a reply. Instead, she started rifling through his stuff some more, possibly looking for more old books.

"I've never seen that before," he said immediately. He knew cops sometimes planted stuff so they could frame a suspect. It now seemed to him that this woman had planted that book, whatever it was.

"A likely story," the cop said as he placed a pair of shiny handcuffs on his wrists.

As he was led from the camper, much to his surprise he saw those same two cats sitting and staring up at him, almost as if this was a spectator sport and he was the star attraction.

Well, maybe he was. For if it was true what those cops said, he was in a great deal of trouble!

* * *

"It seems like such a pity, Max," said Dooley as we watched Jerald Exton being led away. "I kinda liked the guy."

"Me too," I said. After all, Jerald had saved me from a particularly untenable position. And he had done it with more grace and kindness than some people would have awarded a cat having strayed onto their private property. "But if he killed Vernon, he should be punished for his crime, Dooley."

"Oh, I know. But maybe he had his reasons, you know. After all, we don't know a whole lot about this Vernon guy.

Maybe he was the bad guy in the story and Jerald is the good guy?"

"Murder can never be condoned, Dooley," I reiterated the line Odelia had impressed upon us on more than one occasion. "Though I have to agree that we don't know a great deal about Vernon, or Jerald for that matter."

"Maybe Vernon was really putting his foot down on that relationship, you know, and so they saw no other way but to get rid of the man."

"If they really wanted to be together, and Gwen's dad was preventing them, they could always have found a different solution. Jerald didn't have to kill him."

"It's almost like that Shakespeare play, isn't it, Max? Romeo and Juliet?"

"Possibly," I allowed. I don't really know my classics, I have to admit, so if there was a resemblance between the Romeo and Juliet story and what Jerald and Gwen were going through, I could neither confirm nor deny the reality of this. I didn't even know if Jerald could sing a serenade. What was absolutely beyond question was that Vernon's precious book had been found in Jerald's camper, so that seemed to leave little doubt that he was the killer we were looking for. And since his lighter had been at the scene of the crime, with the man's fingerprints on it, that pretty much clinched the deal.

Jerald Exton was our killer. And the fact that he was kind to animals and strangers—and strange animals—didn't change that fact. Maybe he liked cats and hated people—that was also possible.

The young man was carted off to the pen, and more officers flocked to the scene, along with the crime scene people who were going to go through his van with a fine-tooth comb—possibly literally—to find more evidence linking Jerald to the crime he had committed. The murder weapon still hadn't been found, so the hope was that it would be in that van. Jerald's clothes would be checked for gunpowder residue and blood. And of course, Vernon's laptops and phone were items that still needed to be found, along with the contents of the safe and the money from the register.

All in all, it was going to be a busy couple of hours for a lot of people—our own humans included, as Jerald needed to be interviewed and charged.

Soon we were on our way back to the station, and as I touched a paw to my sensitive midsection, Dooley gave me a look of concern.

"Does it still hurt, Max?"

"A little," I confessed.

"Maybe you should have it checked out. Maybe you cracked a rib or something."

"I did not crack a rib, Dooley," I protested. "Just some minor bruising maybe."

"You should still have it checked out." He raised his voice. "Odelia, Max hurt his ribs when he got stuck in that window. We should take him to see Vena."

"There's absolutely no need," I hurried to say.

But the damage was already done. Odelia turned around to face us—we were riding in the back of Chase's squad car while the suspect was being transported in a second car with armed officers—just to be on the safe side—and gave me a look of worry. "Does it hurt badly?"

"No, just a little," I said. "So there's absolutely no need to—"

"We'll go and see Vena," she determined. "But first, we have to go to the police station so Chase can interrogate Jerald Exton about the murder. But once that's done, I'll take you to the vet. Can you wait that long, Max? Or do you think I should take you first?"

"You don't have to take me to Vena," I said. "It doesn't hurt so much."

But the decision was made, and as I looked into my future, the notion that I was about to see the scariest nemesis known to cat-kind was writ large.

Could things *be* any worse?

CHAPTER 14

By the time we got to the police station, a lawyer had already arrived there, eager to represent Jerald, whom he called his client, against any false allegations Chase was about to make. It was obvious that Chase wasn't too well pleased with this wrinkle in an otherwise clear-cut investigation, for he grumbled a good deal under his breath and even voiced his dismay by asking the lawyer how he had gotten there so fast.

The representative of the legal trade gave a sort of smirk. He was a rail-thin man dressed in a perfectly cut and no doubt expensive suit, with a clean-shaven face and not a small amount of confidence in his own abilities. "My services were engaged by Mrs. Blair Beacock," he said. "Mr. Exton's parents work for Mrs. Beacock, you see, so she thought it prudent to assist the young man in trying to prove his innocence in this most distasteful matter."

"The Extons work for Blair Beacock?"

"That's right. Mrs. Exton as a cleaner and Mr. Exton as a gardener. So in that sense, Jerald is practically part of the family." He directed a self-satisfied smile at the detective. "Do you still wish to interview my client, or will you admit that you've made a grave error of judgment and release him immediately?"

"I will interview him," said Chase curtly and led the way to one of the interview rooms. Jerald had already been fingerprinted and his mugshot had been taken, and the young man was seated in the rather unpleasant room, waiting nervously for the detective to arrive. When he saw the lawyer enter the room, he looked pleasantly surprised. And when the lawyer explained that he had nothing to worry about and that he would get him out of there in no time, he visibly relaxed, safe in the knowledge that he had an ally by his side who would do his utmost to bring about the happy ending.

"Look, I had nothing to do with this, all right?" said Jerald as he tapped the table with an irate finger. "I never even came near the guy last night."

"So where were you?" asked Chase, not impressed either by the presence of the fancy, expensive lawyer or his suspect's protestations.

"In my van," said the young man, settling back again.

"Can anyone verify that?"

"Well... no," Jerald admitted. "But that doesn't mean I wasn't there."

"Can you prove that my client was at The Mighty Pen?" asked the lawyer.

This was the moment Chase had been waiting for. He placed a transparent plastic bag on the table. It contained the lighter found at the scene. "Do you recognize this, Mr. Exton?"

Jerald studied the lighter for a moment. "I think I've got one just like it," he admitted. "Where did you find it?"

"Six feet from the body of Vernon Langridge."

"How do we know this is my client's lighter?" the lawyer

argued.

"Because it has his fingerprints on it, and only his fingerprints."

Jerald frowned. "Well, I've been at the bookstore, of course, to pick up Gwen. So I could have lost it then." He turned to his lawyer. "They can't prove I was there last night, can they? I mean, I could have lost it last week or last month." The lawyer seemed to regret having allowed his client to speak freely, for he now advised him to adopt a strict 'no comment' policy. Unfortunately for him, Jerald Exton wasn't a 'no comment' type of guy. So when Chase took out the book that was found in the young man's van and placed it on the table, instead of keeping his mouth shut, he immediately said, "Someone planted that in my van. Someone is trying to frame me, can't you see?"

The lawyer leaned in and urgently whispered something in the man's ear.

"But I had nothing to do with this whole business!" He directed a pleading sort of look at the detective. "You gotta believe me, buddy—I'm being set up here!"

"You are currently in a relationship with the victim's daughter, are you not?" asked Chase.

"Well, yeah. I suppose. I mean, we've been seeing each other, but it's all purely platonic."

"Are you quite sure about that? You could be charged with seducing a minor, Mr. Exton."

"Absolutely. I'm not an idiot, detective. I would never get involved with a girl of Gwen's age. We're great friends and we like each other a lot, but we've decided to wait until she's of age. But that didn't stop her dad from accusing me of all kinds of things and telling her she couldn't see me anymore."

"She wasn't overly concerned about her dad's warnings, though, was she?"

"No, she decided to ignore the old man's ravings. It's her

life, and she wasn't going to allow him to decide for her who she was and wasn't allowed to meet."

"So it's safe to say that Mr. Langridge was no great fan of yours?"

"He was no fan of mine, no. And I wasn't a fan of his either." The lawyer leaned in again, and there was more whispering, presumably reminding Jerald that adopting a strict 'no comment' stance was in his best interests. As it was, Jerald decided differently. "Look, I know how it looks, but I didn't do this, all right? Okay, so maybe the old man didn't like me, and I wasn't too fond of him either, for the way he treated Gwen and tried to stop her from seeing me, but that doesn't mean I killed him. Gwen loved her dad. He meant the world to her. Why would I try to get rid of the guy and hurt her in the process?"

"This book," said Chase, patting the Mark Twain volume, "is worth twenty-five thousand. Plus the contents of the safe, the cash register, two laptops, a phone, and whatever else was stolen—I'd say that gives you plenty of reason to break into the store. Especially since you have an illegal substance habit to finance."

Jerald held up a warning finger. "That's in the past, detective. I'm done with all of that, and you know it. Okay, so I got in trouble a couple of years back, but I'm clean now, and I've put all of that behind me. You understand?"

"So what happened, Jerald?" asked Chase. "You figured you'd rob your sweetheart's dad, lift a couple of nice first editions from his shop and sell them, only you hadn't counted on him catching you in action? So you felt compelled to shut him up once and for all? I can certainly appreciate your point of view. The guy was a nuisance, trying to stop his daughter from being involved with you, so getting rid of him was a prospect you couldn't pass up?"

"No!" said Jerald, springing up from his chair before

settling down again. "You've got it all wrong, man! I would never do such a thing. Not the break-in, or the murder, or anything."

"So how do you explain the lighter? And the first edition found in your van?"

He shook his head. "I don't know, man. Like I said, someone must have planted it there, trying to implicate me in this terrible business. I mean, I don't keep my van locked. Anyone could have snuck in and put that book there. And as far as my lighter is concerned, I must have dropped it when I last set foot in the place—and it wasn't last night, because I was home when it happened."

Chase now placed a number of pictures on the table. They offered a stark view of the murder victim as taken at the scene. Jerald winced, and even the lawyer looked shocked. "Can you explain this?" asked Chase, as he tapped a picture of the dead man.

"I don't understand," Jerald admitted.

"This piece of paper. It was found stuffed in Mr. Langridge's mouth," said Chase. "According to Gwen, it's a page from the manuscript he was working on."

"I... I have no idea," Jerald said.

"Where did you find the manuscript, Jerald? And why did you find it necessary to put this in Mr. Langridge's mouth? It was a very cruel thing to do, wouldn't you agree?"

"Like I said, I had nothing to do with this, so I really can't help you."

The lawyer now piped up, "I think this interview has gone on long enough, Detective Kingsley. I would like to consult with my client now, if I may."

Chase, who felt he had a strong case against the kid, granted the request and left the room. For a moment, the lawyer and Jerald conducted a whispered conversation, then Jerald hung his head. He knew how much trouble he was in.

CHAPTER 15

"What I find odd," said Odelia when Chase had joined us in the little room that granted a good view of the goings-on in the interview room next door, "is that nothing else was found in Jerald's van. No murder weapon, no contents of that safe, laptops... Only the book and nothing else."

"He must have hidden the rest of the items," said Chase. "Or disposed of them."

As it was, the van was being turned inside out at that very moment, and also the Exton home, so there was still a good chance that the other items would be found.

But Odelia didn't look convinced. "It's all a little... too convenient, don't you think? I mean, what killer would be stupid enough to leave his lighter lying around for us to find? Not to mention that book? Jerald doesn't strike me as stupid, so why wouldn't he have hidden the book as well? He must have known that he was one of the first people we would look at in connection to the murder of his girlfriend's dad, considering their fractious relationship. So why didn't he take more precautions to hide his involvement?"

"You think he's telling the truth?" asked Chase. He was leaning against the desk located in the corner of the small space. "That he was framed?"

"It's possible," said Odelia. "At any rate, I wouldn't discount the possibility."

"Let's wait and see what the search turns up, and the house-to-house." Chase's officers were going door-to-door to talk to the Extons' neighbors to see if they could shed some light on Jerald's movements of the night before.

"If I were you, I wouldn't close the investigation just yet. I'd keep looking at possible other suspects."

Chase shrugged. He was an old-fashioned detective in that sense: when it looks like a duck and quacks like a duck, chances are that it is a duck. And obviously, in his opinion, everything pointed to Jerald because he was the killer. But to humor his wife, he was willing to go the extra mile and keep his options open. Which meant he wouldn't be closing the case just yet.

Which also meant we had to keep investigating. And I was just about to offer my personal opinion when Odelia carefully scooped me up, looked me deeply in the eyes, and said warmly, "And now let's take our patient to see the doctor, shall we?"

* * *

IT DIDN'T TAKE us more than ten minutes to arrive at the vet, and in spite of my protestations, it soon became clear that I was going to receive the full treatment—yet again!

"It's for your own good, Max," Dooley said as we sat in Vena Aleman's waiting room. It reeked of the desperation and the cold dread of countless pets who had gone before me. Like lambs being led to the slaughter, hundreds, if not thousands of our brethren and sistren must have sat there just like me, images of the horrors that were about to be perpetrated on them passing before their mind's eye and turning their spines to jelly and their insides to a maelstrom of naked anguish and terror.

"It's all very easy for you to say, Dooley," I said with a touch of asperity. "But you're not the one who's about to be poked and jabbed and subjected to untold torture."

"I'll hold your paw if you like," Dooley suggested. "And Odelia can hold your other paw while you're being examined."

The only paw I was prepared to extend was to the person who could get me out of there, but by now I was starting to suspect such a person didn't exist. Before long it was my turn, and as Vena hoisted me up on her examination table, and addressed me in that hale and hearty manner of hers, designed to put the fear of God into any pet that was unfortunate enough to cross the beefy vet's path, I was ready to commit my soul to the heavens and my mortal remains to science.

For a few moments, as she interrogated Odelia on the circumstances of my mishap, as they called it, she proceeded to prod me gently in the tummy, all the while intently looking for any signs of distress on my part. And I have to admit, a few of the spots she prodded were sore, and the treatment disagreeable to a degree.

"Hmm," she said when all was said and done. "I don't think he's broken anything. As far as I can tell, he's got a few bruises, but nothing serious. Though to know for sure, I'd have to take an X-ray, of course."

I directed a look of panic at Odelia. "No X-rays, please!"

"X-rays don't hurt, Max," Dooley assured me. "They might give you cancer, but they don't hurt."

"But I don't want to get cancer!" I cried.

"Better get those X-rays," Odelia advised. "Just to be on

the safe side. According to what I heard, he really got himself stuck in that window, and since he's a pretty hefty fellow, his weight may have contributed to some internal damage."

Vena nodded. She agreed with this diagnosis one hundred percent. Then again, any opportunity for her to run more tests or to subject us to one of her doomsday machines, she will gladly take. That's the kind of woman she is!

And so I was hoisted in front of a machine, strapped in for the duration, since I couldn't be relied upon to stay still, and moments later my picture was taken—and not in a fun way either!

"It won't take long," Vena assured me when she entered the room again and released me from my predicament. I had already pictured myself being zapped by a lightning bolt of doom, my insides lighting up like a Christmas tree before turning to putty, but I have to admit that the whole process of being X-rayed was suspiciously painless and spectacle-free. No sparks had flown, and I hadn't looked death in the eye.

And as she examined the images on her computer, she quickly came to the conclusion that I was A-okay and that her initial determination that I was as fit as a fiddle, apart from some slight bruising, had been correct after all.

"Your Max is absolutely fine, Odelia," she assured our human. "I think all that fat he's carrying around his waistline acted as insulation and prevented further damage. So in a sense, you could say this is the first time his being overweight worked to his advantage. Though I would still advise you to put him on a diet again."

"Oh, dear," said Odelia.

You see? With people like Vena Aleman, you simply cannot win!

CHAPTER 16

While Max was being subjected to the unwanted ministrations of what could possibly be the least popular person in all of cat-dom, his friends Harriet and Brutus were enjoying a leisurely time. After Gran and Scarlett's release from prison and having cleared their names as the possible Pancake Burglar, both women had returned home to lick their proverbial wounds. Gran had decided not to go to work today and had advised her son-in-law, Tex, of same. Scarlett figured she might as well keep her friend company, for they were both feeling aggrieved after a night spent in the lockup but also more impelled than ever to catch the real culprit in the act.

And so, while the neighborhood watch devised schemes and plans to draw out the Pancake Burglar and make sure that this time he didn't get away, Harriet and Brutus decided to do some brainstorming of their own. On the couch. After having eaten their fill. And after taking a refreshing nap. Those brain cells need plenty of rest and recreation, after all, not to mention sustenance.

Harriet was the first to wake up, and as she did, her eye

fell on Gran's tablet that she had left lying around. So Harriet flicked the device to life, eager to check some of her favorite sites—as there were 'Preening Persians,' 'Prettiest Persians in the World,' and of course, 'The Persian Perspective,' which was a hard-hitting news site that purported to offer a look at the world from a cat's point of view. But as she started up the tablet, the site she actually landed on was called 'The Biographer's Dream.' As she studied it, she saw that it offered to write and print an autobiography simply by answering a couple of easy questions for anyone who wished to regale their friends and family with their memoirs.

"Oh, she shouldn't have," Harriet murmured as she saw that an account had already been set up, paid for and everything, and now all she had to do was fill in the questionnaire and voila! In a mere matter of hours, her biography would be ready to be distributed.

Brutus yawned and stretched. "What's that?" he asked.

"Gran. I told her last night that I also would like to write my autobiography, just like she is doing, and she's already gone and set up this whole site for me. All I have to do is answer a couple of easy questions, and the computer does the rest."

"It writes an entire autobiography from scratch? But how?"

"It's called artificial intelligence, snuggle bear. It takes your answers to these questions about your past and turns it into a written text. Isn't that amazing?"

"It is," Brutus said, though he didn't look as impressed as he should have been. Then again, he'd only just woken up, of course, so his brain wasn't yet working at full capacity.

"I'm going to do it now," said Harriet as she clicked the button to commence. "And I'll have my autobiography shipped..." She studied the screen. A pop-up had appeared, asking her if she wanted to delete her previous answers and start afresh. And since she couldn't remember having answered any questions, she decided it must be a glitch and pressed 'Yes.' Before long, she was going through the list of questions, answering each in as truthful a manner as she could, from the moment she was born to the color of her mother's eyes, to the place where she had grown up, and so on and so forth.

"It's a lot of questions," said Brutus, having placed his head on his front paws.

"It's a lot of life I've lived," she riposted. She didn't mind the time spent on this if the end result lived up to her expectations, which she just knew it would.

"What are you going to do with it when it's done?" asked Brutus.

"Um... sell it, of course. Amazon, Barnes & Noble, our local bookstores—put it up at the library. According to this site, it will be made available everywhere—all around the world, in fact."

"Oh, wow," said Brutus. "Ain't that something?"

Presidents and movie stars had written their autobiographies, and they had sold millions of copies, so why not her? She could just imagine her autobiography topping the bestseller charts. She might even be interviewed on live television and be asked to sit next to those late-night chat people who liked to joke so much all the time. Or the morning chat show people, who were so earnest and kind. Before long, she'd be the celebrity and star she had always known she truly was.

She sighed happily as she moved to the next section, dealing with her adolescence, whatever that was. "The good thing is that this is all multiple choice," she told her beloved.

"Multiple choice, huh?"

"Yeah, easy peasy."

"I could do it."

"Oh, sure. Once my autobiography is ready, we should do yours, angel face. Make it a double whammy."

"Maybe you can do it for me," said Brutus, the lazybones. He yawned again.

She laughed. "I can't write your autobiography for you, baby doodle."

"Sure you can. These famous people do it all the time. Or do you really think they write their own autobiographies? They get some ghostwriter to do it for them. It's all the rage. So you be my ghostwriter, all right?" His eyes had drooped closed again. "You can do it," he murmured, then promptly dozed off.

He was right, of course. Celebrities might be good at whatever it was they did, but they weren't bestselling writers, so they got some other person to write their autobiographies for them. So maybe she could turn this into a regular gig? After she had written her own autobiography, she could simply move on to the next one. Brutus first, of course, and then Max, Dooley, Odelia, Chase, Marge, Tex... Heck, why limit herself to her own family? She could write Wilbur Vickery's autobiography or Father Reilly's. All she needed to do was talk to Kingman and Shanille and get all the juicy gossip from their humans' lives, and she was in business. Before long, she'd have an excellent business going—very lucrative! And all for the couple of bucks the site asked for every book it published with the assistance of this nifty artificial intelligence thingamajig. Now who could ask for more?

CHAPTER 17

After my ordeal at the vet, I was glad to be back at Odelia's office where I fully intended to take a prolonged nap and take advantage of the respite. And just as I'd circled my favorite place in the corner of her office three times and was ready to settle down, she piped up. "Listen to this, Max. 'Dear Odelia Kingsley, you should look into Kenton Clarey. He is a nasty piece of filth, and it wouldn't surprise me if he murdered Vernon Langridge. His wife is sick, so he needs the money, especially since his book contract was canceled and no more money is coming in. Just ask that horrible man how jealous he was of Vernon's success!'" She looked up from reading the letter. "Arrived just now."

"Who sent it?"

"A well-wisher."

"Sounds absolutely legit."

She grinned. "It's still worth looking into, wouldn't you say?"

I have to admit I was still a little annoyed with my human after having put me through the wringer with Vena.

And I had this sneaking suspicion she had done it in retribution for the cheese incident. But since basically I'm a kind and forgiving sort of cat, I decided to let bygones be bygones and focus on this email that had arrived. "Mickey didn't mention anything about a sick wife when we talked to him. Or the fact that Kenton's book contract was canceled."

"Who's Mickey?"

"Mickey 5. Kenton's pug."

"Even dogs don't always tell the truth, Max," she pointed out. "They might lie to protect their humans, or it's possible Mickey simply didn't know."

"Oh, he would know," I said. "If Kenton had a sick wife and was in financial trouble, a loyal dog would know. Which means he lied to us."

"Or he could have decided not to tell us the truth," said Dooley.

"That's the same thing as lying, Dooley," I said.

"No, it's not. If I don't tell you that you've got a fresh freckle on your nose, that doesn't constitute a lie, does it? That's simply me choosing not to tell you."

I stared at my friend. "Do I have a fresh freckle on my nose?"

"No, you don't. It's just an example."

"Well, if Mickey knew about the book contract and the sick spouse and didn't tell us, it was a lie by omission," I said determinedly. "And I would very much like to talk to him again."

"That's quite the coincidence," said Odelia. "Because I would like to talk to Kenton again." And with these words, she picked up her phone and called her husband. And since she put her phone on speaker, we could follow the conversation.

"So Kenton had a motive, huh?" said Chase.

"Looks like it. At least if this well-wisher is to be believed."

"I wonder who he is. Better give me that letter. I'll ask our techies to take a stab at establishing the letter writer's identity. Could be the Extons trying to deflect blame away from their son."

"What did Uncle Alec say?"

"To throw the book at him. He feels we've got our man and didn't agree to keep our lines of inquiry open for now."

"He's ordering you to close the investigation?"

"Strongly suggesting is how I would interpret it. But he trusts our judgment, so he's agreed to look at the other suspects and see if we can't build a case against them."

She smiled. "So you trust my judgment, and my uncle trusts your judgment."

"Pretty much," he said. He paused. "I've looked at Jerald Exton's arrest record, and it's true what he said. Last time he was picked up is three years ago, and he hasn't put a foot wrong since. Looks like he really did turn his life around. I also talked to Gwen, and she confirmed that Jerald insisted they shouldn't start dating until she turned eighteen, much to her frustration."

"Jerald isn't going anywhere," Odelia pointed out. "And neither is the evidence against him. So it doesn't hurt to look at other people. Like this Kenton Clarey. If he really is in dire financial straits, he had an excellent motive for the murder. Though why he would stash that book at Jerald's camper instead of selling it beats me."

"We still don't know what was in that safe," Chase pointed out. "Maybe there were other, even more valuable first editions, and Jerald is right, and that Mark Twain book was planted at his van to throw us off the scent."

They arranged to pay another visit to Mr. Clarey, but first, Odelia had an article to write about last night's murder.

She might be a police consultant, but her main job is still as a reporter for the *Gazette*. And if she hoped to keep that job, there were articles to write, especially when a prominent member of our community had been found dead under suspicious circumstances.

Before long, she was hard at work, and Dooley and I were fast asleep. In other words, after our world was turned upside down, things were back to normal. And a good thing, too!

CHAPTER 18

Scarlett had decided to take her great-nephew Kevin to the zoo. Even though Kevin was basically a nerd and liked nothing better than to spend his time holed up in his room playing computer games or working out complicated mathematical problems, he had one secondary passion, and that was the animal kingdom. It didn't exactly seem congruent with the nerdy side of his personality, but his mom and dad, and in fact the entire family, were greatly pleased and relieved, for it offered him the opportunity to be out and about in nature—or, as was the case today, the zoo.

"So you actually got arrested last night?" Kevin asked.

"I was. Thrown in the slammer along with the other crooks," Scarlett confirmed.

"Cool! And how was it? Did you only get water to drink and moldy bread to eat?"

"Oh, no. We got a nice cup of coffee from the police precinct coffee machine, and in the morning we even got breakfast delivered by Vesta's son." Alec had looked slightly aggrieved, but then that was often the case when he had to spring his mother from prison yet again. That was the problem with the neighborhood watch: it operated on a fine line between legality and illegality, and even though they tried hard to stay on the right side of that line, they simply couldn't help but stray into the world of crime from time to time. When you're trying to catch a crook, sometimes those lines blurred, and that couldn't be helped.

"So are you going out there again tonight?" asked Kevin, who loved this side of his great-aunt's life to such a degree that he had been instrumental on numerous occasions in helping them out in their pursuit to rid their lovely hometown of crime and criminals of all forms.

"Of course. The Pancake Burglar got away, and since there are still people out there who seem to believe that Vesta and I are the Pancake Burglar, we have to catch him in the act. If only to clear our own names."

"It's silly of people to think you could be a criminal, Auntie Scarlett," said Kevin. He was licking from his ice cream cone and enjoying this afternoon at the zoo tremendously, as he always did. "I mean, you don't even look like a criminal."

"And what do criminals look like?" she asked, vastly amused by this conversation.

"Well, like crooks, of course. You're entirely too pretty to be a crook."

She smiled. "Why, thanks for the compliment, Kev. But I'll have you know that there are also very pretty crooks. Femme fatales, for instance."

"Oh, I know all about that," he said, as if he was the world's foremost expert on the phenomenon of the femme fatale.

"You do, do you?"

"Of course." He cast a quick sideways glance at her. "Okay, so now that you mention it, I guess you could pass as a pretty effective femme fatale. But only if I didn't know you."

She laughed. "Thanks, bud. Now let's go and see the tigers, shall we?"

Ever since he was little, Kevin had loved the big cats. They were so majestic and mysterious that he could look at them for hours. And though he was a teenager now and no longer a little kid, that fascination hadn't left him.

They arrived at the big cat pavilion, and Scarlett saw that some kind of commotion was taking place. Several zookeepers were standing around, and of the tigers themselves, there was no trace. She hoped nothing bad had happened. Tigers might look pretty cool, to use Kevin's parlance, but they were also dangerous when approached in the wrong fashion. She addressed one of the female zookeepers who stood leaning against the fence. "What's going on?"

"It's one of the tigers," she explained. "Someone broke in here last night or early this morning and shaved off part of his coat."

"Shaved a tiger? But who? And why?"

The zookeeper shrugged. "No idea. Must be a madman, though. Who in their right mind would voluntarily enter a tiger's cage to shave off part of their fur? It's a crazy thing to do. But of course we're all very upset. If they could get into the cages so easily, who knows what they might do next."

"Have you told the police?"

"We have. But they don't seem all that interested," said the woman. "The chief of police is getting married, and also, there's been a murder, so they're busy with that. Too busy to bother with us."

"Oh, that's too bad," said Scarlett, who felt for that poor tiger and also the zookeepers who were understandably upset. "Is there anything I can do?"

The woman eyed her strangely. "I'm sure we can handle it, miss..."

"Canyon. Scarlett Canyon. I'm a member of the neighborhood watch, you see. We patrol the streets at night and try to catch bad people in the act of doing bad things so good people can sleep easy."

Hope made the zookeeper's eyes sparkle. "The neighborhood watch?"

"That's right. Last night we almost caught the Pancake Burglar, only he managed to get away. So we'll be out on patrol again tonight to look for him. And while we're at it, we might as well pass by the zoo if you like."

"Oh, could you?" said the woman. "The police don't seem to care, and we're seriously understaffed as it is, so we can't cover the entire zoo by ourselves."

"Don't you worry about a thing," said Kevin. "My great-aunt is the best at what she does. If this crazy person comes back tonight, she'll catch him for sure."

"Well, thanks for the vote of confidence, Kev," said Scarlett with a laugh. "But yeah, we'll give you a helping hand."

The woman, whose name was Shara Jarram and had been a zookeeper at the Hampton Cove Zoo for ten years now, was happy to give her all the information she needed. A couple of her colleagues had volunteered to keep an eye out tonight, covering the big cat pavilion. But that left a huge swath of the zoo unobserved. And that's where Scarlett and Vesta would come in. They would plug the holes in the zoo's security, so to speak, and try to catch this... animal shaver person.

Though how they were going to cover both the Pancake Burglar and the zoo, she didn't know. But then she got it. Lately, their two other members of the watch had been more absent than not. Wilbur Vickery claimed he had to get up early to open his store, and Father Reilly often had early mass. But this time there would be no excuses. The neighborhood watch had been called upon to jump to the rescue, and so Wilbur and Francis would have to heed that call.

As she and Kevin left the big cat sanctuary, the teenager asked if he could also join tonight's patrol. "I'll ask your mom and dad," said Scarlett. "And if they agree, of course you can join."

"We have to save those poor tigers from being shaved," Kevin said earnestly. "Otherwise, pretty soon they won't have any fur left, and then where will we be?"

"We'll have to knit them a sweater," Scarlett quipped, but she could tell that Kevin didn't take this lightly. He really cared about these animals and would do whatever it took to keep them safe from harm. She rubbed his back. "We'll make a neighborhood watch member of you yet."

"We'll catch this man, Auntie Scarlett. Just you wait and see."

CHAPTER 19

To say that Alec Lip wasn't feeling on top of the world would be a serious understatement. Even as the most beautiful day of his life approached, he was starting to feel that he was part of a great wave that rolled on like an avalanche with him merely a hapless participant—a minor cog in a big wheel. When he had asked Charlene if she wanted to be his wife, he had envisioned a small wedding. A family affair. Just the ceremony at Town Hall and then perhaps lunch at a nearby restaurant for both their immediate loved ones. But then Charlene said she would love to get married in church, and even though technically that wasn't possible, since they both had been married before and divorced, a quick word with Father Francis Reilly had revealed that there was a way they could pull it off.

And then, of course, Charlene had indicated that because she was the mayor, she couldn't very well pretend that her wedding wasn't a major event in the lives of her citizens, so she pretty much owed it to them to organize something. A reception at Town Hall, maybe, or a party in Town Square. And so the thing had started growing beyond their control and snowballed into the beast they were now contending with. First, the wedding at St. John's Church, then the reception at Town Hall, spilling over into Town Square where a great picnic was to be organized, and in the evening, the big feast people had all been waiting for, though fortunately that would be restricted to a smaller crowd.

All in all, Alec felt he would very much like to skip his own wedding at this point, or maybe fall asleep on the morning and wake up when it was all done and dusted. He had suggested to Charlene that they might elope, just like his niece Odelia had done when her wedding to Chase had gotten out of hand in a similar way. But Charlene said they couldn't possibly do that. She was the mayor, and he was the chief of police, and what kind of example would that set for the community they had both sworn to serve? Well, this wedding was part of that commitment, whether they liked it or not, and it would go down in history as the grandest affair.

Okay, so maybe not as grand as some of the society or celebrity weddings they sometimes got, but a big to-do nevertheless. She had also assured him that things would work out since they always did, and that the wedding planner they had hired would make sure everything ran smoothly.

He now stared at himself in the mirror and didn't like what he saw.

"I look like a clown," he grumbled to his sister.

"I think you look great," said Marge, who stood eyeing him critically, like the expert she professed to be. "Though you'll probably have to hem those pants."

The salesperson who was assisting them seemed to agree. "It's not easy to find something that fits," she revealed, unintentionally indicating that Alec's body shape was unusual. It was true that he looked more like a bowling pin than an actual person. Even though Charlene had told him that he should go on a diet to look his best on his wedding day, what with the pressures of work and figuring he had plenty of time, that hadn't happened. On the contrary, it now looked as if he had gained many pounds instead of losing them.

"I think it might work," Marge said as she bit her lip.

It didn't add to his sense of well-being and self-confidence, he had to say. When had their wedding become a fashion show with him in the role of the star model? He knew he wasn't the world's most handsome man, but Charlene had never seemed to mind and loved him anyway. And now, all of a sudden, his many physical defects were being highlighted, and frantic efforts were being made to hide them as best as possible. But it was too late now. The top of his head: hairless to a degree and no more time to get a hair transplant. His belly: rotund! His legs: short! His pallor: ruddy!

He sighed deeply. "I'll never be able to pull this off, will I, Marge?"

"Oh, you'll pull it off all right," his sister assured him, and even the salesperson seemed to agree that things weren't at the hopeless stage. Yet.

"You could always wear Spanx, sir," the girl suggested.

"Spanx? What's Spanx?" he asked.

"It's designed to make you look... tighter," Marge said.

"Tight is good, right?" He did want to look tighter. A lot tighter, actually.

"Do you sell Spanx?" asked Marge.

"We do. Mostly for women, but we have a small assortment for men."

She disappeared into the bowels of the store and returned with a box from which she took a funny-looking item. It was black and looked like a T-shirt, only thicker and with a zipper in the front. "Try this one," she said and handed him the strange contraption.

So he disappeared into the fitting booth for a moment, where he tried in vain to squeeze into the thing. He now realized what a sausage must feel like.

"And? How are you doing?" Marge shouted from behind the curtain.

"It's very... tight," he said.

"That's the idea. The tighter the better."

He pulled in his belly, took a deep breath, and tried to zip up the thing. "I think I did it," he said in a high, strained voice. "But is it normal that now I can't breathe anymore?"

"I'll ask if she's got a bigger size," Marge said.

And as he tried to unzip again, he discovered that the zipper was stuck. Try as he might, he simply couldn't get the thing off! And to add insult to injury, suddenly the zipper broke off. As he held the implement in his hand, he wondered if he was going to die. Death by Spanx. Was that even a thing?

"Alec?" said Marge, who had returned. "Are you still in there?"

"I'm stuck!" he said in a high, reedy voice.

"Are you decent?"

"Stuck!" he squeaked with some effort.

She threw the curtain wide, and he found himself looking into the startled faces of both his sister and that same salesgirl. For a moment, they simply stared back at him, then their faces colored as they tried not to laugh at his predicament.

"It's not funny!" he squeaked. "Not funny at all!"

"Let's get you unstuck," said the girl.

It took the concerted effort of herself, two of her colleagues, and Marge, but finally they managed to save him from his harrowing situation. The upshot was that he could breathe again. The downside was that they'd had to cut him out of that 'shapewear' as the thing was called, with a pair of scissors, which meant he'd have to pay for it since it was now kaput. And when Marge suggested he try a larger size, he quickly said no way, thank you very much!

Faced with a client who had almost died on their premises, the three salespeople decided to use their creativity and their combined experience to make the best of what they had to work with. Two hours and many iterations later, Alec stood admiring himself in that same mirror. Instead of looking like a clown, he actually looked almost distinguished. He even looked... hunky. Or so Marge claimed.

"Charlene is going to be over the moon," she gushed.

And it had to be said that they had performed miracles. It was all down to the cut of the clothes, according to the head saleswoman, who had been most instrumental in making him look presentable. "You can hide a lot if you pick the right design," she said.

He was grateful—partly because this meant that his ordeal was almost over, but also because they had made him look more handsome than he had looked in years.

"Thank you, ladies," he said brokenly. "I was starting to despair."

Their smiles told him that they, too, had experienced defeat staring them in the face. But they had managed to wrestle it down and turn the situation around in an unparalleled display of determination. And so he invited all three of them to the wedding. What did it matter now? The whole town had been invited at this point, and besides, he was feeling magnanimous.

CHAPTER 20

"You look absolutely wonderful, darling!" Corinne Butterwick caroled as she admired her daughter's dress in the full-length mirror at Baskerville's, the well-known ladies' fashion store at the Timpermall. "Doesn't she look wonderful, Horace?"

Charlene's dad had been reading his newspaper and now looked up. For a moment, he seemed unsure where he was, then gave her a smile and nodded. "Your mother is right. You do look stunning, darling."

Charlene wasn't so sure, though. The original dress she had ordered weeks ago had unfortunately not been ready on time, and so at the last possible moment, she had to come into the store to pick a replacement. She felt truly sorry, for that original dress had been sublime—perfection. This one... Wasn't bad. But nothing could compare to her dream dress. When questioned why they couldn't get it ready on time, the woman who ran the boutique had given her some vague answer about the fabric not being available in sufficient quantities. Which was odd, since she thought the dress had been pretty much ready and only needed a few minor alterations to get it ready for the big day.

Then again, what could she do? If it wasn't ready, it wasn't ready. At least the store had offered her a handsome discount on this replacement dress, and if her mom's words were to be believed, it wasn't a bad choice. Not bad at all.

"I'm so excited that we're finally going to meet our in-laws," said Charlene's mother. "Aren't you excited, Horace?"

Charlene's dad had once again become engrossed in his paper, detailing all the latest financial news from Wall Street. "Mh?" he said distractedly. As a retired financier, he still kept a close eye on the financial markets, not least because he had a substantial investment portfolio that needed his attention, and also because it was a hobby of his. Throughout his long career as an investment banker at one of the bigger financial securities firms, Horace Butterwick had lived for his job, foregoing partaking in any other endeavor. While his colleagues worked on their forehand or their handicap or went fishing in Lake Ontario or hiking in the Adirondacks, all he ever cared about was the market. And now, a few years into his well-deserved retirement, that was still the case.

"Oh, just leave it," said Mom with a throwaway gesture. She was used to Dad's vagueness and the way he could get fully absorbed in his own affairs. Contrary to her husband, Corinne Butterwick did have hobbies. A lot of them, in fact. She was a member of so many clubs and charities it was hard to keep track. She also loved the enthralling wonders of the arts and went to the opera at least once a month, visited gallery openings, was a patron of several emerging young artists, and generally kept herself busier than ever. Today her project was to make sure her daughter looked her absolute best and that Charlene's wedding was the society event of the season, even though she wasn't entirely sure about her husband's antecedents. The few things Charlene had told them hadn't inspired a lot of confidence that marrying into 'that' family was the blessing Charlene thought it was.

"So tell me about the grandmother," said Mom. "I've heard so many stories... Is she really as eccentric as they make her out to be?"

"Well, she is a little eccentric, I guess," Charlene admitted.

"A little or a lot?"

"Just a touch."

"Mh." She gave her daughter a look of scrutiny. Clearly, Mom had heard a lot of gossip that had convinced her that Vesta Muffin was some kind of crazy person. And even though she might be eccentric, Vesta was far from crazy, Charlene felt. She could talk to cats, of course, which probably constituted eccentricity, but she wasn't going to tell her mother that, now was she?

"You'll find out all about her when you meet at the rehearsal dinner," she told her mom as she twirled around. The dress was a simple affair, quite without the usual frills and add-ons, but then that had been the store's point. Charlene wasn't the fresh-faced ingenue she had been when she had married her first husband Ricky and she had been fresh out of college and madly in love. Charlene's mom had warned her the marriage wouldn't last because Ricky was too wild for her, but she hadn't listened. It had soon transpired that Mom had been right all along, especially when Ricky had been arrested for fraud and embezzlement. The worst part was that the company he had stolen from was the same outfit Charlene's dad worked at. Ricky's father-in-law had put in a good word for him, and so when the young man turned out to possess a certain disinclination for honesty and had been on the verge of running away with ten million in an offshore account and his secretary, it had reflected quite badly on Charlene's dad, Ricky's mentor, whose career had hit a stalemate as a consequence.

An internal investigation and external audit had cleared Horace Butterwick of all wrongdoing, though, and the only blame that could be put squarely at his doorstep was that he was too naive, which wasn't a good quality for a banker, of course, but hardly constituted criminal intent.

"At least Alec isn't a crook," Mom said, her eyes shiny as she surveyed her daughter in the big mirror. "Quite the contrary. He's the one who catches them!" She laughed at this, pleased with her own little joke. Charlene wasn't laughing. She didn't enjoy being reminded of Ricky, who had betrayed not only her but also her father. Fortunately for them they had both come back from it, with Dad's career going from strength to strength in the final stretch, even becoming head of his division.

And Charlene had found Alec, of course. Her rock and the man she knew was the one for her and whom she loved with all her heart. And even though she knew that Alec wasn't all that crazy about the wedding as it was taking shape, figuring it had turned into an out-of-control juggernaut, she also knew that the only reason he went along with it was because he loved her in return.

"Will there be a lot of police at the wedding?" asked Mom with a touch of nervousness.

"I guess so," said Charlene. "Alec is the head of the police, so it stands to reason he would have invited his colleagues. Why?"

"Oh, nothing," said Mom as she wiped her nose with a tiny handkerchief. She plastered another smile onto her face. "I'm sure it will all go swimmingly!"

CHAPTER 21

As I could have predicted, our sojourn at Odelia's office was unfortunately cut short by the arrival of that letter. Moments later, Chase picked us up in front of the *Gazette* offices, and we were covering familiar terrain as he drove us to the home of Kenton Clarey. Odelia had taken a picture of the letter and had handed the original to Chase so he could glean possible fingerprints and all of that stuff.

"What puzzles me is why anyone would send a letter like this," Chase confessed as he drove his squad car with a steady hand along the streets of our fair town. "I mean, in this day and age and the ubiquity of the internet, nobody writes letters anymore, do they? So why didn't this anonymous letter writer send you an email instead?"

"Because emails are easier to trace?" Odelia suggested.

"Or maybe our letter writer is an older person," Chase suggested. "They're still used to writing letters, whereas the younger generation probably doesn't even know that letters exist. Or stamps, for that matter."

"Whatever the case, we'll know soon enough if the things

written in that letter are true or not. It might very well be the case that it's nothing but a pile of empty accusations and lies."

Somehow I had a feeling it wasn't. This letter writer, whoever he or she was, seemed to know a great deal about Kenton Clarey. Which once again led us back to Dooley's question: why hadn't Mickey told us the truth?

Chase parked his car in the driveway, right behind Kenton's BMW, and as we trudged up to the front door, the cop paused for a moment to admire the bestselling writer's wheels. Even though the pickup Chase drives isn't an old jalopy like Odelia's own specimen, it's not exactly a luxury car either. But then I guess Uncle Alec's budget doesn't exactly stretch to providing his officers with German luxury brand automobiles.

Like before, it didn't take long for Kenton to answer the doorbell, though when he saw us standing on his doorstep yet again, within hours of the first time, he seemed highly surprised. Presumably, he'd hoped to be rid of us after answering Chase's litany of questions. "Detective Kingsley," he said. "What brings you back so soon?" His brow was furrowed, so he must have realized that a return visit from the local constabulary is never a good sign.

"We have some more questions for you, Mr. Clarey," Chase explained. "May we come in?"

"Yes. Yes, of course," said Kenton, and stepped aside to allow us entry. "What questions would these be?" he asked once we had installed ourselves in his living room once more. I looked around for a sign of Mickey, but he appeared absent from the scene.

"We've received this letter," Odelia said and handed her phone to the writer.

He put on his reading glasses and took his time to study the letter. Then he shook his head. "Who wrote this?"

"We have no idea."

"Anonymous, huh? I should have known." His lips had turned into a fine line of dismay. For a moment, he rubbed his cheek, clearly trying to buy time while he pondered his response. Finally, he must have realized that only the truth would suffice, so he nodded. "It's true. My wife is very ill, and we are faced with certain financial constraints."

"What about your book contract? Has that been canceled?" asked Chase.

"It has," Kenton admitted. "The last book didn't sell as well as the ones before, and the publisher said that under these circumstances, they wouldn't renew the contract." He sighed. "Six books in, and I'm left without a publisher. My agent has contacted other publishing houses, but so far nobody seems willing to pick up the series. It's a tough time to be a writer, detective, and no mistake."

"Meanwhile, Vernon had sold *his* book. That must have stung."

"It did sting," said the author. "Especially since I was always the one who 'had it made,' so to speak. I was the one the others turned to for advice or to get in contact with my agent or my publisher. And now, all of a sudden, I was without a publishing deal, and if I'm not mistaken, my agent might drop me as well. If there's no money to be made, what's the point in keeping me on?"

"What about your wife?" asked Chase.

"What about her?"

"It says in the letter that her medical bills are costing you a small fortune and that you're in urgent need of a serious financial injection. Is this true?"

A pained look came over him. "It is. My wife... Well, I won't bore you with the medical details. Suffice it to say that her treatment is both costly and necessary. Without it…" He grimaced. "Let's just say I can't afford not to pay for the medical treatment she's currently receiving. But also, I can't afford the treatment, period. Which leaves me in a very difficult position indeed."

"The Mighty Pen had a lot of very valuable first editions on display. Did Vernon keep any of them in his safe?" asked Chase, seemingly changing tack.

Kenton looked puzzled. "Um, I guess he did. Yes, I believe so. Some of the books he had on offer were so valuable he kept them behind lock and key. Why?"

"The safe was emptied out by his attacker. Only one book has been found so far, with the others still missing."

"One book has been found?" Now this was news to the man.

"So if I understand you correctly, you find yourself in serious financial trouble, Mr. Carey. Not only that, but you need that money. It's not too much to say it's a matter of life and death, am I correct?"

"You are correct," said Kenton, shuffling uneasily.

"You told us that you were out walking your dog when Vernon was murdered. Do you still stand by that statement, sir?"

"I do, yes."

Chase exchanged a glance with Odelia, who looked down at her notes. Her meaning was clear: we needed to talk to that dog again—pronto!

"Where does your route take you, sir? Exactly?"

Kenton clearly saw the way the wind was blowing, for his features reddened considerably, and I could see beads of sweat forming on his brow. "Look, I had nothing to do with what happened to Vernon. It's true that I could use the money from the sale of those rare first editions of his, but I'm not a murderer or a thief, Detective Kingsley. I liked Vernon. He was a friend and a colleague. If worse comes to worst, I would have swallowed my pride and asked him for a loan, just to tide us over until I could sell my next book. I wasn't going to rob the man and then murder him. I still have options."

"But you also have your pride. The prestige you derive from being a published author. And now that's no longer the case, and the roles have suddenly been reversed, I can imagine how that must have felt to you."

"Rotten," he said. "It feels pretty rotten. Especially since I've spent years honing my craft and building the Marvin Amis brand, just to see it all go to waste." He wrung his hands, which were soft and perfectly manicured, not a callus in sight. "Look, I may be in a bad way right now, but I will come back from this. I still have my six-book series, which is still selling reasonably well, so I have royalty checks coming in on a regular basis. And I will find a new publisher. Maybe not one of the big five, but I have my readership, so all is not lost. It's a setback, not the end of the world." He gave us a pleading sort of look, and it was clear that the man was in some serious trouble. But did that mean he was also a murderer?

At that moment, Mickey sauntered in. He looked as surprised to see us as Kenton had. "Back already?" he asked. "I thought you asked all the questions you had to ask?"

"You haven't exactly been entirely truthful with us, have you, Mickey?" I asked.

The look of embarrassment he gave us spoke volumes.

"I know," he admitted. "Look, the thing you have to understand is that Kenton wasn't my first human. That was Mrs. Hardcastle, and she did not like dogs. Not in the least. I was supposed to be a guard dog, you see, after her house had been burgled. Her kids told her to get a dog, and so she did, against her better judgment. And I may be many things, but I'm not a guard dog. So after the honeymoon was over, Mrs. Hardcastle quickly became disenchanted with me and decided to drop me off at the pound. Where I languished for three long months—the worst time of my life, I don't mind telling you—until finally, the Clareys came along and adopted me. They'd just lost Mickey number four, and so I became Mickey number five. A name I like a lot better than the name Mrs. Hardcastle christened me."

"What was the name?" I asked.

"Fluffy," he said ruefully. "I mean, do I look like a Fluffy?"

Dooley and I both suppressed a grin. "Mickey definitely suits you better," I admitted. Then I turned serious again. "But you still haven't told us why you lied."

"Well, isn't it obvious? I love the Clareys. They saved my life. So why would I go and blab about their private affairs to the first cat that comes along? No offense."

"None taken," I said because I could understand where Mickey was coming from. If a dog dropped by the house and asked me a lot of questions about Odelia, I very much doubt if I would tell them anything likely to cause trouble for my humans either. "Look, the only thing we need to know is if Kenton really did take you for that walk. And if at any point he went into The Mighty Pen."

Dooley and I waited with bated breath while Mickey took his time to respond. It almost felt like one of those game shows where the presenter deliberately stretches out the response to build up suspense!

Finally, Mickey shook his head. "He got home from his writers' group meeting, looked in on his wife, and took me for a walk. This must have been around ten-thirty. We walked for about half an hour and then returned to the house."

"And did you at any time go anywhere near The Mighty Pen?"

"No, we did not. And Kenton was never out of my sight. Does that answer your question?"

I gave him a smile. "It does. It does indeed."

"Look, I know the guy, all right? He's not the murdering type. He can't even kill a spider in the bathroom. Captures it in a glass jar and puts it out. He might look tough and talk tough, but he's a softie through and through."

"Odd, for a person who used to be in the military."

He grinned. "Oh, but he was never in the military. That's just something he made up to give himself credibility with the fans. Thriller readers love that stuff, you see. They gobble it up. And since he writes military thrillers, I guess he figured it couldn't hurt to add a flourish to his author bio."

"It's not a flourish when it's an outright lie," I pointed out.

"So what did he do before he became a writer?" asked Dooley.

"He was a used-car salesman. And a good one, too. So if push comes to shove, and nobody wants his books anymore, he could always go back to his old profession. Though I have a feeling he'd consider that a personal defeat."

I studied the man's profile. He might not be ex-military, but he did have that military bearing: back ramrod straight, eyes blazing with a certain authority. Even the way he spoke sounded clipped and self-assured. I could imagine that Kenton Clarey was an intensely proud man, so having to admit defeat probably wasn't in his dictionary.

"Look, can I give you a piece of advice?" Kenton said now. "Go and talk to Marina Steele." He shook his head. "I hate to talk bad about a colleague, but if anyone wrote that nasty letter, it's her."

"She knows about your canceled book deal?" asked Odelia.

"I think she suspects. I was on the phone with my agent before the last meeting of our writers' group, and I think she must have overheard. The thing is, she shouldn't throw stones at other people because she has her own secrets that she hasn't shared with anyone."

"What secrets, Mr. Clarey?" asked Chase.

He took a deep breath. "Marina was in love with Vernon. Crazy about the man. But Vernon was still in love with his wife, which didn't sit well with Marina, who had hoped that after the divorce, she might become the new Mrs. Langridge. But Vernon didn't see it that way. To him, she was just a friend and a colleague. And Marina hated that. She hated it so much that…"

"That she might have murdered the man she loved?"

Kenton nodded. "You know what they say: if I can't have you…" He gave the detective a look of significance. "…nobody can."

CHAPTER 22

We had just gotten into the car when Odelia got a call from her editor, Dan Goory. He told her that another letter had arrived at the office, this time hand-delivered, though unfortunately he hadn't seen who had slipped it through the mailbox. The letter writer encouraged Odelia to talk to Marina Steele in connection to the Langridge murder.

"I'll quote from the letter, shall I?" Dan's voice suggested.

"Please do," Odelia said as she darted a look of concern at her husband.

"Okay, here goes. 'Marina and Vernon were passionate lovers—at least in Marina's vivid imagination! In every single one of her ridiculous and ridiculously atrocious bodice rippers, Vernon is the dashingly handsome hero, and Marina the comely heroine who throws herself at his mercy, chest heaving and cheeks blushing. Pity she lacked the courage to confess her great love to the man himself, or otherwise the world would have been spared such an odious display of bad taste!'"

"Obviously not a fan," Odelia remarked.

"No, I would say not," Dan agreed. "So have you talked to this Marina Steele person yet? If her romantic aspirations were rejected by Vernon, she may have lashed out. She may even have killed the man she was in love with."

"We have talked to her," Odelia said. "But she didn't mention being in love with Vernon."

"Well, I'll let you get on with it," said Dan and rang off.

Chase started up the car, and I had the distinct impression I knew where we were headed next. Obviously, the romance novelist had lied to us, or at least not given us the full picture. But then that was hardly surprising since most people hate to admit the truth, especially when it incriminates them in any way.

"We should have talked to Meena," Dooley said. "When she said Meena was staying with a friend, it was obviously a ruse to throw us off the scent. Meena was probably there when Marina was standing over the dead body of her lover, the smoking gun still in her hand, tears streaming down her face as her heart broke into a million pieces as she watched him huff out his final breath."

I grinned. "Have you been reading romance novels again, Dooley?"

He gave me a shamefaced look. "Marge had one lying around that she'd brought home with her from the library, and I may have leafed through the pages."

"It wasn't one of Marina's herself, was it?"

"It could have been. If it was, she's not as bad a writer as this letter person seems to think."

"I wonder who this well-wisher could possibly be," I said as the car lurched into motion. "Whoever it is, they seem to know an awful lot about the people who were in Vernon's life."

"Could it be his daughter?" asked Dooley. "After all, she

was closest to Vernon because she actually lived with the man for seventeen years."

"It's possible. But if she really wants to help us find her father's killer, then why do it in such a roundabout way? Why not simply tell us straight out what she knows?"

"Maybe she feels it's more effective this way? These letters do grab our attention, don't they?"

"That, they sure do."

For the second time that day, we met Marina Steele, only this time we found her at home and not at the restaurant since she only worked mornings, so she could have the afternoons and evenings to work on her novels. She must have been hard at work on her next book because when she opened the door to admit us into her apartment, she looked distracted and her hair was a mess, as if she had been twisting it around her finger, trying to come up with ideas for drama to put her characters through.

"Yes?" she said as she stared at us. "What do you want?"

"Some new information has come to our attention, Miss Steele," Chase explained. "Information that unfortunately compels us to have another little chat with you."

She sighed deeply, and I felt for her. She probably had been in the midst of a passionate scene, and now she had to talk to the cops again. It was enough to dampen anyone's spirit, especially one as artistic as this young novelist. "Come in," she said, but I could see that her heart wasn't in it.

Contrary to what I had expected, her apartment was tidy to a fault. No dust bunnies under the couch, no remnants of a meal in the kitchen sink, and even her windows had been washed. Clearly, Miss Steele was a very neat person. My main objective in this visit was to find and talk to Meena, of course, the dog Marina had mentioned at our earlier meeting. We finally found the Maltese terrier hiding underneath one of the couches, as reluctant to speak to us as Marina was to talk to our humans. They say dogs take after their owners, or is it the other way around, and this was clear evidence of this peculiar fact.

"Hey there," I said to the doggie once we had discovered her hiding place. "Could we please have a word with you? We're not going to harm you, you know."

"We like dogs," Dooley added for good measure. "Some of our best friends are dogs."

"I don't believe you," said Meena, who was obviously the shy and retiring sort. "Cats hate dogs, everybody knows that, and you two look really vicious."

It was the first time anyone had called me vicious, and even though I hastened to dissuade the doggie of this notion, it's hard to prove that you're not vicious. I mean, how do you disprove a negative? I tried to point out that we had never in no way, shape, or form hurt any dog in the furtherance of our mission statement, which obviously is to solve crimes and assist our human in the same. But that didn't convince Meena even in the slightest. On the contrary, she retreated even further underneath that couch until she was stuck against the wall.

"Okay, so this is the problem we're faced with," I said finally. "Our humans work for the police department, and they've been tasked with solving a murder case. The murder of Vernon Langridge, who was one of your human's dearest friends. As things now stand, Marina is one of their suspects in the murder. Which means she might be arrested and tried for this crime and go to prison. If that happens, you won't have a human anymore, Meena, which is not something you would enjoy, I can imagine. So please answer a few questions and help us clear Marina's name. That's all we're asking."

For a moment, Meena simply stared back at us, with a touch of defiance if I wasn't mistaken, then finally she said,

"What makes you think that Marina would murder this man?"

"Well, she was in love with Vernon, wasn't she?"

"And what if she was?"

"He didn't love her, which gives her a clear motive for his murder."

"I don't see how she would want to murder the man she loved, even if he didn't love her in return. And by the way, how do you know all this?"

"A little birdie told us," said Dooley.

"What bird? Who is this bird?"

"Look, all we need you to do is to confirm Marina's story," I said. "She told us that she was home with you at the time of the murder, watching Netflix."

"It's true," Meena quickly said. "Absolutely true!"

Somehow her words didn't have the ring of truth, but since she refused to say more, we decided to follow the conversation between our humans and Marina, hoping this would bring us further than our own botched interview.

"It's true that I was in love with Vernon," Marina admitted. She was sitting on the couch, looking prim and proper, but I could tell that she was badly shaken at the realization that we knew all about her romantic crush.

"But he didn't love you, is that correct?" asked Odelia.

Marina shook her head. "I had hoped that in time he would come to see me as more than just a friend. He was an amazing man, you know. So talented, but also kind and warmhearted, and the best friend anyone could ever hope to have. We saw each other often, outside the monthly meetings of the writers' group that he had set up. We were each other's critique partners, you see. I would read the things he wrote, and he would read my stuff and provide feedback. There were times I saw him every day, and a connection like that obviously creates a bond."

"But not a romantic bond."

"No, not a romantic one. Last week, I was at his place and I overheard him talking to his ex-wife on the phone. It soon became clear to me how much he still loved her. He had told me that he wanted to get back together with Diana, but I figured it was for Gwen's sake. Vernon felt that the separation had a devastating effect on Gwen. Her grades had suffered, and she had started seeing this extremely unsuitable young man—a drug addict, as he described it, even though Gwen said that wasn't true. And so Vernon had been trying to convince Diana to give their marriage another try. But it wasn't until I overheard that phone call that I understood how much he still cared for her and missed her."

"Which made you realize that he didn't love you."

"Yes. We would never pass beyond the friend stage."

"That must have made you very upset."

"It did upset me a great deal."

"Is that why you killed him?" asked Chase.

Marina looked up as if stung. "What? No!"

"You said yourself how upset you were when you understood that Vernon didn't love you—and probably never would. How he wanted to give his marriage another chance. So it's understandable how you would have gone over to his place last night, maybe to confess your love to him? To plead with him to see you as more than just a friend? And when he rejected you, you shot him. Is that what happened, Marina?"

A high blush had settled on her cheeks. "Absolutely not," she said determinedly. "And I can't believe you would even think such a thing. I loved that man. I could never do anything to hurt him." She had become emotional and brought shaking fingers to her face. "I think I want you to leave now."

I glanced underneath that couch again, but Meena was still in hiding.

"I also want you to leave now," the Maltese terrier told us.

And since there seemed no other option, we did as we were told.

"We still don't know if she did it or not, Max," Dooley said as we walked out. "But if that dog's behavior is anything to go on, I think she's guilty."

"It is possible that Meena simply doesn't like cats, Dooley," I pointed out. "That doesn't mean Marina is a murderer. It means we'll never get anywhere with her. Unless..."

"Unless what?"

"Unless we get one of our canine friends to talk to her. Maybe she'll open up to them."

And so a plan formed in our minds to ask our neighboring dogs, Rufus and Fifi. If anyone could get Meena to open up to us, it might be them. After all, Meena was the only one who could confirm Marina Steele's alibi, so it was important.

But as Odelia was about to pull the door closed behind us, Marina came hurrying up and said, "Look, I know how this must look, but I promise you that I didn't murder Vernon. But I can tell you who did."

Odelia and Chase gave her a look of expectation. She kept us in suspense for a moment, but then good writers do that. At least she didn't suddenly close the door in our faces and end our conversation on a cliffhanger!

"It's Diana," the young writer now claimed.

"Vernon's ex-wife?"

She nodded. "Vernon once told me that this new guy Diana is dating has political ambitions. But to pull that off, they'll need a lot of money. And ever since Vernon sold his book to a publisher, Diana has been on his case to loan her the money. Vernon refused, of course. He wasn't going to bankroll the man he saw as his romantic rival. But Diana insisted. Simply would not let up."

Chase nodded. "That's very valuable information, Miss Steele. Thank you."

"I know I don't have an alibi for last night, but that doesn't mean I did it," she insisted. "Like I said, I could never hurt the man I loved. Even if he didn't love me."

Dooley and I had been listening to this conversation and looking for signs of deception in the young woman's face, but it's very hard to read a person and know if they're lying or not. But if she was lying, she was very good, for she sounded absolutely convincing. And as we sat there, suddenly Meena came tripping up. When she saw we were still present and accounted for, she hesitated, then hid behind the leg of her human.

"I've been thinking about what you said," she now revealed. "Is it true that Marina will go to jail if I don't speak up?"

"She is one of the suspects, yes," I confirmed.

"One of the main suspects," Dooley added.

Meena chewed on this for a moment. "Okay, so it is true that we sat on the couch together last night, as we do most nights, watching television. But it's also true that I nodded off at some point, since these shows are all so incredibly boring. So I'm afraid I can't really answer your question."

"You mean that Marina could have slipped out of the apartment at some point without you noticing it?" I asked.

She looked shamefaced as she nodded in confirmation. "I'm a terrible dog, aren't I? I can't even provide my human with an alibi!"

"I think it's very brave of you to admit the truth, Meena," I said, touched by the dog's honesty. She could have lied through her teeth, but she hadn't.

"What was she watching?" asked Dooley, much interested.

"Oh, I don't know. Some show about men and women shouting at each other and doing bad things to each other. She loves that stuff even though it puts me to sleep."

"I know what you mean," said Dooley. "My human loves to watch soaps, and they're exactly like that. People doing mean things behind each other's backs."

"So, are you going to arrest Marina now?" asked Meena in a small voice.

"Oh, no," I assured her. "Marina is only one of the many suspects we're looking at. And besides, we already have a man in custody. Gwen's boyfriend?"

"I remember Marina mentioned him," Meena confirmed. "And so did Vernon when he paid us a visit not so long ago. He wasn't happy with that boy. Said he was a criminal and he was trying to remove him from Gwen's life." She sighed deeply. "Look, I can't be sure that Marina didn't sneak out of the apartment last night, but I can tell you that I don't think she's a murderer. She's such a nice person, and I'm sure she wouldn't go around shooting people, especially Vernon since she liked him so much."

"Is it true that he was in every single one of her books?"

Meena smiled. "Who told you? Yes, it's true. You should see her office. She has a corkboard on the wall that's full of Vernon's pictures, and every time she writes a romantic scene, she stares at those pictures for what seems like hours."

"Maybe now that Vernon is dead, she will stare at you for hours," Dooley suggested, "and instead of writing a romance, she will write funny books about a Maltese terrier instead."

Meena practically vibrated with joy at these words. "Oh, wouldn't that be amazing?!" she breathed.

CHAPTER 23

As far as I could tell, Diana Ludick and her new beau didn't seem to experience the kind of financial constraints Marina Steele had mentioned. Quite the contrary, in fact. The sizable mansion they inhabited must have cost them a pretty penny, and the security measures that were in place were impressive. Before we finally got to speak to Vernon's widow, it took a lot of doing and we had to pass a lot of hurdles. And when we were sitting down with the lady in question on her patio, which offered a stunning view of a smooth lawn that sloped down to the beach beyond and then the Atlantic beyond that, it took a while before we had heaved our collective jaws up from the floor where they had dropped and could engage the woman in conversation.

"Pretty nice, isn't it?" said Mrs. Ludick—she had reverted to her maiden name after the separation—with a little smile of satisfaction at her visitors' stunned expressions. "One of the perks of getting involved with a real estate mogul who's entertaining political ambitions."

"Mr. Roughsedge wants to go into politics?" asked Chase,

who was the first to get a grip of himself and remember why we had come there.

"Yeah, I guess after a lifetime of being as successful as dear Cesar is," she said, plucking a piece of lint from her floral summer dress, "one starts looking for a new challenge. So he wants to become our next governor. And I don't blame him. The way this current administration is running things, it's a miracle the state is still on its feet and not staggering from one financial pothole to the next." She looked up. "Cesar has some great ideas, and it will be an honor to help him see them through."

She was definitely a classy lady, I thought, though there was something hard about her expression that told me she could also be very tough if she needed to be. She had certainly adapted to her new lifestyle impeccably, for she looked as if she had been born wealthy instead of having passed into it only a short while ago.

"What can you tell us about your ex-husband, Mrs. Ludick?" said Odelia.

"What can I tell you?" she said with a languid gesture of her hand. "Vernon was a lovely man, but ultimately we drifted apart. I think I finally realized I was destined for greater things, and he was holding me back. But when all is said and done, I'm forever grateful to him, not least because of the daughter we had together. Gwen is such an amazing young woman, and even though her father and I didn't see eye to eye at the end, we were united in the determination to give Gwen the childhood she deserved and tried to shield her from the fallout of the separation."

"So the divorce hadn't been finalized?" asked Chase.

"No, like I told you this morning, Vernon refused to sign the papers. He said he was trying to save our marriage, even though I told him there was nothing to save. But he would have signed the papers eventually. What else could he do?

You have to both want to stay married, Detective Kingsley, and obviously I had moved on. With Cesar. And happily so, I might add." She ostentatiously admired a large rock on her finger, causing Odelia to go a little goggle-eyed for a moment.

"So... now that your ex-husband is dead, will there be a wedding in your near future?" asked Chase, making it sound a little blunt.

Diana must have felt the same way, for she looked displeased. "If you're trying to suggest that I killed Vernon so I could marry Cesar, you're very much mistaken, detective," she said coldly. "I may not have loved the man anymore, but there was still a lot of affection there. We parted on amicable terms and remained friends. Last time we spoke, he even told me that he was going to sign the papers, so there was absolutely no reason for me to murder the man."

"Isn't it true that you had asked your ex-husband for a loan, Mrs. Ludick?" said Odelia. "So that you and Cesar could launch his political campaign?"

The woman laughed a throaty laugh. "Look around you, Mrs. Kingsley. Do you really think we need Vernon's money? Cesar is a very wealthy man. He'll launch his campaign when he's good and ready and doesn't need anybody's money. He's independently rich—do you understand what that means?"

"Political campaigns are extremely costly, so it stands to reason that Mr. Roughsedge would be looking for donors," Odelia said, proving she wasn't to be fooled by the bluster. "And since Vernon had sold his book to a publisher in a lucrative deal, it stood to reason that you would turn to him."

The woman's eyes narrowed, and I had the impression she would have lashed out at Odelia if she could have gotten away with it. "Of course Cesar is looking for donors. And naturally I approached my ex-husband and asked him to be a part of the wave of the future for our beloved home state."

"And what did he say?"

"He turned me down," the woman admitted reluctantly. "Said he was going to support the other candidate if Cesar entered the race." She shrugged. "Simply to spite me, of course, for wanting a divorce. Vernon could be petty that way." She turned to Odelia, eyes blazing. "But if you think I was going to kill him over such a trifling matter, you are very much mistaken, Mrs. Kingsley!"

"Can you tell us where you were last night, Mrs. Ludick?" asked Chase. "Around eleven o'clock?"

"I was here."

"Doing what?"

She hesitated. "Gardening."

Immediately we all looked at the woman's long nails. Perfectly manicured and garnished in a delectable cherry red, it was hard to imagine they would look this immaculate if she had been gardening. And besides, Diana Ludick didn't exactly look like the gardening type.

She must have realized her faux pas, for she quickly added, "I assist our gardener. Tell him what to do. I don't actually root around in the earth myself. I mean, are you kidding me?" She produced a weak laugh that convinced no one.

"You were gardening at eleven o'clock at night?" asked Chase, and didn't hide his incredulity at this statement.

She raised her head defiantly. "Absolutely. I'm devoted to this house and its stunning gardens, and once I'm busy, I lose all track of time."

"So if we ask your gardener, he'll be able to confirm this?"

"Of course." Chase and Odelia exchanged a look of surprise. It didn't escape Mrs. Ludick, for she added, "You don't possibly think I could have killed my ex-husband, do you? The father of my daughter? I may have stopped loving the man, but Gwen adored him. When I walked out on my marriage, she was given a choice: to move in with me or to stay with Vernon, and she chose the latter. She was always a daddy's girl, and that hasn't changed." She pressed a hand to her chest. "I'm a mother, detective. And as a mother, I feel deeply about my child and want what's best for her. So I would never want to deprive Gwennie of her beloved daddy. So get this silly notion that I'm somehow responsible for my ex-husband's death out of your head right now." She settled back again and placed a pair of oversized sunglasses on her nose, adopting the movie star look. "Now if there's nothing else…"

"There's the matter of your daughter's boyfriend," said Odelia. "Gwen's father wasn't a big fan of her relationship with Jerald Exton."

"Now that's an understatement," she scoffed. "Vernon hated that boy. And I have to say that I fully agreed with him. That horrible young delinquent had no business coming anywhere near our little girl." She raised a finely penciled eyebrow, causing it to go a little squiggly. "I hear he's been arrested?"

"He has," Chase confirmed.

"Do you think that Gwen and Jerald could have conspired to murder your ex-husband, Mrs. Ludick?" asked Odelia. "Because he was standing in the way of their being together?"

The sunglasses were removed again so Diana could direct one of her icy looks at the reporter. "You are mad," she said in a low voice. "Stark-raving mad!"

"Gwen wanted to be with Jerald, and her father was dead set against it."

"Well, of course he was! Would you want your daughter dating a criminal? A drug dealer? Of course not! We were all shocked when Gwen announced she and Jerald were an item. And desperately hoped the girl would come to her senses. But that doesn't mean she would *murder* her dad!" She suddenly rose in a sort of imperious way. "This interview is over. If you want to ask me more of your stupid questions, you'll have to arrest me." And with these words, she strode off, every inch the offended diva.

For a moment, we just sat there, wondering how to proceed. But then, a thickset man joined us, looking a lot less irascible than Vernon's ex-wife. He introduced himself as Cesar Roughsedge, the new man in Mrs. Ludick's life. "You'll have to excuse Diana. Vernon's death has hit her hard. They may have had their problems, but she was still very fond of the man."

"This is a police investigation," said Chase. "So we do have to ask some difficult questions from time to time."

"I know, I know," he said placatingly. "And I'm sure that Diana will answer all the questions you have once she's had time to process what happened. In the meantime, if there's anything I can do..."

"Could you tell us where you were last night, Mr. Roughsedge?" asked Chase. "Let's say around eleven o'clock?"

"I was here," said the man, looking startled by the question. "I was working on my campaign—meeting with my campaign manager. He will confirm it."

"At eleven o'clock in the evening?"

"Absolutely. You'd be surprised how time-consuming a political campaign really is, detective. I have to say I was surprised. It's a full-time job. But worth it—absolutely worth it," he hastened to add, lest we got the wrong idea.

They chatted for a little while longer, but nothing more was gleaned from the conversation. And since it soon became clear that Diana had done a bunk and wouldn't be back, we said our goodbyes, with Cesar pressing Odelia's hand warmly and clapping Chase on the back as if they were long-lost brothers.

"Too bad they don't have a pet," said Dooley as we made

our way back to the car. "Which is strange, don't you think? Rich people often have pets."

"Maybe Cesar Roughsedge is allergic," I suggested.

"It would help him a lot in his campaign. People love pets. And they love people who love pets."

"Maybe he'll get a pet. Just so he can win his election."

"It's entirely possible, Max. He looks like a man who'll do anything to win."

I wondered if he would be willing to commit murder. If Vernon had insisted on stopping the divorce, it might have thrown a spanner in the works for Cesar's campaign. A man dating a married woman, even though recently separated, probably doesn't look good in the eyes of the electorate. It would be better for the divorce to come through so Cesar and Diana could get married. And now that Vernon was dead, nothing stood in the way of a big, glamorous wedding that would be in all the papers.

* * *

THE MOMENT the cops were gone, Cesar breathed a sigh of relief. He was still going through media training to learn how to respond to tough questions in interviews, so he saw this whole interaction as part of his learning process. But boy, it hadn't been easy to keep a straight face and lie to those people!

The fact of the matter was that Vernon's death couldn't have come at a more fortuitous time. He hadn't officially launched his bid for governor yet, so the intense media scrutiny hadn't begun, and hopefully by the time it had, he and Diana would be happily married, and the murder would have passed from the collective consciousness. And with Jerald Exton arrested for the crime, hopefully Gwen would have second thoughts about her connection to that no-good kid and would move on to a better prospect. Diana already had a couple of possible suitors in mind she would introduce to her daughter the moment she moved in with them.

Before long, they'd be able to play the happy family, which meant the governorship was in the bag, and they'd be moving house to Albany!

CHAPTER 24

We had arrived back at the police station, where Chase would touch base with the other officers working on the case. Under normal circumstances, he would also have discussed the case with Odelia's uncle, but since the Chief was busy fitting his tuxedo, that wasn't going to happen. Odelia should have returned to the *Gazette* offices, but first she wanted to get all the updates on the case that she could, which is why we found ourselves drifting into Dolores Peltz's ken again. The desk sergeant gave us a critical look when we entered the vestibule, which she considers her personal domain. And it's probably true that in most police stations, you'll be hard-pressed to find a pair of cats wandering in as if they belong there. But then this is Hampton Cove, and we do things differently around here.

The moment we set paw in the main room, where all the action takes place, we became aware of a loud sort of ruckus. As it turned out, it was Gwen Langridge who was causing all the commotion, as she was demanding at the top of her voice that her boyfriend be released.

Chase hurried to join his colleague Sarah Flunk, who was bearing the brunt of the teenager's onslaught. The young officer was red in the face, almost as red as Gwen herself, and the two stood practically nose to nose.

"What's going on here!" Chase boomed as he intervened.

Gwen stepped back. "She won't let me see Jerald!" she said, pointing an accusing finger at Sarah.

"He's been arrested for murder," Sarah insisted. "You can't just barge in here and demand to speak to him!"

"Jerald is not a murderer! He's the sweetest boy on the planet!"

"Be that as it may," said Odelia, also coming to the officer's aid, "evidence was found in his van that points to his guilt, Gwen."

"I don't care! I want to see him—now!"

Dooley blinked. "I think she's going to stomp her foot now, Max."

He was right. The teenager did stomp her foot. Both feet, in fact, though not simultaneously. So it was a good thing that Chase decided to lead her away, before either Gwen or Sarah said something they would later regret. That's what happens when things get heated: people say stuff they don't necessarily mean. One thing was clear, though: Gwen felt very strongly about her would-be boyfriend. Which made me wonder if there was any truth to the suggestion Odelia had made to the girl's mother that she and Jerald might have set up that murder together. After all, if she had practically attacked Sarah for not letting her see her boyfriend, what might she have done when her dad told her she couldn't see Jerald anymore?

It certainly was something to consider.

"What was Gwen's alibi again?" asked Dooley, who must have come to the same conclusion.

"She doesn't have an alibi. She was upstairs, asleep in bed."

"Mh," said Dooley meaningfully. If he'd been human, he would have rubbed his chin. And if he'd lived one hundred years ago, he might even have polished his monocle in a significant manner.

It didn't take long for Gwen to cool down. And when she finally left, she didn't even say, "I'll be back," only to return half an hour later with a truck to demolish the entire police station and murder everyone inside because she wasn't allowed access to Jerald.

I think we all breathed a sigh of relief when the teenager had vacated the premises, and I could only imagine what life must have been like for poor Vernon, forced to endure the girl's temper tantrums on a regular basis.

We were standing at Sarah Flunk's desk, now that the officer was free to devote her little gray cells to the actual investigation again. She informed her boss that she had checked Vernon's phone records and also his internet search history, as gleaned from the man's cell phone provider and his internet service provider, respectively.

"Regular calls to his agent," she said as she showed the printed-out listings where she had marked the most frequent correspondents of the dead man in yellow marker. "In fact, the last person he called was that same agent. Name of Oliver Levy. He's got an office in downtown Manhattan, but when I contacted him just now he said he's in town today to handle his late client's affairs. He's staying at the Star Hotel."

"Great work, Sarah," said Chase appreciatively. "What about the search history?"

"Well, it seems he was looking for a lawyer, sir."

"A lawyer?"

"Yes, more specifically an entertainment lawyer, or at least someone specializing in royalties."

"Huh."

"Probably something to do with this book deal of his," Odelia suggested.

"Could be," said Sarah. "He had been looking at a lot of websites devoted to royalty rights. And if he was in the process of signing a book deal, that would be understandable."

She handed Chase the documents she had printed out and marked up, and he took them back to his office to pore over. And since having to watch people read stuff is probably the most sleep-inducing thing in the world, apart perhaps from watching grass grow, we decided to take a nap.

But first, a nibble. On Odelia's instigation, and since we seemed to be spending a lot of time recently at the police station, Chase had decided to keep a bag of kibble in his desk drawer. And so Dooley and I now gave him the kind of piteous look cats are rightly famous for. Unfortunately, he was so busy checking those documents, and so was Odelia, we decided to add our brand of sad mewling to the mix, hoping it would attract their attention. When that didn't do the trick, Dooley volunteered to jump up onto the detective's desk and place himself squarely on top of those very same papers, planting his tush right in the center.

Chase uttered an annoyed grunt but still didn't make the connection, which is when I rolled my eyes and said, "Food! We're starving here, people!"

Finally, Odelia got the picture, opened the desk drawer, and took out the food in question. And so, before long, we were well-fed and ready to take a nice, long nap on top of the windowsill. It offered a view of the patch of weedy derelict land located behind the police station, and as I looked out, I thought I saw Clarice's head stick out for a moment before disappearing again.

Our formerly feral friend may have found a permanent

home, but that hasn't stopped her from reverting to her old ways from time to time to go on the hunt. The next time her head popped up, she caught sight of us and gave a cheerful wave. We returned the wave, then put our heads down and dozed off.

CHAPTER 25

We met the late Vernon's literary agent in the lobby of the Star Hotel. He looked very young for such an important job, I thought, and for a moment I got the impression he was still in his teens. Then again, maybe he simply had mastered the art of staying young forever, like some of those billionaires who spend all of their money on ways to stem the passage of time. He greeted us in an ebullient fashion, which told me that he was probably good at what he did, in spite of his young age, for being an agent is all about networking and pressing the flesh, and what better way to go about that than with some vigor.

Mr. Levy led us out of the lobby, through the bar, and into the dining area, where he proceeded to secure us a table near the window. He ordered himself a martini while Odelia and Chase opted to go alcohol-free for the moment, as did Dooley and I. I'm not big on booze, you see, and neither is my friend. Apparently, alcohol kills brain cells, and that's bad for any detective worth his or her salt. Oliver Levy didn't seem to have that particular qualm, for when his drink arrived, he downed it in one gulp and immediately ordered a refill. Maybe he had a surplus of brain cells in his young noggin.

"So my client," he said, placing his elbows on the table and his hands together until his index fingers touched. "I'm not going to lie to you, detective. Vernon Langridge was a very unhappy man. Extremely unhappy, even. That's what that call was about. I had just got word from the publisher that they were canceling his book deal, and he wasn't happy about that, as you can probably imagine."

"Vernon's book deal was canceled?" asked Odelia.

"Yes, it was. I'll give you the timeline of events, shall I? Make things clearer." He frowned as he collected his thoughts. But then the waiter arrived with his second martini, and he quaffed once more, a little less greedily this time. "Okay, so we signed the contract a year ago, and Vernon received his advance, to the tune of fifteen thousand dollars, which was pretty good for a first novel from an unknown writer. But then the publisher believed in the book, and so did I. Vernon delivered the final draft last week, I read it, and immediately sent it on to the publisher. Yesterday they got back to me and told me the book didn't live up to their expectations. They said it was a mess, and they were extremely disappointed. They weren't going to publish it, and that was that."

"What about the advance?" asked Chase.

"It was agreed that Vernon could keep the advance."

"But no book."

"No book," the agent confirmed.

"He must have been devastated," said Odelia with feeling.

"Oh, he was. Extremely disappointed, in fact."

She turned to her husband. "That's why he was looking for an entertainment lawyer."

"He was?" asked the agent, arching his brows. "It wasn't going to do him any good, you know. It was all in the contract Vernon signed. Upon delivery of the manuscript, the publisher has the right to refuse publication if they feel the book isn't up to their expectations. So Vernon didn't have a leg to stand on, I'm afraid. Which is what I told him."

"But why? You read the book yourself, didn't you?"

"Of course. I'd read all the different drafts and had worked with Vernon to whip the book into shape. But final approval lies with the publisher, and if he feels the book isn't publishable, that's his prerogative."

"Was this the thriller Vernon was writing?" asked Odelia. "About the antique dealer who turns amateur sleuth?"

Mr. Levy smiled. "That's right. Why, have you read it?"

"No, I haven't. But the members of his writers' group have told us about it. Apparently, Vernon had been reading snippets of his new book to them."

"Yes, and he also worked with a critique partner, I believe. One... Marina Steele? According to Vernon, she also loved the new book. Said it was great."

"So why the publisher's refusal?"

The agent shrugged. "As I understood, the final product didn't correspond with the novel as it had initially been sold to them. Words like 'badly written,' 'amateurish drivel,' and 'sentimental bilge' were used, though I refrained from passing them on to Vernon. He was down in the dumps enough as it was without having to be subjected to such harsh criticism of his work. Though if I'm honest with you," he said, leaning forward, "I think it had less to do with the quality of the book or the writing and everything to do with a recent shift in the market away from books about amateur sleuths and toward the police procedural kind of stuff. Less cozy and more serious, you know."

"We met a cozy crime writer," said Odelia with a frown, "who complained about the same thing. Said she couldn't get her books published."

"It's all about the trend," the agent claimed. "You can't buck the trend. And that's exactly what Vernon was up against. A year ago, the kind of book he wrote was all the rage, and now, when it was finally ready for publication, the market has shifted away from cozy crime, and he was going to be left by the wayside. Unless he adapted, of course, and wrote a nice bleak crime thriller instead."

"But isn't it possible that by the time his bleak thriller was ready, the market might shift again?"

"Of course. That's what makes this business so infuriatingly hard. It's very well possible that in a year's time, cozy crime will be all the rage again."

"Tough business," Chase murmured sympathetically.

"Anyway, I told him not to give up and that I would try to shop his book to other publishers. Not that I held out a lot of hope, mind you."

"What does this mean for you personally?" asked Odelia. "No deal means no money for you, right?"

"No, that's absolutely correct. No deal, no commission. But you don't have to worry about me. I've decided to fold my own little shop and join Michael Holden's outfit. I start on Monday." When his interlocutors didn't immediately react, he added, "Only the biggest literary agency in the business! Michael Holden is an absolute legend. Represents ninety percent of the world's bestselling authors."

"Wow, that's a pretty big deal," said Chase without a lot of excitement. Clearly, the world of publishing wasn't really his jam.

"It is a pretty big deal," said the young man with satisfaction. "And something I've worked very hard to accomplish. But enough about me. Did you have any other questions about Vernon?"

* * *

Oliver watched as the two cops made their way past the bar and into the lobby. He held up his hand to order himself another drink. He could definitely use it. At least now this whole business with Vernon was finally over, and he could focus on his new job. And as he sat nursing his drink, he smirked a little and congratulated himself on a job well done. These cops didn't have a clue!

CHAPTER 26

Because The Mighty Pen was understandably off-limits for the time being, at least until the investigation into the murder of its owner was concluded, the writers' group that Vernon had founded met at Kenton Clarey's apartment. It wasn't really a regular meeting, for how could it be now that a tragedy of such major proportions had befallen its members? In his own mind, Kenton saw it as a wake, a way of commemorating their friend and sharing in the sorrow of his passing. The first thing he did was pose a question to Marina that had been burning on his lips ever since those cops had paid him a second visit.

"The police received a letter accusing me of murdering Vernon," he told the young romance writer. "It said that I was jealous of Vernon because my book contract had been canceled and he was just about to hit the big time, so I murdered him out of spite." He paused as he fixed her with an intent look. "Did you write that letter, Marina? I'm sorry but I simply have to know."

But Marina seemed shocked. "Of course not!" she said. "I

didn't even know that your contract had been canceled, Kenton. Are you serious?"

"Sadly, yes. They published the first six Marvin Amis thrillers, but they won't publish number seven. Which leaves me in quite a pickle, as you can imagine, with Mikaela in the state she's in."

They were in his living room, just the three of them, and he had served them drinks, which they were all in need of after the events of last night and that day. Mikaela was resting in the bedroom, and he had closed the door so she wouldn't be disturbed.

"It's such a terrible tragedy," said Tarsha, shaking her head. "And then there are people trying to push us even deeper into the mire. It's disgraceful. And wicked."

"It is disgraceful," Kenton agreed. "But I have to wonder how they even knew that my book deal was canceled. I didn't tell anyone. Though of course, word quickly gets around. But to link that to Vernon's murder is simply outrageous."

"At least they've already found the killer," said Tarsha.

"Yes, at least there's that," Kenton agreed.

The story about Jerald's arrest had been posted on the *Gazette* website, and since it was written by the same person who had paid all three of them a visit, it was probably safe to trust that it was true.

"If only Vernon had taken more precautions," said Marina, who seemed the most affected by the tragedy, which was only to be understood, Kenton thought, since she had been so in love with the man. "He knew that Jerald had a criminal record and that he was upset that Vernon wouldn't allow him to see Gwen."

"What could he have done?" asked Tarsha. "Hire a bodyguard?"

"Tell the police, at least."

"But what could the police do? And besides, if I understood the article correctly, Jerald hasn't confessed. He's being accused of the crime, but he claims it's got nothing to do with him and he's being framed."

"They found that book in his van," Kenton pointed out. "So that tells me all I need to know, and I guess the police feel the same way."

"They were back this afternoon," said Marina. "The second time in one day. Said they'd received a letter accusing me of being in love with Vernon and murdering him."

Now this was news. Immediately, they were all ears while Marina told them about the ordeal she had suffered through. It sounded exactly like what Kenton had experienced himself. Some poisoned pen willy-nilly accusing people.

"I told them that I couldn't possibly have done it, for I loved him so."

"I know you loved him," said Tarsha warmly. "I think the only one who didn't was Vernon himself."

"You should have told him," said Kenton. "Maybe he felt the same way?"

"No, he didn't," said Marina with a violent shake of the head. She seemed on the verge of tears again. "He was still in love with Diana and could never love another. Oh, what he ever saw in that awful woman I will never know!"

"Diana is the kind of woman who can wrap a man around her little finger," Tarsha said. "A real femme fatale."

Kenton suppressed a smile. Tarsha always thought she knew all there was to know about crime, even though she had never been involved in it, and every single one of her books contained at least one femme fatale. Then again, in her case, that was understandable. It was one of those secrets he had no trouble keeping to himself, since to pass it on would be like planting a dagger in the old woman's back. And he might not consider these people friends, but he still appreciated them too much to use their own secrets against them in any way. Well, apart from telling those cops about Marina, of course. But then he had only lashed out because he thought she had written that horrible letter.

"I think Diana was involved in this somehow," Marina revealed. "It's what I told that detective. Cesar Roughsedge wants to become our next governor."

"God save us all," said Tarsha.

"So he needs money. A lot of it."

"But I thought he was rich," said Kenton. "Vernon said he's rolling in money."

"Then why was Diana so interested when Gwen told her about Vernon's book sale? And that fifteen thousand advance he got? Gwen told me her mother was like a dog with a bone. Kept asking about Vernon's big sale and how he was going to sell millions of books and become a best-selling author. No, I think Roughsedge isn't as rich as he says he is, so they were counting on Vernon bankrolling the man's bid for the governor's seat. And when he refused, they paid Jerald to kill him." She had gone very still, and her cheeks were flushed, her eyes glittery. Clearly, she had given this a lot of thought, as of course they all had. "That's why Diana never divorced him. She knew that as long as they were still married, she was the main beneficiary if he died. And now that he's dead, all of those millions will go to her and Cesar. Enough to put them in the Executive Mansion."

"But there are no millions," Kenton pointed out. "Not yet, at least."

"Exactly! But there will be. And now that he's dead, even more than when he would have been alive. We all know that book sales pick up when an author passes away, and especially under such tragic circumstances."

"She really thought this through, didn't she, our Diana?" said Tarsha.

"Oh, yes, she did. She's probably been planning this for months."

"But why isn't Jerald talking?" asked Kenton. "All he has to do is tell the police that it was, in fact, Diana who was behind the whole thing. Instead of taking the rap like he's doing now."

"Maybe he doesn't know Diana was the one who hired him," Marina suggested. "Maybe she used a middleman. Isn't that how it goes?" She was eyeing him intently, as if he was such an expert on violent crime. He was a writer of thrillers, of course, so it was true he knew a little bit about it. But that didn't mean he was as well-versed in the ways of the underworld as she thought.

But since he wouldn't be caught looking like a fool, he nodded intelligently. "Yes, that's exactly how it's done. You hire a contract killer through an intermediary." But where could Diana possibly have found such an intermediary? She wasn't exactly a criminal mastermind. Before she had linked her lot to Cesar Roughsedge, she had worked at The Mighty Pen, alongside her husband, so all she knew was how to sell books, not hire contract killers.

Then again, maybe Cesar himself had seen an opportunity and taken it. That man certainly had the connections to pull this off. And he wouldn't have enjoyed watching the woman he wanted to marry still being married to Vernon and refusing to sign the papers. She was going to have to take him to court if she wanted a divorce. But instead of taking him to court, Diana and Cesar had found a cheaper and easier solution, one that solved all of their problems in one go: to murder the man.

Marina had broken into tears again, with Tarsha trying to stem the flood by pressing tissue papers to the girl's face. Good thing Kenton had stocked up on the stuff, for he'd known tonight's meeting would be fraught with sadness.

He felt pretty sad himself. Though in his case that had nothing to do with the death of their friend and everything to do with the end of his career as a published author. But then he decided to shelve his personal problems for once and be there for Marina. After all, they had lost a friend, but she had lost a loved one.

CHAPTER 27

"Oh, but you have to come, Max!" said Harriet.

"But we've been on our paws all day!" I lamented.

"On your paws! And what do you think we've done? Tell him, sugar bear."

Brutus gave her a look of uncertainty. "Well..."

"We've been so busy you wouldn't believe it!" said Harriet.

"What did you do?" asked Dooley curiously.

"Well, for one thing, I've been working on my autobiography."

"Oh, you're writing your autobiography?"

"That's right. And yours, too, by the way. In fact, I'm writing everybody's autobiography, but don't go blabbing about it now, you hear? It's supposed to be a surprise. For the wedding, you see. Everyone will get their own autobiography, and it's going to be just grand," she smiled a pleasant smile. "I can just see those happy faces. People will be so thrilled!"

"I don't get it," I admitted. "How can you write another

person's autobiography? Isn't the person themselves supposed to write it?"

"Oh, but I know them all so well after all these years that I'm perfectly capable of writing it for them. And that's exactly what I'm doing."

It didn't seem to make a lot of sense to me, but then Harriet can prove to be something of an enigma. I decided not to pursue the matter and simply let it go. After all, I hadn't been kidding when I told her we'd been on our paws all day. And I was really looking forward to having some downtime.

But apparently, Harriet had decided differently.

"Look, it's the animals, see?" she said. "We have to save the animals!"

"What animals?" asked Dooley.

"At the zoo, of course! They're being shaved!"

"Saved?"

"No, shaved!"

Dooley was thoroughly confused. "So... do we have to save the animals or shave them?"

"Save them from being shaved," Brutus clarified.

The four of us were in Odelia's backyard, and as far as I was concerned, we would stay there. Nothing nicer than a pleasant nap on the lawn. Okay, so maybe not as pleasant as lying on a flowerbed, but relaxing all the same. But as I said, Harriet had other plans, and they included us.

And so, as soon as the family had sat down for dinner, Gran announced that she was off to the zoo, and she was taking the cats along with her.

"What do you need the cats for?" asked Marge.

"And why are you going to the zoo?" asked Uncle Alec suspiciously.

But Charlene thought she knew. "You're working on some kind of surprise for the wedding, aren't you, Vesta?"

"Oh, no," Gran assured her future daughter-in-law. "Nothing to do with the wedding at all. The animals are being shaved, you see, so we have to stop that man."

Long association with Gran had taught her relatives never to question her statements, and they didn't do so now. Instead, their attention turned to Uncle Alec, with Odelia inquiring about the suit he had chosen for the wedding.

"I did pick a suit, actually," her uncle announced proudly. "And I have to admit it looks really great."

"They tried to dress him in shapewear," Marge revealed. "But it made him look like a sausage."

"And nearly killed me," Uncle Alec said.

"So we decided to go in a different direction. It's a suit that makes the wearer look slimmer, and even though I was skeptical at first, it actually works."

"It does," said Uncle Alec. "And the best part is that I don't have to diet anymore. The suit does all the dieting for me."

"Charlene patted her betrothed's rotund belly. "I like a bit of heft on a man," she confessed. "My big soft teddy bear."

Uncle Alec beamed. Being out of the office for a day agreed with him. He already looked a lot more relaxed than he had been before. Of course, the downside was that Odelia and Chase looked more stressed. But that couldn't be helped. I still wondered if Uncle Alec needed to be saved from his wedding, but since he looked happy and relaxed, maybe he didn't mind getting married.

"Do you still think we need to stop the wedding, Max?" asked Dooley, whose thoughts often run along the same lines as mine. "He doesn't seem to mind so much anymore."

"You're right. He doesn't look like someone who needs to be saved."

"Let's take a wait-and-see approach," my friend suggested.

"So how are your parents settling in?" asked Tex.

"Yes, and why didn't they join us?" asked Marge.

"Oh, they're fine," said Charlene. "A little tired, you know, after the trip. So they decided to stay at the hotel and get an early night. You'll all see them tomorrow at the rehearsal dinner."

Charlene's parents lived in Florida and seemed to like it there so much they very rarely came up to the Hamptons to pay their daughter a visit. Like Charlene, they hailed from Hampton Cove but had escaped the cold winters to become snowbirds in Florida. Charlene was fine with that. After all, she had a lot of friends in town and also her new adopted family: us!

"So about the Pancake Burglar," Gran now began.

"Oh, not that again!" Uncle Alec said, throwing up his hands.

"He still hasn't been caught, Alec!" Gran pointed out. "And I'm starting to think that the only people who care are we of the neighborhood watch. Which is why tonight there will be two patrols going out. Me and Scarlett will try and catch the Shaver. And Wilbur and Francis will look for the Pancake Burglar. You don't have to thank me," she said when her son made to speak. "All in a day's work."

"I wasn't going to thank you," the Chief grumbled. "I was going to tell you to be careful. And more importantly, not to get arrested again! The last thing I need is for my mother to be in jail on my wedding day."

"I won't be in jail if you don't put me there," said Gran with unfailing logic. She picked up her napkin and wiped her lips. "And now if you'll excuse me, I have a shaver to catch. And a pancake man!"

And with these words, she beckoned the four of us, and we were on our way. As if it wasn't enough that I had a day job catching killers, now I had a night job catching shavers and pancake people!

. . .

PURRFECT BOOKSHOP

THE TRIP to the zoo didn't take all that long. First, we picked up Scarlett at her home, and she wasn't alone. Claiming she felt for her poor baby being left all alone in that empty apartment, she decided to bring Clarice along. We welcomed our friend, who didn't look all that excited to go to the zoo, but then sometimes you have to make allowances for your humans, even as they get carried away by their big ideas.

"I don't even know what a shaver is," Clarice grumbled.

"It's a person who shaves animals," Harriet explained.

"But why?" asked Dooley. "Why does he do it?"

"Beats me," said Harriet with a shrug. "Why does any human do anything?"

"Because they're crazy," said Clarice pointedly, and that was true enough.

Next, we passed by the General Store to pick up Wilbur Vickery, and since he felt it wouldn't do to leave Kingman all alone at the store, he brought him along for the ride.

"I was just looking forward to a nice evening at home," said the voluminous cat plaintively. "And now they're dragging me to... where are we going, exactly?"

"Not sure," I said. "We're going to the zoo, and Wilbur is going pancake hunting or something?"

"I'm sure Kingman will stay with us," said Harriet.

"As long as I can nap," said Kingman. "I've been on my paws all day."

I couldn't imagine Kingman being on his paws at any moment, since mostly his days consist of lying around in front of his store and chatting with fellow felines, preferably of the female persuasion.

Next, we found ourselves at St. John's Church, where we met up with Father Reilly. Father Reilly owns his own car, and he and Wilbur would be riding together. And since the priest didn't like the idea of leaving Shanille at home, he had decided to bring her along with him, or at least with us.

The upshot was that no less than seven cats were riding in the back with Gran and Scarlett, with Wilbur and Francis Reilly going their separate ways. I had the impression both men were looking forward to their vigil. The fact that Father Reilly had rubbed his hands with glee and said, "I love pancakes!" was probably a good indication of that.

"I'm not sure this is such a good idea, Vesta," said Scarlett as she glanced at the seven of us. "Are you sure the zoo will allow seven cats?"

"Of course they will! Are you kidding? It's the zoo. They love animals!"

As it turned out, they weren't overly pleased to find that the neighborhood watch was disproportionately represented by the feline element. Preferably they would have liked to see more humans and fewer cats. Then again, you can't look a gift cat in the mouth, so Shara Jarram, as the zookeeper's name turned out to be, decided to allow it. "I thought there were more members of the watch?" she asked as she escorted us to the pavilion where the big cats were kept.

"The others are on a separate mission," Gran explained. "Catching the Pancake Burglar."

Shara smiled. "What a fascinating life you lead, Mrs. Muffin."

"Tell me about it."

Scarlett's great-nephew Kevin was waiting for us at the pavilion. He looked excited, since this was his first foray into neighborhood watch territory. And then Shara left, and our long vigil commenced. I could have told Kevin that he was in for a rude awakening since these stake-outs are mostly extremely boring, and the chances of something actually happening are slim to none. But lucky for him, he didn't speak my language, and Scarlett wasn't going to scare him off by giving him the benefit of her experience.

"Okay, so I think you guys should spread out," Gran now

announced. "There are ten of us, so five teams of two should suffice. Let's post a team at every pavilion to keep an eye out. Too bad we don't have walkie-talkies..."

"Oh, but we do!" said Kevin, the nerd. He shrugged out of his backpack and surprised his great-aunt and the rest of us with an array of gizmos. They didn't look like walkie-talkies, but that was because they were even better: they were ear mics that would allow us to stay in constant contact.

Before long, all seven of us had been outfitted with the nifty gadgets, and then he offered the same service to Gran and Scarlett. After an initial test and some fiddling, we could all make ourselves understood, which was quite an innovation, I have to say. I almost felt like I was in a James Bond movie.

And so we spread out. I teamed up with Dooley, Harriet with Brutus, Shanille with Kingman, and Clarice with Gran. That left Scarlett and Kevin, and they were happy to keep each other company and stake out the big cats.

Dooley and I had been assigned to the giraffes, and since I gave little credence to this whole shaving business, I figured we'd settle in for the night and have a nice long nap. After all, the giraffes were also napping, so why not us? Unfortunately, it was not to be. As it turned out, the others were all feeling pretty chatty, and since we had those darned ear mic thingies on, we could hear every single word of every single person and every cat in our company. Yikes!

CHAPTER 28

Vesta was in her element. This was what it was all about: being a force for good at the heart of her community and spreading plenty of sweetness and light. And if she had to make the odd sacrifice from time to time, that couldn't be helped. Like now, for instance. She could have assigned Wilbur and Francis to zoo duty while she and Scarlett staked out that dreadful Pancake Burglar—she hadn't stopped thinking about those delicious pancakes since last night—but instead, she had decided that their co-watch members should also have the benefit of sampling the burglar's rare talent for pastry.

"I hope they'll save some pancakes for us, that's all I'm saying."

"They'll have to catch him first," Scarlett pointed out.

There was a crackle, and Vesta adjusted her earpiece.

"Oh, they'll catch him all right," she said. "After all, Francis has the benefit of having the Lord's ear. All he has to do is say a quick prayer or two, and he'll be guided directly to the burglar's door."

"If that's the case," said her friend, "then Francis should

join the police. A quick prayer or two, and he'd solve all the crimes on their roster."

"And put my son and all of his officers out of work? Are you crazy?"

Shara Jarram had selected the small enclosure the zookeepers employed to keep an eye on their charges as the location for this stake-out, and even though by now Vesta was an old hand at this watch business, she was still having a hard time staying awake. It's one thing when being in the neighborhood watch is your only pastime, but she also led a busy life during the day, and after a while, a lack of sleep makes itself felt, especially in those of a certain age. Though if anyone had put it to her in those terms, she would have vehemently denied age had anything to do with it. On the contrary, she had never felt better or more energetic. With every decade, she was getting younger!

She glanced down at Clarice, who was languidly licking her visage. "And how are you holding up, toots?" she asked. "Happy to join the watch, are you?"

Clarice gave her a face that spoke volumes. In her case: are you kidding me? "I'm only here because Scarlett asked me to," Clarice clarified.

"It's important that we catch this man," Vesta argued.

"Is it? Is it really? As far as I can tell, this person's only crime is that he likes to shave animals. And is that so bad? Maybe they like it. Maybe he's doing them a service. Maybe," she said as she stretched out, "he's a retired vet."

"How do you reckon that?" asked Vesta, intrigued by this point of view.

"Isn't it possible that this vet enjoys visiting the zoo, and he just happens to notice that certain animals aren't being as well cared for as they should be? And isn't it also possible that he decided to do something about it? So he shaves the animals and has their fur examined in the lab to make sure they're not carrying certain diseases, for instance, or are infested with parasites, as many animals are?"

"It's possible," Gran allowed. "Though unlikely."

"It's not only possible, it's very probable," Clarice argued.

"But if he really thought that the animals weren't being handled properly, shouldn't he go to the zoo administrator and point out the deficiencies in the organization?"

"Who would listen?" said Clarice, indicating a distinct lack of trust in the powers that be. But then Clarice always had a fractious relationship with authority.

Vesta checked the monitors that showed the zebras that had been assigned to her and Clarice in their sleeping quarters, and saw that all was well and not a creature stirred—for the moment at least. She relaxed and wished, not for the first time, that she had brought more provisions. She was starting to develop a serious appetite, and the idea that Francis and Wilbur were out there enjoying those delicious pancakes right now didn't help.

She now spoke into her mic. "Team one, come in. Please report."

"Team one here," Dooley spoke. "Everything fine, Gran. No Shaver activity."

"The big cats are also resting peacefully," said Scarlett. "No Shaver here."

One by one, the different teams reported that nothing was happening out there and that it looked as if the Shaver would be a no-show. Perhaps it had been a one-time thing, and they had organized this whole stake-out for naught.

"So, are you looking forward to your rehearsal dinner?" asked Scarlett.

"You bet," said Gran. "I'll finally be meeting Charlene's parents, so that should be a hoot."

"I wasn't invited," said Clarice with a touch of pique. "Not that I'd come, of course. I hate large gatherings, especially of humans. But it would still have been nice to be invited, you know."

"Charlene sent over the guest list," Vesta pointed out. "And I guess she's not as cat-minded as the rest of the family is."

"But *your* cats are invited, correct?"

"Well... I guess it's sort of implied that they'll be there," she said.

"We didn't get an invitation, if that's what you think," Harriet's voice sounded over the system. "We simply choose to show up on the day. Crash the party, if you will."

"Does it hurt, Harriet?" asked Dooley. "To crash a party like that?"

"It doesn't hurt if you land on top of the wedding cake," Kingman pointed out. He sighed in a sort of wistful way. "I would love to crash straight into a wedding cake. And then have to eat my way out of it. Now wouldn't that be something?"

"You won't get the chance," Shanille said. "Those wedding cakes are pretty small, and there are usually a lot of guests at those shindigs, so by the time you reach the cake, there will be nothing left but crumbs."

"Oh, I don't know," said Harriet. "I have it on good authority that Charlene ordered a gigantic cake. She knows how much her future husband loves to eat, so she made provisions."

"I don't even like cake," Max grumbled. "Except maybe chicken pie."

"I don't think they serve chicken pie as a wedding cake," Brutus indicated.

"What's with all this meowing?" asked Kevin now. "Is something going on?"

"Just the cats getting all excited," Scarlett said. "They get like this when they're excited."

"Excited about what, though?" asked Kevin. "Maybe they know something we don't? Cats do have an instinct about this stuff, so maybe they have smelled the Shaver?"

"I don't smell anything," Clarice said as she put her nose in the air and sniffed. "Except for the stench of cigarettes. One of these zookeepers is definitely a smoker."

Vesta had momentarily forgotten that Kevin wasn't *au courant* that she could talk to cats, and she wasn't about to explain it to him either. Good thing he couldn't see her. He probably thought she was just another one of her cats meowing. Then again, it wasn't essential to their mission that he knew. Need-to-know basis and all that.

"Do the cats know something that we don't, Vesta?" asked Scarlett now.

"No, they don't," Vesta said. "So far, I have no eyes on the Shaver. You?"

"Nope. Nothing happening here either."

She sighed. "Maybe it's all for the best. After the hullabaloo of last night, maybe we need a quiet night for a change."

"Especially with the big wedding coming up," Scarlett said, clearly in agreement.

"I hope he shows up," said Kevin. And she could understand where he was coming from. After all, this was his first-ever stake-out, and if nothing happened, that would be a major disappointment for the young man.

* * *

"I WONDER why these giraffes have such a long neck," Dooley said. "Doesn't it get uncomfortable, you think, Max?"

"You tell me, Dooley," I said. "After all, you're the Discovery Channel person."

"I don't think I've seen a documentary about giraffes yet,"

he confessed. "So maybe we should ask them? They'll be able to tell us, right?"

"I think we should probably let them sleep," I said, not wanting to rock the boat or cause a stir. As far as I could tell, the giraffes were all fast asleep, and I much preferred to keep it that way.

We had positioned ourselves underneath a tree across the little pathway that led past the giraffes' enclosure. The animals themselves were resting peacefully, and so far, the Shaver, if such a person even existed, and if the loss of fur hadn't been self-inflicted or the consequence of an unfortunate run-in with a sharp rock or something, hadn't shown his face yet.

"So, are we going to gatecrash the wedding, Max?" asked Dooley.

"I suppose so. At least drop by to show our faces, you know. If only out of respect."

"So, none of you received a formal invitation?" asked Clarice, who still couldn't get over the fact that she hadn't been invited.

"No, we did not," I confirmed. "As a rule, cats are not invited to weddings, Clarice. At least not officially."

"So, if I wanted to, I could also gatecrash this wedding?"

"Of course. Join the rest of us while we pop round to chuckle at the groom's attire and marvel at the bride's dress. It's going to be a fun day for all."

Though maybe not for the groom. Even though Uncle Alec was happy to have finally found a suit that fit, I got the impression that he would much rather have worn casual clothes to his own wedding. But Charlene wouldn't hear of it. She wanted a classic wedding with people dressing up and making an effort to look their absolute best.

Maybe she was right. If you're not even going to dress up for your own wedding, then when are you? I think she was even slightly disappointed at this moment by the groom's lack of excitement about the whole thing, possibly mistaking his reluctance to star in a show that he felt had spiraled out of control for a lack of interest in her. Brides are sensitive that way.

"Mayday, mayday!" suddenly Brutus's voice sounded over the airwaves. "We have a possible sighting of the Shaver. I repeat: a possible sighting of the Shaver!"

I wasn't sure whether 'mayday' was the correct term to be used on this occasion, but at least Brutus had made his meaning perfectly clear and also its urgency.

"What do we do, Max!" Dooley cried. "We can't leave our post!"

"All hands on deck!" Gran bellowed—too loud for my taste.

"What's with all the maritime references?" I asked with a touch of pique but still did as I was told and got up from my perch to join the others.

"Where is Brutus?" asked Shanille.

"The elephants," I said.

"Who in their right mind tries to shave an elephant!" Kingman said.

"He's already shaved a tiger," I said. "So why not try an elephant?"

"Because it's dangerous, that's why! He'll get himself killed!"

Before long, Dooley and I were racing along in the direction of the elephant enclosure. When we got there, we searched around for Brutus and Harriet, and when we couldn't immediately locate them, my earpiece crackled, and Brutus hissed, "Look up!"

So I did, and much to my surprise, found Brutus and Harriet located on a branch. It was some good thinking on their part as they had a perfect view of the enclosure from their position.

"Do you see him?" I asked.

"I do, yeah," said Brutus. "He clambered over the fence, snuck up to one of the elephants, and he's in the process of shaving the poor creature's leg!"

Dooley and I approached the enclosure, and lo and behold, Brutus was right. A man sat crouched next to one of the elephants, who was fast asleep, and was carefully shaving the elephant's leg with what looked like a cordless beard trimmer, catching the trimmings in a little plastic bag.

We were soon joined by Kingman and Shanille, and when Gran and Clarice arrived, followed by Scarlett and Kevin, the Shaver had quite the audience.

"We have to make sure he doesn't escape," Gran whispered to her friend. "Maybe you go round the back and guard the exit. I'll stay out here and try to catch him as he tries to leave."

"Will do," said Scarlett. Kevin, who looked extremely excited now that the action had begun, practically stood dancing from one foot to the other.

"What shall I do?" he whispered.

"You go with Scarlett."

"Oh, this is so great!" he said. "I love the watch, Vesta!"

"Looks like we've got another recruit," Scarlett said with a grin.

We watched as the man methodically shaved part of the elephant's leg, closed the ziplock bag, and tucked it into his backpack. Then he carefully made his way back to the fence. As he did, he tripped over a branch and stumbled into the shallow pool that the elephants use to cool off on a hot day. The splash he made must have alerted the animals of the presence of an intruder, for they both woke up and looked in the direction of the Shaver.

"Uh-oh," said Gran. "He's in trouble now."

One of the elephants now pointed with her trunk to the leg of her mate. "You're missing some fur, honey bunch."

The second elephant uttered a squeal of dismay. "Aaaaaargh!" he said.

Then the first elephant caught sight of the plastic baggie containing part of her mate's missing fur. "He stole it!" she said. "That little man stole it, sugar plum!"

It was at this moment that the elephants saw that a captive audience stood watching the scene. And since I figured this would prevent a lot of awkwardness later on, I decided to introduce myself. "Hi, my name is Max," I said. "And we're here to stop this man from shaving you."

"Well, you did a pretty lousy job, didn't you, Max!" the male elephant bellowed. "He's gone and shaved me, hasn't he!"

"Yes, he has," I agreed.

"I'm going to squish him," said the elephant. "I'm going to squish that fella like a bug!" And he got up from his position with a view to carry out his promise.

"Maybe don't squish him," I suggested. "If you do, there will be a lot of trouble, Mr..."

"Jack," said the elephant. "And I don't care! He's the one who started this!"

"Sugar plum, don't," said the female elephant. "You know what humans are like. They get so upset when you stomp on one of them. Remember your uncle Henry?" She turned to me. "Some kid once shot at him with a toy gun, so Uncle Henry got really upset and grabbed the kid and dragged him through the fence. You should have seen the reaction from the zookeepers. You'd think Uncle Henry had committed mass murder! All he did was kick this kid around a little."

"He didn't even kill him," Jack grumbled. "Henry always was a softie."

He had approached the Shaver now, but the latter had decided not to stick around and was now running around the enclosure, trying to get away from the very large animal he'd pissed off. When he tried to climb the fence, Jack simply dragged him down again with his trunk and stood over him in a sort of menacing fashion, causing the Shaver to scream out for help.

"Now you've gone and done it," said Gran.

The Shaver looked over and located the source of the statement. When his eyes met Gran's, he cried, "Get me out of here, miss. Please get me out of here!"

"You shouldn't go around shaving wild animals, buddy," Gran admonished him. "They will get upset, and then where are you?"

"Don't give me a lecture, just get me out!"

Gran bridled a little at this. "I'll give you a lecture any time I please. You shouldn't be in there!"

"Please help me!" cried the guy.

"Don't stomp on him," I told Jack. "It will end badly for you."

"The cat is right, Jack," said his partner. "They threatened to put down Uncle Henry after he gave that kid a good thrashing, remember? He was only saved because he was a gift from the Maharajah, and there would have been a diplomatic incident. But you're not a gift from any Maharajah, Jack!"

"I know, Diane," said Jack as he reluctantly took a step back. "But look at my leg! I look ridiculous!"

"It will grow back," I said. "Won't it?"

"Or you could always wear a leg wig," Dooley suggested.

"A leg wig!" said the elephant. "You're pulling my trunk, aren't you, little fella?"

"No, I'm serious," Dooley assured him. "Or you could wear a leg scarf. Make it look fun. Or they could tell visitors that you hurt your leg. That way, people will sympathize and give you all kinds of presents. They could even do one of those crowdfunding campaigns. Make it a thing."

"He's right, Jack," said Diane. "You can turn this around. Make it a moment of triumph."

"Oh, hell," said Jack, who didn't look entirely convinced. But at least he wasn't going to stomp on the Shaver until he was as flat as a pancake.

Gran now assisted the Shaver in clambering over the fence, but once he was safely on the other side, she immediately fastened a pair of handcuffs on his wrists. "Mr. Shaver," she declared solemnly. "You're under arrest!"

"Oh, hell!" said the Shaver, inadvertently stomping all over Jack's copyright.

And as Gran placed a heavy hand on the man's collar, she asked the question that had been puzzling us all along: "Why did you do it, eh? Why did you feel the need to shave these poor creatures?"

The man, whose name turned out to be Roosevelt Toal, hung his head in shame. "I just wanted to know, all right?"

"Know what? What are you talking about?"

She had fished the plastic baggie from the man's backpack and now held it up. Along with this one, there were several more baggies, and all of them had been labeled: tiger, elephant, giraffe. Some were filled with fur, others empty, and it looked as if he had planned to take a sampling of every single animal in the zoo. "I mean, what do you need all these for?" she demanded.

"It's my mom," said the man reluctantly. "She keeps telling me my dad was an animal."

"Why would she say that?" Scarlett inquired.

The guy sighed. "I guess she decided to come clean? I mean, I've known for a long time that I'm different, you know. I wasn't like the other kids in school. And I keep getting arrested, for one thing. Mostly for petty stuff. Stealing cars and such. And every time it's my mom who has to bail me out. And she doesn't like it. So last week, when I was arrested again, and she came to bail me out, we got in the car, and she started shouting at me. Telling me I was just like my dad, who was an animal, just like me! But when I asked her what kind of animal, she clammed up. And it just wouldn't leave me. Kept going round and round in my head. And finally, I decided that I simply had to know."

Gran exchanged a blank look with Scarlett. Clearly, they were at a loss.

Mr. Toal noticed the look and shrugged. "Wouldn't you want to know?"

"Know what?!" Gran practically screamed, losing her patience.

"What kind of animal my dad was, of course. A lion, a giraffe, an elephant? My mom wouldn't tell me, so I just figured I'd find out myself. So I'm sampling all of these, and I'm giving them to this buddy of mine, who works at some lab somewhere that does something with DNA and all, and he's going to test these against my DNA and find out what kind of animal my dad really was." He looked pained. "I just hope it's not a hippopotamus. I really don't like hippopotamuses. They're scary."

CHAPTER 29

Wilbur Vickery and Francis Reilly weren't exactly enthusiastic or even experienced members of the neighborhood watch. In fact, the only reason they had gone along with this particular mission was because Vesta simply wouldn't let up. The Pancake Burglar had played her and Scarlett for fools last night, and she wasn't going to let that happen without some repercussions for the man in question. And so both men now sat in Francis's black Peugeot while they patrolled the neighborhood where the burglar had last been seen.

"I don't mind telling you that I don't like this, Wilbur," Francis confessed as they passed through the same street they had passed three times before at a snail's pace. "I don't like it one bit."

"Do you think I like it?" his associate grumbled. "I've got stock to check, boxes to unpack, labels to print. And here I am, driving along looking for this elusive Pancake Burglar, who probably is sitting at home right now laughing his ass off for the neat trick he played on Vesta and Scarlett."

"I have a sermon to write," Francis said with a sigh. He knew people thought these sermons wrote themselves, but that was hardly the case. Some colleagues plucked them off the internet, of course, ready-made, but he wasn't that kind of priest. Every sermon he had ever given, he had agonized over, sweating bullets in the process. He wasn't a gifted writer, and every word had to be wrung from his imagination and coerced out practically at gunpoint. "And a wedding to prepare."

"I saw Alec this morning," Wilbur commented as he slipped down a little more in his seat. Pretty soon now, he'd probably fall asleep. "He didn't look so happy. Are you sure he even wants to get married?"

"He proposed," Francis said. "And when he and Charlene came to see me last month, they both looked as happy as can be. Why? Do you know something I don't?" He had almost said, 'If you object to this wedding, speak now or forever hold your peace,' but had stopped himself just in time. Force of habit, of course.

"Oh, no," said Wilbur. "I'm sure they'll be very happy together. It's just that..." He hesitated, gave his compadre a quick sideways glance, then continued, "Charlene's first husband..."

"Yes? What about him?"

"Well, he was a crook."

"He was?"

"Defrauded the company he worked for out of a lot of money. Which makes me wonder if Charlene isn't overcompensating now by marrying a cop."

"I'm sure Charlene loves Alec very much, and vice versa," said the priest, who was determined to always see the best in people. "And besides, Charlene's husband may have been a crook, but that had nothing to do with her."

"I wouldn't be too sure. The guy couldn't have pulled off what he did without a little support from the home front, if you know what I mean."

Francis's lips tightened, and a foreboding look stole over his face. The worst part about living in a small town was the gossip, he had decided long ago. And he was relentless about pulling that type of pernicious vice out by the root. "That's nothing but foul gossip, Wilbur, and frankly beneath you."

"Oh, it is, is it?" said Wilbur with a touch of belligerence. "Well, I'll have you know that it was a member of Charlene's own family who told me, so it's not gossip if it's true."

"Charlene's own family believes she colluded with her criminal husband?"

"Yes, they do. So there." He had folded his arms across his chest and looked like an angry toddler.

"I don't think Charlene is a crook," Francis said carefully.

Wilbur relented. "Well... no, I don't think so either. It's just that... where there's smoke, there's fire, right? She must have known what her husband was up to and didn't act on it. Which in itself is criminal behavior."

"Mm," said Francis. He decided not to dignify these accusations with a response. He happened to be very fond of both Charlene and Alec and thought theirs was a match made in heaven. But still, if this type of gossip was making the rounds, perhaps it behooved him to take it up with the couple, just to make sure they knew what they were up against and take measures to address it.

"Look!" suddenly Wilbur yelled and pointed to a house across the street.

While they were engrossed in their conversation, Francis had stopped the car and parked it across from the Waverly place, one of his most faithful and devoted parishioners. There was no light on inside, so what was that man dressed in black from head to toe doing sneaking across the front lawn?

"It must be the Pancake Burglar," Wilbur said.

"Are you sure?" said Francis, suddenly feeling a little queasy. It's one thing to agree to go on patrol, but quite another to actively intervene when a person is signaling their burglarious intent by entering a place under the cover of darkness. One never knows if this person is carrying a gun and is willing to use it on whoever stands in their way. "Maybe we should call the police?"

"And miss our chance at tasting those pancakes? Vesta said they're delicious. The best she's ever tasted." Wilbur pounded his hand with his fist. "I'm having pancakes tonight, Francis. Whether you like it or not!"

And with these words, he put his hand on the door handle.

"Wait!" said Francis, staying his partner's departure. "There won't be any pancakes if we catch him now, will there? The man follows a strict procedure: first he burgles the place, stashing the loot, then he bakes the pancakes. So if we go in now—no pancakes."

Wilbur gave him a shrewd look. "Good thinking, Francis. You're right. We better wait until he's had time to collect the loot." He checked his watch. "How long does it take to whip up a bowl of batter? Fifteen minutes? Twenty?"

"Half an hour at least—or more. You want your batter to set. It makes the pancakes light and fluffy. And we like light and fluffy, don't we?"

"Oh, yes we do," said Wilbur, licking his lips with glee. "We love light and fluffy!"

And so they settled in for the duration, making sure they kept a close eye on the place, lest their pancake supplier escape before the deed was done.

"I really hope it's the guy we're looking for," said Francis.

"Of course it is. Who else could it be? The Waffle Burglar?"

The shopkeeper laughed loudly at his own joke, but Francis wasn't laughing. If they had sat out an actual burglary without intervening, there would be hell to pay if the Waverlys found out.

CHAPTER 30

Charlene darted a look of concern at her soon-to-be husband. Alec hadn't been his usual sunny self these past couple of days, and it worried her. A man who's on the verge of linking his lot to the woman he loves shouldn't look so downcast. Which told her that maybe he wasn't as in love with her as she had previously thought. So far, she had held off on addressing her concerns, but now she felt she could wait no longer. Tomorrow was the rehearsal dinner, and the next day they'd stand up in front of their families and loved ones and pledge their troth. If they didn't thresh this out now, it would be too late, and Alec might make the biggest mistake of his life. And she, too, of course.

They were in bed, with Alec reading a book about fly fishing and Charlene reading a bridal magazine for some last-minute tips. She removed her reading glasses and chewed on the temple tip for a moment as she wondered how to broach this most delicate subject. Finally, she gathered her courage and cleared her throat. "Alec?"

"Hm?"

"Is something the matter?"

He didn't look up. "Hm?"

"You seem troubled."

"I'm fine."

This was going to prove harder than she had anticipated. But she was nothing if not persistent, so she decided to tackle the topic head-on. No prevarications. "It's just that you seem very unhappy. Are you having second thoughts about the wedding?"

This time he did look up and even put down the book. He eyed her with a touch of astonishment. "Second thoughts? Why would you think that? Are you having second thoughts?"

"No, of course not. But you have been so distracted lately that I thought..."

"I'm not having second thoughts about marrying you, sweetheart," he assured her. "But..."

She knew there would be a 'but.' So she steeled herself. "But?"

"It's just that... I'm going to look like such a fool. In my penguin suit, standing up there in front of all those people. What are they going to think of me? I'm the chief of police. I'm a person who should be projecting authority. And now they'll finally see me for who I really am: a fraud, a fake, a fool."

Her heart melted. "Oh, honey. Is that what you really think?"

"When I saw myself in the mirror at the store today, I could just imagine what people will think when they see me standing there in that church. They'll laugh at me, make jokes at my expense. Maybe they'll even shoot a video on their phones and share it. They'll turn me into a meme, honey, I just know they will. I'll be the laughingstock of this town, and I'll never have their respect ever again. Next time I arrest some young punk, he'll show me a TikTok video of me, and laugh in my face."

"But sweetie, I saw the pictures Marge took of you in your suit."

His head jerked up. "You saw me in my tux? But you shouldn't have. It's bad luck to see the groom before the wedding."

"Oh, that's just a load of superstition," said Charlene. "I saw the pictures, and I have to say, you look absolutely gorgeous in that suit. Marge did a great job picking it out for you." She squeezed his arm. "No one is going to laugh at you. On the contrary, they're all going to think you're a real catch."

"And you caught me," he said with a half-smile as he tapped the cover of his book. An angler had caught a large fish and posed with it for the camera.

"I did—and I'm never throwing you back. Just so you know."

"Oh, I wouldn't want you to. I'm glad you caught me—or I caught you."

"We caught each other," she corrected him and pressed a loving kiss to his lips. She had picked the wrong one the first time around, but she was making up for it big time now. Greatly relieved, she put her reading glasses back on and soon was reading up on the latest bridal fashion. Then, since she wasn't really interested in what other brides wore at their weddings, she put down the magazine and snuggled up to her big bear of a man. Soon she was asleep.

* * *

ALEC WATCHED as his bride-to-be slept peacefully and thought he was probably the luckiest man alive. And if she was correct and he didn't look like an idiot in that tux, maybe he'd be able to go through this ordeal with some equanimity and emerge unscathed. He couldn't remember having been this nervous at his first wedding, but then he'd been a lot younger and hadn't been chief of police. When you assume a position of authority, you step into the limelight and people suddenly look at you differently. Then again, with Charlene by his side and his family occupying the first couple of pews, he should be fine.

And he was just about to join his fiancée in the land of nod when his phone made its funny noise, announcing that a message had arrived and required his attention. When he grabbed it from the nightstand and checked, he saw that it was from the night dispatcher.

'Trouble at the station. Please advise.'

He frowned as he slipped from between the covers, careful not to disturb Charlene, then tiptoed out of the room, closing the door behind him, and headed downstairs. At some point, they'd have to decide which house they were going to live in, he thought. For now, they spent some nights at his place and some at Charlene's, though he had to admit Charlene's was probably the better option.

He walked into her large living room and looked out through the sliding glass doors into the backyard. The dispatcher picked up on the first ring. It wasn't Dolores, who could handle any trouble without involving the Chief, but a new recruit who had immediately been thrown in at the deep end.

"What's all this about trouble at the station, Mortensen?" he asked.

"A neighbor called nine-one-one, Chief. Said she thought she'd seen two burglars. So a patrol car was sent out, and they arrested Wilbur Vickery and Francis Reilly. They claim they were staking out a house, but the officers are both new and didn't know the arrangement with the neighborhood watch, so they ignored their protestations and brought them into the station. They're not happy."

"Oh, God. Not again."

"And your mother made a citizen's arrest at the zoo. A guy who's been illegally shaving the animals."

"Shaving the animals?!"

"Yes, sir. He says his mom told him his dad was an animal, so he wanted to find out what animal this could possibly be and asked a buddy to test the fur against his DNA."

"Tell me this is a joke."

"It's not. Though it's safe to say the guy isn't the smartest tool in the shed."

"Name?"

"Roosevelt Toal."

Alec groaned. "I know Toal. Probably the dumbest criminal in Hampton Cove. Him and his brother Taft. So now he's out harassing animals, huh? Wonder whether the judge will laugh him out of the dock or throw the book at him for contempt of court."

"So what about Vickery and Reilly, sir?"

"Let them go. And enlighten those officers on the activities of the neighborhood watch." He waited for his dispatcher to hang up, and when she didn't, he asked reluctantly, "Is there anything else?"

"Well... Vickery and Reilly claimed they were on the verge of catching the Pancake Burglar. And as it turns out, they weren't lying."

"Tell me it isn't so."

"Delicious pancakes."

"You tasted them?"

"The officers who responded to the victim's call brought some to the station. And your mother wasn't kidding, sir. They really taste fantastic. The guy may be a lousy burglar, but he's one hell of a pancake chef."

He cursed under his breath and ended the call. Even on the eve of his wedding, they simply could not leave him in peace, could they? At least Ma hadn't been arrested this time, so that was progress.

He returned to bed and inadvertently woke up Charlene.

"Who was that?" she asked.

"You don't want to know."

She smiled. "Cheating on me already, are you? And we aren't even married yet."

He grinned. "At least you know what you're signing up for."

"Oh, I know what I'm signing up for. My big sweet teddy bear."

Soon they were snuggling, and before long, they were both fast asleep.

CHAPTER 31

Even though he should have been fast asleep, against his better judgment Tex Poole was still up. He had recently become enamored with the trials and tribulations of a well-known writer who had lived in Great Neck, Long Island, and now he couldn't stop reading the man's work. Already, he had read all of the books available at the library, which Marge had been so good as to bring home for him, and now he was reading the remainder of the man's oeuvre on his e-reader. And as he was thusly engrossed while his wife lay asleep next to him, he wondered why nobody had ever bothered to tell him how enjoyable reading could be.

As a doctor, he had read plenty, of course, but mostly textbooks and voluminous medical tomes that he had to learn by heart. Frankly speaking, he thought that perhaps all of it had put him off reading. But now it had returned—with a vengeance! It wasn't as though the household he was a part of was fully devoid of reading material, though. With his wife a librarian and his daughter also an avid reader—even his mother-in-law enjoyed perusing the odd book from time to time—there were always plenty of books lying around. And as he now chuckled his way through another pleasant little tome, he was already dreading the moment he had gone through all of the writer's vast output.

Just as he had glanced at his bedside clock and told himself he really should go to sleep now, a peculiar sound reached his ears. It seemed to come from downstairs and sounded like the clanging of pots and pans. Knowing that Vesta was out on one of her patrols again, he figured she must have returned and was making herself some hot milk before she went to bed. And since he enjoyed hot milk as much as the next person, he decided that maybe it wasn't a bad idea to join the stalwart watch member.

He yawned as he slowly made his way down the stairs, but when he entered the kitchen, much to his surprise, he found himself staring not into the familiar face of his mother-in-law, but at a man he had never seen before. He was youngish, had bulbous eyes and a jutting jaw, and seemed as surprised to see the doctor as Tex was to see him.

"Who are you?" said Tex immediately.

The man blinked, then aimed the frying pan he was holding at Tex's head and made a run for the kitchen door. The doctor ducked the pan and lunged for the man's legs. The moment he grabbed them, he held on for dear life as the nocturnal marauder bucked and writhed in an attempt to get away from him. But Tex wasn't the kind of homeowner who was prepared to let just anyone enter his home unannounced and start throwing pans at his head. And since he had considerable strength in his hands and arms, due to the countless operations he performed as a matter of routine, the man must have felt his legs had gotten trapped in a particularly enthusiastic vise.

After a while, he stopped moving, knowing he was licked.

"If you've come for a consultation," Tex said, panting a

little, "you should really make an appointment. I don't like it when people simply show up."

It had often been the way these past couple of years. Patients would first drop by the office, and when they didn't find him there, they would come to the house. In the beginning, he had welcomed them into his home and provided them with whatever it was that they needed. He had even performed minor surgical procedures on his kitchen table. But after a while, he had tired of the invasion of his privacy and had put up a sign next to the doorbell that Doctor Poole was only available at his office. It was the first time, though, someone dropped by in the middle of the night.

Vesta chose that exact moment to enter the house via the kitchen door and for a moment stood staring down at the two men. Then she grinned. "You are a dark horse, aren't you, Tex? I didn't know you were into wrestling?"

"I'm not. Either this man is a patient, though I've never seen him before, or he was up to something. He threw a pan at my head, so I'm starting to consider the latter explanation as the most likely one."

Vesta frowned. "A pan? What kind of pan?"

"A frying pan. It's lying over there by the wall. I just hope it didn't make a dent." It certainly had been the man's intention to make a dent in his head.

Vesta picked up the pan and studied it. "You're not by any chance the Pancake Burglar, are you?" she said. "I've been looking for you, buddy."

The man seemed to have lost his tongue, for he didn't respond.

"You do make some really great pancakes, though. I had some last night and they were absolutely delicious. You have to give me your recipe."

This seemed to appeal to the young man, for he smiled. "You really liked them?"

"Absolutely," said Vesta. "They're the best ones I've eaten —ever."

"It's my ma's recipe," said the man. "She got it from her ma, and so on down the generations. It's a secret, though, so I can't give it to you."

"Oh, that's too bad."

He thought for a moment. "Though if you promise to let me go, I'll consider it."

For a moment, Vesta seemed to waver. "No way," Tex said. "Don't even think about it."

"They are really good."

"This man is a burglar!"

"I know, but he's also a very talented pancake chef." She sighed. "No, I guess you're right. We shouldn't set a bad example. That's a no, sonny jim," she said. "I'm afraid you're under arrest."

"Darn it," said the kid. "I knew I shouldn't have gone out again."

"Oh, this isn't your first house, is it?"

"No, I hit this other place. But they didn't have a lot worth stealing, so I figured I'd try another one."

"There isn't a lot worth stealing here either," Vesta pointed out.

"No, I noticed that," said the kid, sounding disappointed. He turned to Tex. "Are you poor, sir?"

"No, I'm not poor!" said Tex.

"But not rich either," said Vesta.

"It's just that I don't like ripping off the rich," said the kid. "They always got these Dobermans or Rottweilers and an army of armed guards. It takes the fun out of the profession."

Vesta's lips curled up into a smile. "You're a very intriguing young man, aren't you? What's your name?"

"Taft Toal."

"No, but really."

"No, that's my name. All the male members of our family are named after presidents. They started with the very first one, and by now they're somewhere in the middle, I guess. My brother is called Roosevelt, and I'm Taft."

"I think I met your brother," said Vesta. "At the zoo."

"Possible," said Taft. "He's got this obsession with animals. No idea why."

"Well, pleased to meet you, Taft," said Vesta, and actually held out her hand!

Tex shook his head. He liked pancakes as much as the next man, but he couldn't imagine shaking the hand of a crook just because he was good at making pancakes.

"Could you… make some for us?" Vesta now asked. "Just a couple?"

The kid smiled. "Only if you promise not to press charges."

Vesta darted a look at her son-in-law, who shook his head. "No!" he said.

"You heard the man," said Vesta.

"Are you a cop, sir?" asked Taft.

"No, I'm a doctor."

"Oh, is that right?" He rolled up his pants leg. "Could you take a look at this weird spot? It wasn't there before, and suddenly it appeared. Could it be cancer?"

If he'd heard this question once, he'd heard it a thousand times. But when he took a closer look at the spot in question, he had to admit it did look a little suspicious. "You better have that checked by a dermatologist," he suggested.

"Thanks, sir," said the kid. He wavered for a moment. "Okay, so I'll make you some of my mother's famous pancakes. Just because you were kind enough to check my spot. But just this once, you hear?"

And before long, Taft Toal was whipping up a nice batch of batter, and Tex had to admit he knew his way around a kitchen. And as both he and Vesta sat around admiring the man's skills, he asked, "Why do you burgle houses? You could be a pastry chef, or a cook, or anything you like."

Taft shrugged. "Well, it's my job, sir. I mean, my dad was a crook, my granddad was a crook, and so were all my ancestors. So it just stood to reason that both me and my brother would follow in their footsteps. Dad would be very disappointed if we didn't, see. He was big on tradition, my dad was."

"That would be the animal your mother refers to?" asked Vesta.

Taft grinned. "Dad was a force of nature, all right."

"He died?"

"Yep. Fell off the roof of a house he was burgling."

"But isn't it annoying that you get arrested all the time?" asked Tex.

"That's also part of the tradition, sir. My granddad used to boast that he spent half his life in prison, and my dad only one third of his life. But then my dad claimed he still had plenty of time to make up for that, though as it turned out he didn't. So it's almost like a competition with us."

The smell of the pancakes wafted through the kitchen, and Tex's stomach was rumbling with anticipatory delight. He couldn't wait to sink his teeth into the delicacy. Marge must have been awakened by the noise and the delicious smell, for she now appeared at the door, stretching and yawning. "What's going on here?" she asked. But when she saw Taft expertly flip a pancake into the air, she pressed her hands together with delight. "Oh, will you look at that? Is he a friend of yours?"

Vesta hesitated, then nodded. "Yeah, this is Taft. Taft, meet my daughter Marge. And this is her husband Tex. I'm Vesta Muffin, by the way."

Taft laughed. "I make a mean muffin, Mrs. Muffin. Just so you know."

Some people called Vesta a mean muffin, Tex thought ruefully, but wisely kept his tongue. He wasn't going to risk Vesta's ire now that he was so close to tasting 'the best pancakes in the world.'

"Dig in," said Taft, and placed a plate of steaming pancakes on the table. Tex picked up one and took a bite. Immediately the taste captured his senses and made him close his eyes in delight. "Now this is a good pancake!" he cried.

Taft grinned as he wiped his hands on a dish towel. "My mom is a pastry chef, and so was her mom, and her mom before her. So I guess it runs in the family."

It sure did. Crooks on his father's side, pastry chefs on his mother's side. What an odd combination. At least they got to enjoy the pancakes, not the burglary!

They all ate their fill, and when they were full, for a moment Tex wondered how to proceed. By rights, he should call the police so they could arrest Taft on the spot. Then again, the boy had given them a culinary treat without compare. And he hadn't actually stolen anything.

He shared a look with Vesta, whose eyes were sparkling. Finally, he nodded, causing his mother-in-law to shoot him a grateful look that went a long way to alleviating his sense of guilt.

"Promise me to behave from now on, Taft," said Vesta as she wagged a finger in the kid's face.

"I will, Mrs. Muffin," said Taft easily.

"No more…" She darted a quick look at her daughter. "Well, you know."

"And have that spot looked at," Tex said.

"I will, Doctor Poole," said Taft. "Thanks."

And with these words, he took his leave.

"That was the Pancake Burglar, wasn't it?" said Marge the moment the kid had left.

"It was," Vesta confirmed.

"Too bad he's a burglar. He could make me pancakes every day."

"He's very talented," Tex agreed.

"I'm sure he'll walk the straight and narrow from now on," said Vesta.

Somehow, Tex wasn't so sure about that. He made a grab for the final couple of pancakes, but Marge snatched them from under his nose. "These are for Odelia," she announced and placed the plate in the fridge.

They'd enjoyed a rare treat, but Marge was right: it's important to share.

And then it was time to go to bed, so they all turned in. He just hoped Taft wouldn't be back to rob them blind—without leaving a batch of delicious pancakes this time.

CHAPTER 32

It had been an eventful night for all of us, save perhaps for Odelia and Chase, who had spent a relaxing time at home. As the four of us sat on the couch, still a little bleary-eyed, I have to admit, we watched the human procession in the breakfast nook as they got ready for their day. First, Gran dropped by and announced that last night's bust had gone off without a hitch.

"We arrested Roosevelt Toal, aka the Shaver, and also received a visit from his brother Taft, aka the Pancake Burglar. So all in all, a good night."

Chase had looked up sharply at the mention of the Pancake Burglar. "You finally nabbed the Pancake Burglar?"

"I didn't say that. I said he paid us a visit. Delicious pancakes, by the way. Wouldn't you agree, Marge?"

Odelia's mom had entered through the sliding glass door and gave her mother an uncertain look. "They were delicious," she confirmed.

"A guilty pleasure, wouldn't you say?" Gran added with a wink.

"So why didn't you have the guy arrested?" asked Chase.

"He didn't steal anything," said Gran. "Just showed off his pastry skills."

"Which are impressive," Marge said, then quickly changed the subject. "So today is the day, huh? Rehearsal dinner? Are you all as excited as I am?"

"Okay, but you knew he was wanted by the police, so why didn't you call it in?" asked Chase, who can really be like a dog with a bone sometimes.

"It's called compassion, Chase," said Gran. "It's a Christian thing."

"All well and good," said the cop. "But this guy has got a string of burglaries to his name, so I would very much like to put him behind bars. Pancakes or no pancakes. So next time you see him, you call it in. Is that understood?"

"Aye aye, sir," said Gran, giving the cop a two-fingered salute.

"He's been very busy, this pancake man of yours," said Odelia.

"He's not *my* pancake man," said Gran.

"He also burgled a house on Forster Street. Unfortunately, it wasn't the pancake man who was arrested but two innocent neighborhood watch members instead." We all watched as Gran's eyes went wide as saucers.

"My watch members? Arrested? Say it isn't so!"

"It is so," Odelia said. "Wilbur Vickery and Father Reilly. Try as they might, they couldn't convince the arresting officer that they weren't burglars casing out a house but law-abiding members of the public on neighborhood watch business. But then the desk sergeant notified my uncle, and he instructed them to release the two men."

"I guess he didn't want to jeopardize his wedding," said Marge. "With Father Reilly in jail, he would have had to call the whole thing off."

"Oh, dear," said Gran. "This is what you get when you

don't hold their hands. The one time I send them out into the field all by themselves, and immediately they get themselves in trouble."

It seems to be a recurring theme for watch members to be arrested. At least they had been sprung from prison. Otherwise, poor Shanille and Kingman would have been parentless for the foreseeable future.

Breakfast over, our humans all went their separate ways: Grace to the daycare center, Marge to the library, Gran to the doctor's office to assist Tex, Chase to the police station, and Odelia to the offices of the *Gazette*. As for the rest of us… Frankly, I felt like staying home and having a nice long nap. But unfortunately, fate decided differently. No sooner had Odelia left than she was back again, waving her phone.

"We're off to interview Tarsha Kettles," she announced. "Are you coming?"

"But we already interviewed Tarsha Kettles," I protested.

"Mrs. Kettles has been lying to us," she said curtly.

"Oh, go on, Max," said Harriet.

"You're not coming?" I asked.

"I have my autobiography to finish," she pointed out. "I want to have it ready in time for the wedding, and I still have my adult years to cover."

"And I'm also staying put," said Brutus. "I'm Harriet's autobiography-writing assistant."

"Every star author needs an assistant," said Harriet. "And I've got the best assistant of all."

Outside, the sound of a car honking could be heard, and judging from the way Odelia stood twitching, I had a feeling it was Chase's way of letting us know that time was of the essence.

And so we said goodbye for now to the autobiography-writing pair and took our leave.

Once we were in the car, Odelia explained that another

letter from the 'well-wisher' had arrived at the *Gazette*, and this time it targeted Tarsha Kettles. Turned out that Tarsha wasn't the cozy mystery writer's real name. Kay Parker was. Turning to us, she said, "Kay Parker killed her mom and dad in a house fire in Chicago fifty years ago when she was a teenager. She later confessed that she had argued with her mom and dad the night before about a party she wanted to go to, and they wouldn't let her. She said she never wanted to kill them or even burn down the house. She just wanted to teach them a lesson, but things got out of hand. She called the fire department, but it was too late, and her parents died. She spent a couple of years in a juvenile jail and was released without fanfare, changed her name, and moved to Hampton Cove."

"But what does that have to do with the murder of Vernon Langridge?" I asked.

"The well-wisher claims that Tarsha was angry with Vernon because he had criticized her work in progress. The well-wisher implies that Tarsha has a short fuse, and that Vernon's critique set her off, the same way her mom and dad's refusal to let her go to the party did all those years ago. The letter writer calls her a psychopath who never truly repented what she did to her parents."

"Where does he get this information?" I asked.

"Beats me," said Odelia, turning back to face the front. "But if this is true, she just shot to number one on our list of suspects."

"You bet your life she has," Chase grunted in agreement.

It didn't take us long to reach our destination, and when Tarsha opened the door, it wasn't too much to say she was surprised to see us. She had probably hoped to see the back of us—especially me, with my flower-destroying tendencies. This time I took great care not to come anywhere near her precious flowers, and when Min toddled up to us and greeted us affectionately, I thought that at least one person in this household enjoyed our company.

"Why are you back?" asked Min.

"More questions," I explained.

"Apparently, your human killed her parents," said Dooley.

Min's eyes widened in shock. "What? No way!"

"It appears to be true," I said. Odelia wouldn't simply take this letter writer's word for it. She would have looked up the name Kay Parker and found that she had indeed been responsible for the death of her parents. But whether Kay Parker and Tarsha Kettles really were one and the same person remained to be seen.

"It's true," Tarsha now confessed. She had clasped her hands together in her lap and bowed her head. Seated on the couch, she looked old and frail, I thought, and I could imagine this business of the arson had hung over her head all these years. Over half a century is a long time to ponder a crime. "I didn't think anyone would find out," she said, "but obviously someone has gone to great lengths to dig into my secret past. But I didn't lie to you the first time. I had nothing to do with Vernon's death. Even the death of my parents was an accident. I never meant for them to die. I was an angry kid, lashing out because they had forbidden me from doing what I wanted, so I decided to teach them a lesson by setting fire to my dad's shed. He loved woodworking and had transformed the shed into a small workshop. So I figured I'd burn some of his stuff, only I hadn't counted on the fact that the whole shed would go up in flames in no time. The fire then spread to the main house, and before I knew it, our home was ablaze. I rushed to get help—this was before the age of the mobile phone—but by the time the fire department arrived, it was too late. My parents were trapped upstairs and died in the blaze. I spent the next ten years in jail, but I've spent the last fifty years in my own prison, my own hell, repenting and trying to make amends for what I've done." She looked up, a haunted look in her eyes. "And just when I thought that was all behind me, it's being dredged up again."

"How do you think this well-wisher knew about your past?" asked Chase.

"I have no idea. The only person I ever told was Vernon. He used to organize these New Year's parties for his customers and his writers' group members? One year, I drank a little too much and told him the story. He swore he wouldn't tell a living soul, but obviously, he must have. Whoever this letter writer is, clearly it's a vile person. Absolutely vile." She spoke with some heat. "Accusing me of murder. I could never murder anyone, least of all Vernon, who was a dear, dear friend, an extremely talented writer, and a man I admired very much."

"He claims that you killed Vernon because he criticized your work in progress," said Odelia.

Tarsha frowned. "Well, he did criticize my writing, and I admit that I felt upset about it at the time. But as I let his words sink in, I realized how right he was. He said it didn't live up to my previous work, and that I was better than that. So I set about to rewrite the sections he had flagged, and the book got a lot better for it, I have to say. So even though I was upset at first, I soon saw that he had done me a big favor. So it's simply preposterous to claim that I killed him because of that."

"So you still stand by your statement that you were home alone two nights ago?"

"Absolutely. I stayed in, along with Min. You could ask her," she added with a smile. "If cats could talk, I'm sure she'd be happy to confirm my alibi."

Dooley and I both turned to Min. "Can you confirm her alibi?" I asked.

"Yes, I can," said Min. "We were here all night. Tarsha

likes to read in the evening, and I like to keep her company. I fell asleep in the crook of her arm, so if she would have left at any point to murder this man, I would have known."

It seemed as good an alibi as any, even though it probably wouldn't stand up in court. Then again, we didn't need it to stand up, either in court or anywhere else, since at this stage we were simply trying to figure out what was going on and who could be in the frame for Vernon's murder.

"I'm still trying to come to terms with this whole well-wisher business," Tarsha said. "The things they said about me in that letter... I mean, the only people who would know about Vernon's critique of my work are the members of the writers' group. Which means one of them must be writing these foul letters. That means either Kenton or Marina. But try as I might, I just can't imagine either of them being evil enough to do such a horrible thing—I simply cannot."

CHAPTER 33

Odelia dropped us off in the heart of town. She had an article to write, and we had a lot to digest ourselves. Chase, meanwhile, returned to the police station, which felt a little desolate, he admitted, now that the Chief was absent from the helm. Almost as if the driving force behind the force, if you will, had downed tools. It wouldn't be long, of course. The moment the wedding had taken place, things would return to normal—which is just the way I like it.

"Do you think Min was telling the truth, Max?" asked Dooley as we traipsed along Main Street.

"I'm not sure. Pets do make unreliable witnesses sometimes, just like humans do. It could be that she's simply trying to protect Tarsha."

"I was thinking the same thing. She could be lying to protect her human. In which case, we have no idea what actually happened, do we?"

"No, we certainly don't."

"Maybe we should bring some pressure to bear on her? Like Chase sometimes does? Lock her up? A small space with nothing but the suspect, a powerful lamp shining in their eyes, and two cops hovering over her in a menacing fashion? Get her to crack under the pressure, you know."

I grinned at this odd image. "I very much doubt that kind of thing still exists in any police station, Dooley. If it ever did. Sounds more like something from a thirties gangster movie."

"It might work," he argued. "I could be the bad cop, and you could be the good cop, and together we might be able to break down her defenses."

"We don't even know if she was lying," I pointed out. "So there's no reason whatsoever to come down all hard and heavy on her."

"Yes, and I'm not sure I could do the bad cop part," he admitted. "That sounds more like something Brutus would enjoy." He looked up as if he'd just gotten a brilliant idea. "Now wouldn't that be something? Harriet could play the good cop, and Brutus the bad cop, and together they might be able to get at the truth."

"I have the impression Brutus and Harriet have better things to do right now than to assist us in our inquiries."

"Like writing that autobiography, you mean?"

From Harriet's words I got the impression that she was putting the finishing touches on her memoirs, and it was only a matter of time now before her masterpiece was ready. Following online instructions, she had taken a picture of herself with the tablet camera that would serve as the cover for the book, and the rest was all being handled behind the screens. Very soon now, the first copy of her autobiography would land on our doormat, and we would all be able to enjoy her life story. Some light reading, she called it. And on par with the kind of autobiography a real diva would pen.

We had arrived at the General Store, and much to my relief, Wilbur was in his usual spot behind the checkout counter, ringing up his customers' wares with a smile on his face and a quip on his lip. Clearly, his momentary incarceration hadn't dampened his typically upbeat spirits in the slightest.

"So he's been sprung from the pokey, has he?" I asked Kingman.

The voluminous cat looked sleepy, and I shouldn't wonder. Like us, he had spent half the night looking for the Shaver, and now he needed his rest.

"Yeah, he's right as rain again," Kingman confirmed. "He seems to feel it was a big adventure, though I'm not sure Father Reilly feels the same way."

Shanille now came ambling up and endorsed this point of view. "Father Reilly is very upset," she revealed. "He feels it's beneath his dignity as a man of the cloth to spend his night in a police jail. He's afraid that once word spreads about this misadventure, his parishioners will desert him en masse. Already the bishop has summoned him for an urgent tête-à-tête, so there will be consequences."

"But he did nothing wrong," I said. "It was all a big misunderstanding."

"Even to partake in an activity such as this stake-out is a big no-no for a priest," said Shanille. "Or at least that's how the bishop feels about it. So it looks as if Father Reilly's career as a neighborhood watch member is over. Until the whole hubbub has died down a little."

"Well, at least we now know who the Pancake Burglar is," I said.

Both Kingman and Shanille looked at me with consternation written all over their features. "You caught the Pancake Burglar?" asked Shanille.

"Not caught him exactly," I said, and explained what happened after the Pancake Burglar evaded capture and decided to burgle Marge and Tex's place instead.

"So the Pancake Burglar is the brother of the Shaver?" asked Kingman.

I confirmed this, causing my interlocutors to utter words of surprise. "Well, what do you know?" said Shanille. "Roosevelt and Taft Toal. I hope they both rot in jail for the rest of their miserable lives."

"Roosevelt didn't actually commit a major crime," I pointed out. "And Taft's pancakes are to die for, if Gran is to be believed. She's actually the one who decided to let him walk free."

"Just because he makes such delicious pancakes? But that's not fair!" said the choir director.

I shrugged. "Gran works in mysterious ways," was all I could say.

"Blasphemy," Shanille determined. "Please don't take the Lord's name in vain, Max."

"What did I say?!"

"You know."

I didn't, but then I wasn't particularly interested in getting into a theological argument with Shanille, so I wisely kept my tongue. "Look, all I'm saying is that maybe these men deserve a second chance. And Taft did promise Gran he would change his ways, and he seemed sincere about it."

"A leopard never changes its spots," Shanille said, taking the harsh view. "Especially a pair of career crooks like the Toal brothers."

Dooley derived a lot of jollity from this statement. "But Shanille, the Toal brothers aren't leopards. I'll bet they don't even have spots."

"All the same, they will never change their ways. Mark my words."

I marked her words and decided to move on since I felt we had exhausted the topic. "So another letter from the well-wisher arrived," I said, "and this time he revealed that Tarsha Kettles once killed her parents in an arson attack. She wondered how this person could know this, and I also wonder." I eyed my friends hopefully. "Maybe you've heard something that could shed light on this letter writer's identity?"

But both Kingman and Shanille confessed they had no clue either. "It's a fascinating world, though, isn't it?" said Kingman. "The world of literature? Take Wilbur, for instance. He doesn't look like a big reader, but he is."

"I know, you told me," said Shanille dryly. "Blair Beacock, right?"

"That's right. He's only the woman's biggest fan. She's such a major talent, isn't she? Writes bestseller after bestseller, and the quality never diminishes."

"That's because she hasn't written a book in fifteen years," said Shanille.

We all turned to our friend. "What?" I said, not hiding my astonishment.

Shanille nodded with satisfaction. Like Harriet, she enjoys being at the center of attention, though she's more circumspect about it. "That's right. Blair Beacock hasn't written a single book in fifteen years. All of those Chanel Birdsey books she brags about writing? Not a letter. Not one iota."

"But then who writes them?" I asked. "Her husband? Her son? Her daughter?"

"Vernon Langridge," said Shanille. "He was Blair's ghostwriter."

Sheer astonishment rendered us all mum for the moment, then we all burst into speech at the same time. Kingman got the upper hand since his dismay was more palpable than ours, considering the fact that Blair is Wilbur's favorite writer—perhaps the only writer whose books he reads, since

Wilbur is not exactly a voracious reader by any stretch of the imagination—quite the contrary.

"But that's impossible!" Kingman wailed. "He couldn't have—it's outrageous what you're suggesting, Shanille—simply beyond the pale!"

Shanille fixed him with a kindling eye. "Are you calling me a liar?"

Kingman quickly backtracked. "Oh no, of course not. But... Vernon? Max told me he couldn't even write. His own book was rejected by his publisher because it was unreadable. Trash."

"I don't know anything about that. All I know is that Father Reilly and Vernon were close friends. They both loved books, and one evening, when Vernon was over at our place, he and Father Reilly got to talking about Blair's books, and Vernon said he had a big secret, and if he told Father Reilly, would he promise not to tell anyone. And that's when he revealed that he had been writing the Chanel Birdsey books for the past fifteen years. As a ghostwriter."

"But that's not fair!" said Kingman. "Blair has signed Wilbur's copies. He has at least twenty signed copies of the Birdsey books in his library. Are you telling me that Blair has been lying to us about writing them herself?"

"That's exactly what I'm telling you," said Shanille, pleased as punch that she had been able to give us a scoop that none of us had been aware of. "Blair Beacock has been lying to people for years, claiming to write her own books, while in actual fact, she hired Vernon to write them for her."

"Odd that he didn't tell his writers' group," I said with a frown. I was wondering about the bearing this information would have on the investigation.

"Maybe he did," said Shanille with a shrug. "Though from what I remember, he was very insistent that Father Reilly didn't tell a living soul about this. It was all very much hush-hush. He really made him swear, and Father Reilly did."

"So why are you telling us?" said Kingman, still peeved about Blair's deception.

"I'm not Father Reilly, am I?" said Shanille. "I never made any promises."

She was right, of course. People tell all kinds of secrets to each other and never stop to consider that the walls have ears—or rather the pets have. And pets are probably the biggest gossips you can imagine. Which begged the question. "Why haven't you told us about this sooner?" I asked Shanille.

"It slipped my mind," said Shanille. "I mean, who cares who writes what books? I don't. And also, there's only one book that really matters, and that's the Bible. The rest is simply superficial fluff that will soon turn to dust."

"I guess so," I murmured, though I had a feeling not everyone would agree with this point of view, especially the members of Vernon's writers' group.

"Harriet is writing a book," Dooley said. "Her autobiography. And she says it's turned into a real page-turner. Or was it a potboiler? Or a pot-turner? Though it could have been a page-boiler."

"I very much doubt that anything Harriet writes could be considered a page-turner," said Shanille with a smirk of condescension. "For one thing, her life simply hasn't been interesting enough to fill an entire book. And for another, as far as I know, Harriet can't write."

"She's using a ghostwriter," I pointed out.

"That explains it then," said Shanille, who clearly didn't have a high opinion of Harriet's capacity as an autobiographer.

"When can we read it?" asked Kingman. He loves his daily portion of gossip, and if Dooley's words about the book being a potboiler were correct, there might be a lot of juicy gossip having made its way between the pages of Harriet's book.

"Well, it's done, I think," I said. "So it should be out soon."

"She wanted to have it ready for the wedding," Dooley revealed. "Gran was also writing her autobiography as a present to her son, and Harriet wants her book to coincide with Gran's."

"I can't wait," Kingman said fervently.

Shanille rolled her eyes. "Men," she said. "You're all the same, aren't you?"

And with these words, she stalked off, leaving us to look after her with a touch of bewilderment.

"What did she mean by that?" asked Kingman.

"Beats me," I said. I may be a detective, but the female psyche is one of those profound mysteries I have yet to fully plumb. I'm starting to suspect I may very well never succeed.

CHAPTER 34

The time had finally arrived for the big wedding rehearsal. I could tell it was a big thing because all of our humans, without exception, were extremely nervous about the event. Somehow, the parents of the bride had never met the mother of the groom, and from what I had been able to glean in the past few days, there was a general feeling of apprehensive anticipation. It ranged from the disastrous (Chase, Tex, and Uncle Alec himself) to the mildly embarrassing (Marge and Odelia) to the absolutely wonderful (Charlene, as the lone holdout of the positive scenario). As for Gran herself, we could only guess what she thought of the occasion as she was playing her cards very close to her chest.

Charlene had finally extended a formal invitation to Dooley and myself, along with Harriet and Brutus, but that was it. Even though Scarlett would be there, no other pets were expected to be present at this most auspicious occasion. The couple had enough on their plates as it was, and they didn't want the place to be overrun with a clowder of pets.

It had taken some persuading for Odelia to be allowed to

sneak us in since Charlene's mother was allergic to cats. She had requested that no such heinous creatures be present. But Charlene couldn't very well invite her future in-laws and straight off the bat tell them that cats were off-limits. It would set the wrong tone, and besides, Gran had clearly told Charlene that if her cats weren't invited, she would boycott the whole thing.

The wedding rehearsal itself took place at St. John's Church, with Father Reilly officiating the proceedings. Both the bride and groom had opted to wear something more casual for this occasion, which surprised me, I have to say.

The four of us, seated on the last pew to stay as far away from Charlene's mother as possible, commented on this strange phenomenon.

"Where is Charlene's wedding dress?" asked Brutus. "And Uncle Alec's tux?"

"This is the wedding rehearsal, smoochie poo," said Harriet, who must have been reading up on these things. "So people are allowed to wear casual clothes. It's only on the wedding day itself that the good stuff comes out, and the bride is dolled up to perfection."

"Oh," said Brutus. Clearly, he was a novice at this stuff, as was I, I have to admit.

"Where is Charlene's mom?" asked Dooley, craning his neck to catch a glimpse of the woman. "Is that her?"

He was referring to a red-haired woman of sizable proportions standing next to a man of similar heft, both of whom were glowing with pride as they regarded Charlene. Father Reilly had given his little speech, and now it was time for the groom to kiss the bride, or vice versa, which they did with relish. There was a slight diminution of exuberance noticeable on the part of Charlene's mom, which told me she hadn't yet decided whether her little girl linking her lot to this big police chief was a good thing or a harbinger of future doom. Then again, when a couple of a certain age marries, the atmosphere is a lot more subdued than when a pair of youngsters plight their troth. I'm not sure why that is. Possibly because all the parties involved have gone through this exact same ritual at least one time before and are starting to wonder if this is going to be it or if they'll be in this exact situation again a couple of months or years down the line.

"Charlene's mom doesn't look happy," Brutus commented.

"No, I don't think she feels Uncle Alec is a real catch," Harriet added.

"She probably feels that her daughter should be marrying a billionaire or a movie star or something," said Brutus. "And not some lowly police chief from some small Podunk town in the middle of nowhere."

It was a harsh view of the state of affairs, but I couldn't deny that he just might have a point. Even Charlene's dad looked unhappy and certainly didn't display the kind of carefree enjoyment a parent must feel on the happiest day in his little girl's life.

On the other side of the aisle, Gran stood erect and proud, although the glances she kept darting at the party of the second part weren't exactly warm and fuzzy. At all. More like death glances of a nature that was sure to elicit comment from all parties involved. Which is probably why Marge now stepped forward, took her mother by the arm, and led her away. If there was going to be a heated exchange, it was best if it took place in a more quiet and discreet setting.

The service came to an end, and we were all led out of the church and walked the two blocks to the restaurant where Charlene and Uncle Alec had booked a large room for the evening feast. This was the location for the rehearsal dinner, and I was looking forward to the dinner part, which I hoped would involve actual food and not merely pantomime as the wedding had been.

Food had been placed near the back of the large room, and if Odelia was to be believed, the idea was that we would remain in situ and not mingle with the guests, as we might get trampled or, worse, kicked out, or even worse, trigger Charlene's mother's allergies. Our marching orders were to make ourselves scarce and, if possible, pretend that we were invisible.

For me, it wasn't all that hard to accomplish since it was time for a little nap anyway. So after I had dug into my personal bowl, filled with what I have to say was some extremely delicious nosh, I retreated to the corner where Odelia had placed a few baskets and closed my eyes for a pleasant nap. Dooley, who had joined me, confessed he couldn't sleep since he was nervous about the wedding. And when Dooley can't sleep, he substitutes nap time for talk time, which kept me from enjoying my own nap.

Harriet and Brutus had gone off in pursuit of more food since the food may have been great, but the portions were tiny. Before long, I decided to accept the fact that there would be no naps in my immediate future.

"I like Charlene," said Dooley. "I mean, I like her a lot. I think she'll be the perfect wife for Uncle Alec. Don't you, Max? Do you also like her? Charlene, I mean?"

I could tell he was nervous because he was babbling like a brook. "Yeah, I also like her a lot," I admitted. "And I think they're very well-suited for each other and genuinely seem to enjoy each other's company."

"But what about love, Max? Do they love each other? Passionately and unreservedly? Would Uncle Alec go to the ends of the earth for Charlene? Fight a thousand ships just to be near her? Battle a dragon to touch a single strand of her hair?"

"Um..." I have to admit I'm not sure how I feel about this love business people are always going on about. As I understand it, Charlene and Uncle Alec seemed to like each other a great deal and shared genuine affection for the other person. Whether that extended to Uncle Alec battling dragons and the like, well, perhaps not so much. But I wasn't convinced that was entirely necessary.

As we sat there philosophizing about life and love, Charlene's mother suddenly drifted into our nook. Even though we had been forewarned not to go near her, clearly nobody had thought to extend the same message to her. She was clutching a flute of champagne in her hand, and judging from her jerky movements and the way she was awkwardly tottering on her high heels, she was slightly tipsy.

"Ooh, cats!" she squealed with amusement. "Will you look at that big fat orange one! He almost looks like a balloon! Horace, have you seen that fat one?"

The woman's husband now toddled up, looking equally sozzled. He spluttered with marked glee. "He is fat, isn't he? The fattest cat I've ever seen! Like a zeppelin, but without the propellers!"

Both inebriated parents guffawed with abandon as they seemed to find the sight of me most entertaining.

I should have found the entire exchange upsetting, but for some reason, I couldn't be bothered. Possibly because my energy wasn't at its peak, or because I didn't overly like these people. So all I did was mutter a protest. "For your information, I'm not fat, I'm merely big-boned. And I'm not orange—I'm blorange. Now please move along before I make you sick." And before they made me sick.

The woman must not have understood my riposte, for she took another gulp from her drink then came to stand very close to me indeed. "I have to touch it," she announced as she reached out a tentative hand in my direction. With a certain measure of alarm, I watched her finger poke me in the belly. "Like sticking your hand in a bowl of Jell-O!" she declared with a scream of utter relish. "I can even hear the ploink-ploink sound Jell-O makes! You have to try it, Horace." And when Horace seemed reluctant to take her up on this challenge, she lowered her voice and screamed, "Do it!!!"

And so Horace did 'it.'

For a moment, I felt a powerful urge to bite that finger as it dug into my innards, still a bit tender after being stuck in Jerald Exton's van window, but I refrained from doing so. Which is when the sneezing began. It started with a single sneeze but quickly turned into a series of loud sneezes that caused Mrs. Butterwick to double over. And as she did, she accidentally hit her head against the corner of the table, bounced once, and went down like a sack of potatoes.

"Corinne!" Mr. Butterwick screamed as he witnessed this distressing scene. "Corinne, darling!"

But Corinne darling was out for the count.

"Do you think she's dead, Max?" asked Dooley with interest.

"I'm not sure," I said. They do say that alcoholics have a guardian angel watching over them, and I was hoping this would be the case here. For I could imagine that the wedding might be called off if the bride's mother had tragically died during the rehearsal dinner.

Tex was called upon to offer first aid, and he determined that she had bumped her head, which I could have told him, and I'm not even a doctor. Before long, the woman came to, fixed her eyes on Tex, and then placed a hand on his cheek. "My, my," she said. "Aren't you a handsome devil?"

Horace now asserted himself by inserting himself into the conversation before things got potentially embarrassing. "Corinne, darling, how are you feeling?"

She frowned. "I have a slight headache. Now I wonder how that could be." She sneezed again, this time covering both Tex and her husband with a thin layer of froth. Both men closed their eyes, and it was soon determined that Corinne might be better off taking a short break from the festivities by lying down in one of the other rooms. Horace now turned to us with a vicious sort of look on his face. He pointed one of his sausage-like fingers at me. "It's that fat orange one!" he declared with much pique. "He's responsible! If he hadn't come near my wife, she wouldn't have suffered that allergy attack and knocked her head. I want this cat removed from the scene—pronto!"

This time I experienced his words as a personal affront. After all, I hadn't moved from my position at all. "But it is your wife, sir, who is to blame," I said therefore. "She's the one who approached me—not the other way around!"

But of course, the man couldn't be dissuaded from his point of view. But before I could be bodily expelled from the scene, Gran came to the rescue.

"What's all this?" she demanded as she stepped to the fore.

"This cat attacked my wife!" the man declared, still on his high horse, possibly fueled in no small measure by the champagne he'd imbibed.

"I did no such thing!" I argued.

"I think it's better for all concerned if you don't start throwing these wild and unfounded accusations around," Gran suggested. "I'll have you know that Max is the most peaceable cat in existence and he would never attack anyone."

"Well, he did. And I have the witnesses to prove it!" He cast around wildly, then pointed his stubby finger at the nearest person he could see. As luck would have it, this person was none other than Wilbur Vickery, and he looked decidedly unhappy to be dragged into the fray. "I saw nothing," he declared immediately.

"But you must have seen something," Horace said. "You were standing right there, man!"

But Wilbur closed his eyes and repeated solemnly, "I saw nothing."

Clearly unhappy with this failure of his star witness to deliver the goods, Horace now wheeled around in search of a second witness for the prosecution. This time his index finger landed on Fido Siniawski, our local hairdresser. But Fido, too, refused to be dragged into this mess. "I'm afraid I didn't see anything either," he declared. He looked amused by the events as they had unfolded, so I had a feeling he had seen the whole thing but didn't want to get into an argument with the Mayor's father.

"This is an outrage!" Horace fumed. "A conspiracy! Here, darling—come here a minute."

"What's going on?" asked Charlene. "Is it true that Mom has taken ill?"

"She was attacked by that hideous monster over there!" said her father.

"Who, Max? Are you sure?"

"One hundred percent. I want that creature removed from the scene, and I want him put down!"

Now this was too much. And so I decided to let it be known that I protested against this outrage with word and deed. And to show this man that I meant it, I pushed forward and positioned myself in front of him. Now I may not be as tall as all that, but when I'm thoroughly upset, I can project menace like no other. "You take that back!" I now hissed. "You take that back right now!"

Horace recoiled with a look of horror on his face. "See?" he said, his jowls quaking. "See what a dangerous beast we're dealing with here?"

Like me, Gran clearly had had enough of this whole nonsense. "You, sir, are a liar," she said, poking her bony finger into the man's collarbone. "And if you don't apologize to my cat right now, I'm calling off this wedding!"

"You can't do that!" said Charlene immediately.

"Watch me. Alec!" she bellowed at the top of her lungs. "Over here!"

Uncle Alec immediately came running, and so did Marge, Odelia, and Chase. It wasn't too much to say we were now the center of attention, with the whole room watching the scene with bated breath. Even the muzak had stopped pouring from the hidden speakers in the ceiling.

"This man has made threats against Max," Gran announced. "And told us he needs to be put down!"

A gasp of shock rose up from the audience. Clearly, this was the goods. The kind of scene you only see in *The Bold and the Beautiful*, though rarely involving a household pet, of course.

"And if he doesn't apologize right now, I'm forbidding you from marrying this woman! And I mean it!"

Uncle Alec looked a little sheepish, and it wasn't hard to see why. He was effectively stuck between a rock and a hard place. On the one hand, his mother, but on the other hand, his future father-in-law. Tough to take sides!

"And I forbid you from marrying this man," said Horace Butterwick, "if that monster isn't put down!"

I could have told him that I wanted him put down, or his wife, but even though I was upset, I wasn't prepared to stoop to the same level as this man, who clearly was the devil's spawn—though it might also be true that it was the drink talking. Perhaps once he'd sobered up, he wouldn't try and murder me?

"Look, I think we should all take a deep breath," Charlene suggested. "Dad, Max belongs to Odelia, who's Alec's niece, and he's an absolutely lovely cat. So I'm sure he would never attack anyone. Are you sure that's what happened?"

"One hundred percent!" the man blustered.

"Nothing happened," said Fido now as he stepped to the fore. Clearly, he had decided that being Switzerland perhaps wasn't the right course of action right now. "Max didn't move from his spot. Your mother had a sneezing fit and hit her head against the table. There was never any attack."

"Fido is right," said Wilbur, also stepping forward. "The woman seemed crazy to me. Shouting and screaming and behaving like a lunatic. She called Max big, fat, and orange and laughed her head off while she poked him in the ribs and made fun of him and compared him to Jell-O. Until she sneezed and hit her head and then it was all over. So she has no one to blame but herself." He was staring at the Mayor as he spoke these words, clearly expecting some kind of rebuke. But none was forthcoming. Instead, Charlene sighed deeply and thanked both Wilbur and Fido for their testimony.

Horace, who had been panting audibly, still wouldn't budge. "They're liars!" he yelled. "All of them! That cat is..." Suddenly his eyes went wide and he clutched at his chest. I saw that his face was very red and sweaty, and all this shouting clearly wasn't doing him a lot of good. "Ack," he grunted, and then he sort of toppled over.

"Dad!" Charlene cried and hurried to the man's side.

Immediately, Tex was there to take a look at the corpse.

"Oh, dear," said Dooley. "Looks like you killed both of Charlene's parents today, Max."

"I didn't kill anyone," I said indignantly. "They killed themselves!"

"Of course. That's what I meant," he said quickly, lest I turn my ire on him.

I actually felt a little embarrassed that I had allowed myself to get riled up like that. Then again, if people are going to accuse me of things I didn't do, I have every right to defend myself, right?

As it turned out, Horace Butterwick wasn't dead, and it didn't take long for the man to come to, with Tex declaring that it wasn't a heart attack but a malaise, brought on by the emotions of the moment. He advised Horace to rest, and so he soon joined his wife in that darkened room the restaurant was so gracious to offer the bride's parents, both of whom were now out of commission.

Before long, the party was in full swing again, though I could tell that Uncle Alec and Charlene felt bad about the incident. Gran took a seat next to us and grumbled, "I had a feeling Charlene's folks weren't up to snuff, but I hadn't expected them to be this bad. And to think I thought *my* family was nuts. What do you think, Max? Should I call off the wedding or not?"

"You can't call off a wedding that's not your own, Gran," I pointed out.

"Yeah, I guess so," she said reluctantly. "Though when Father Reilly asks if there are any objections, I have a good mind to stand up and tell him there are!"

And with these words, she was off, making a beeline for her son, presumably to warn him against marrying into this family of lunatics.

CHAPTER 35

In all the turmoil of the rehearsal dinner, it had completely escaped my attention that I should have told Odelia about the startling revelation Shanille had made: that Blair Beacock was not actually the writer of her own books, even though she claimed to be in all of the many interviews she gave. I rectified my mistake the moment we got home from the turbulent dinner, and I was gratified to discover that Odelia was as surprised by this information as I was. Even Chase, who's not much of a reader, didn't know what to make of it.

"Does it often happen that people don't write their own books?" he asked as he plunked himself down on the couch. Grace was already fast asleep upstairs, with a baby monitor placed in her cot in case she woke up.

"I'm not sure," said Odelia. "Though it surprises me that Blair wouldn't write her own books. She's always describing in such detail how she's come up with the plot and how she spends months writing the latest Chanel Birdsey book. At the reading, she said she gets up at five every morning and spends her whole day writing. She has no hobbies and writes seven days a week. So all of that was a lie?"

"Has to be if what Vernon told Father Reilly is true."

"Could be that Vernon was lying," said Odelia. "Maybe he was jealous of Blair's success and made up the story that he was actually the writer of her bestsellers? He knew Father Reilly wouldn't tell anyone, so he could tell him whatever he liked. Let off steam, you know. Vent his frustrations."

"Only one way to find out," said Chase with a shrug. "Let's talk to Blair in the morning." He yawned. "That was one hell of a rehearsal dinner. Two in-laws knocked out cold, big fracas, and the bride and groom barely on speaking terms. Are you sure there will be an actual wedding tomorrow?"

"Did Uncle Alec and Charlene get into a fight over this whole business?" asked Odelia.

"I got that impression, yeah. Not a fight, per se, but a general coolness that probably shouldn't exist on the eve of one's wedding." He grinned. "I just wish I was a fly on the wall in that bedroom this evening."

"Oh, I do hope they'll make up," said Odelia fervently. "Charlene's parents may be a little over the top, but she's such an amazing person."

"She is." He frowned. "Odd that things would get out of hand to such an extent, wouldn't you say? Maybe someone put something in their drink?"

"Or maybe that's just the way they are."

"Poor Charlene. Her perfect wedding is well and truly ruined now."

I shared a look with my friends. "Do you think it's all my fault?" I asked.

Harriet and Brutus hadn't been present at the scene, of course, but they had experienced the aftermath and heard the whole story in excruciating detail. "It wasn't your fault, Max," said Brutus. "So you shouldn't feel bad."

"If only we had left," I said. "Then none of this would have happened, and Charlene and Uncle Alec's wedding would have gone off without a hitch."

"I very much doubt that," said Harriet. "Judging from the way those two were behaving, I'd say they were spoiling for a fight. If not with you, then with one of the other people present." She patted my paw. "You shouldn't blame yourself, Max. This had nothing to do with you and everything to do with the Butterwicks."

"Have they apologized?" asked Brutus.

"No, they haven't," I said. Not that I was expecting them to. They seemed to have cemented their position that it was all my fault, even though I couldn't see how that could be. Mostly, I was the injured party. Or at least I thought I was.

"I should have bitten them," said Dooley now. "I should have bitten both of them. They were so nasty to you, Max. Just awful!"

"Yeah, it wasn't a pleasant experience," I agreed. "Not pleasant at all."

But since the whole thing was behind us now, I decided to try and forget it.

I just hoped that the wedding would still go through.

* * *

ALEC REMOVED his clothes in silence and got ready for bed. All evening, Charlene had avoided him, and it had made him feel very bad indeed. He had racked his brain trying to discover what he had done wrong but couldn't see it. He had tried to be a fair arbiter and not pick one side over the other. Charlene herself had made it clear that she didn't believe a word of her dad's story, but the moment the man had removed himself from the scene to take a nap, she had turned her back on her betrothed and been incommunicado the rest of the evening.

It puzzled him, but mostly it unnerved him to a great degree. Was the wedding off now? Was she angry with him? But why? On the drive home, she had stared out of the passenger-side window without uttering a single word, and even when he tried to engage her in conversation, she had refused to respond. Now they were home—her home, at least —and he wondered how to proceed. He hated these tense scenes and never knew what to do. At least she hadn't told him to sleep on the couch or to go to his place so they wouldn't be together.

By all rights, he should be sleeping in his own home, for it wasn't right for the groom to see his bride on the eve of their wedding. But they had both agreed that they were too old to adhere to such a superstition and were simply going to ignore these silly structures. Now that he was seated on the edge of the bed, wondering when Charlene would emerge from the bathroom and what her mood would be, he wondered if they had made a mistake. Maybe they had rushed into things, and they should have waited—or never started it.

But she had wanted to get married and had seemed so happy about it. Clearly, now she was having second thoughts about the whole thing.

The bathroom door opened, and his bride-to-be appeared. The light in the bedroom was subdued, and as he gazed at her profile, backlit by the bathroom light, the sight of her took his breath away, as it did every time.

"Charlene," he said with a catch in his voice. Odd, that. He had confronted hardened criminals and tough crooks by the thousands, and his voice had never failed him. But now that he was faced with this woman, he could barely speak.

Charlene took a seat on her side of the bed, and for a

moment, silence reigned. Then finally, she turned down the comforter and slipped her feet beneath it. He did the same, and moments later, they lay side by side, staring up at the ceiling, and the silence dragged on until it became unbearable.

Finally, she spoke. "Maybe this was a mistake," she said.

He swallowed away a lump. "Do you really think so?"

"My mother needed stitches. She looks like a ghoul. And my dad says he won't come to the wedding if your mother is also going to be there."

"I see." He was quiet for a moment, wondering how to address this. Frankly, he'd never been in a situation like this before. He had heard stories, of course, of in-laws behaving badly, and his own experience with his mother should have prepared him for this, but in all honesty, the Butterwicks were a few degrees worse than Ma ever was. At least she wasn't spiteful like Charlene's folks.

Charlene now turned to him. "I have a confession to make, Alec."

Oh dear. She was going to tell him she had never really loved him.

"Yes?" he said weakly, and he hated how his own voice sounded.

"My mom and dad... they really adored Ricky. Were absolutely crazy about him. So when we got divorced... Let's just say they never got over it. So any man I would marry after Ricky, they wouldn't approve. The reason they liked my first husband so much is that he provided them with anything their hearts desired. And..." She paused for a moment as she composed her thoughts. "If I tell you something, can you promise not to act on it? I mean..."

He had turned to her, and frankly, he could make neither heads nor tails of what she was telling him. But as long as she wasn't telling him the wedding was off, it was all to the good. "Sure. Absolutely. What is it?"

"Mom and Dad—they have a substance abuse problem. They've been in and out of rehab many times, and it doesn't seem to stick. And I'm not just talking alcohol or cocaine, but also pills. Mom pops Xanax as if they're M&Ms, and Dad's drug of choice is Advil. Which explains his stomach problems. And to mix pills with alcohol probably isn't a good idea either." She took a deep breath. "The fact of the matter is that they're both addicted to pills and coke and booze, and Ricky is mostly to blame since he's the one who got them all the stuff they wanted."

"But I thought he was convicted for embezzlement?"

"He was, but he had a nice little sideline as a dealer."

"God. You never told me that."

"I thought that if you knew... Well, that you wouldn't..."

He frowned as he studied her profile. A tear had appeared in her eye. "Wouldn't what?"

"I thought if you knew that my parents are addicts and my ex-husband a dealer... that you wouldn't want to marry me. You being a cop and all." She cast down her eyes and idly plucked at the sheet as he processed this.

"But honey," he said finally, and a little lamely, he thought, "that has nothing to do with you. I mean, the fact that your parents have issues—I would never hold that against you. Ever." He had grabbed her hand and now pressed it in his. "Look, I love you, Charlene, and nothing your parents say or do will ever change that."

She sniffed. "Not even the fact that they single-handedly ruined our rehearsal dinner?"

"They didn't ruin anything. Not as far as I'm concerned."

"Or that they demanded that Max be put down?"

"Well, that was a little extreme, but—"

"Or that your mother decided to call off the wedding if they didn't apologize?"

"You know my mother. She's a little... whacky."

She laughed. "You can say that again. And so are my folks."

"Just a little," he said with a grin.

"We're quite the pair, aren't we?" she said. "Your mom is nuts, and so are my mom and dad. I knew the moment they were put together there would be trouble, but I hadn't expected this."

"Frankly, I thought the universe would implode, so it wasn't as bad as I expected."

She wiped away a tear. "I'm sorry, Alec. I should have told you about my parents. I guess I was too proud to, and too afraid you'd think badly of me."

"I could never think badly of you, honey. You are not your parents, and I am not my mother."

"Thank God for that," she said, and they both laughed at the ordeal they had gone through that evening. It could have been worse, though. Charlene could have called off the wedding. Now that would have been a real disaster.

And so he clasped her in his arms, and even though it was probably frowned upon by the strict rules that governed weddings, they kissed and made up.

The wedding was going through. They might have to seat their respective in-laws as far away from each other as spatially possible, but that was a cinch.

CHAPTER 36

The next morning, we found ourselves as guests at Blair Beacock's beachfront mansion. The Beacocks lived in a gorgeous property that must have cost them a pretty penny. They had some notable neighbors, including celebrities from the silver screen, a renowned film director, and the owner of a successful social media site. It was quite a change from our own humble surroundings. Present at the gathering were Blair Beacock herself, her husband Teddy, and the couple's children Dylan and Carey, who lived nearby. Seated on the sofa, the four Beacocks presented a united front.

On the wall behind them, I noticed several framed covers of the many successful books that Blair had supposedly written. However, it remained to be seen if she had actually written them herself or not. When parking in their driveway, I had clocked a bright red Lamborghini, several Teslas, and a classic Ford Mustang that must have cost a fortune. In other words, the Beacocks were quite well off, and the Chanel Birdsey books must have sold a significant number of copies to afford such luxuries.

"I don't understand," said Carey, a heavyset young woman with blond hair. "What are you accusing my mother of, exactly?"

"We're not accusing your mother of anything, Miss Beacock," said Chase. "But as this is a murder investigation, we're obliged to explore every possible angle that might shed light on the circumstances of Vernon Langridge's death. It has recently come to light that Vernon was the ghostwriter your mother used for her books. So, you can see why this would be of interest to us."

"But... but that's simply not true!" Carey protested. "It's a lie! A filthy lie!"

"Carey," said her mother warningly. She exchanged a glance with her husband, who nodded. "Who told you this?" Blair asked, clearly troubled by the allegations.

"A little birdie," said Chase with a smirk.

The Beacocks seemed uncertain about how to proceed, but then Blair took charge. "It's true," she admitted. "Vernon was my ghostwriter for the Birdsey novels."

"Mom!" Carey cried, dismayed by the revelation.

"There's no use denying it, honey. Clearly, someone blabbed."

"We should sue," grumbled Dylan unhappily.

"It's those letters, isn't it?" said Teddy. "Those poison pen letters?"

Blair lifted her head. "I don't see how this has any bearing on your investigation, detective. It's just a lot of gossip."

"How long had Vernon been writing for you, Mrs. Beacock?" asked Odelia.

Blair eyed Odelia with a distinct lack of warmth. "I hope you won't mention this in your paper?"

"I'm not here in my capacity as a reporter," Odelia assured her, and Blair relaxed, but only slightly.

"Fifteen years," she said. "I wrote the first fifteen Birdseys, and then Vernon took over. He's done a really good job. He learned to write in my voice and has made a marvelous success of the series."

"If I may ask, why did you stop writing them yourself?" asked Odelia.

Blair shrugged. "I guess I got burned out on the characters. I felt I was repeating myself, writing the same book over and over. Then I heard from a fellow writer how he had handed over the reins to a ghostwriter and had never looked back. No more deadlines, no more pressure. It was such a relief. And the sales hadn't suffered—on the contrary, he was selling more each year. So I asked to meet with the publisher, suggesting that we could do the same thing. Turns out half the bestselling authors in their stable use a ghostwriter. So they started looking around for someone willing to do the job and finally came up with Vernon. Coincidentally, someone from my own home town."

"Did you often meet him? Sit down together to work out the plot?" asked Odelia.

"Not really. Mostly Vernon did all that himself. Like I said, he did an amazing job, and we've always been very happy with his work."

"But... you still did the book launches, the book tours, and the press."

"Well, of course. The readers don't know I'm not the one who writes the books. They think I'm the writer, so naturally, I have to go out there and promote them as best I can." She smiled. "I know it may seem strange to you, but that's the nature of the beast. I'm not the only one who gives interviews about a book they haven't actually written. At first, it felt a little weird, but I got used to it. I would read the book the moment Vernon was done, and then I'd go out on tour and promote the hell out of it."

"And how did Vernon feel about that? It couldn't have

been easy to watch you pretending to have written a book that he himself had actually written."

"That's how it goes, Mrs. Kingsley. He knew what he was getting into when he signed the contract. And he was handsomely rewarded for the privilege."

"Vernon had written a novel of his own, which was rejected by his publisher."

"Yes, I'd heard about that. It surprised me a great deal because he was such a good writer. According to what I was told, the book wasn't commercial enough. It didn't hit the right notes to be a bestseller. It's not enough to be a great writer, you know. You have to come up with a killer idea. And apparently that's what was missing from his novel."

"I guess people don't want to read about antique dealers working as detectives," said Teddy.

"But as I told him, he just needed to keep plugging away. Come up with something truly great, and he would get there."

"Did you have a lot of contact with Vernon?" asked Chase.

"Not as much as you would think. Why? You're not suspecting me of this terrible crime, are you?"

Chase ignored her. "Could you tell us where you were three nights ago, Mrs. Beacock? Let's say around eleven?"

Blair laughed a curt laugh. "So you *are* suspecting me. How quaint. Well, I was right here, having dinner with my family and then spending the evening together."

"Do you often dine late?"

"We do. We all lead busy lives, but we like to spend our evenings together as a family if we can."

"So... the four of you were here?"

"Yes, we were," Teddy said in confirmation, and both Dylan and Carey nodded.

"It was pot roast night," said Blair. "If you want to know.

And it was delicious. I cooked it myself for a change, allowing Claude a night off."

"Claude?"

"Claude Drewry," Carey explained. "He's our private chef."

"And a marvelous chef he is. He is the reason we've all gained so much weight these last couple of years. But I can't blame him. He's extremely good at what he does, and we're lucky to have him."

"Can anyone confirm that you were all here?" asked Chase.

The four Beacocks gave us confused looks. "Well, I can confirm that my family was here," said Blair. "And they can confirm I was here. Isn't that enough?"

Chase decided to move on. "How well do you know Jerald Exton, Mrs. Beacock?"

"Oh, we've known Jerald since he was a boy. His parents work for us, you see."

"You have arranged a lawyer for Jerald? Is that correct?"

Blair folded her hands in her lap. "It was the least I could do. That poor boy being accused of murder. His mom and dad are extremely upset. So when they asked us for help, naturally we decided to pay for a lawyer. Is he still under arrest?"

"He is. At the moment, he's our prime suspect."

"But why? He's such a sweet boy."

"We have our reasons," Chase said curtly. He got up. "Could we speak to the Extons?"

"Of course," said Blair, also rising from her seat. She darted another nervous glance at Odelia. "You're not going to write about the ghostwriting thing in the *Gazette*?"

"I won't," Odelia promised. Though it would have been quite a coup if she had. Then again, it was probably none of our concern how the book publishing world organized itself.

If they decided to hire ghostwriters for their stable of bestselling authors, that was their business. It still seemed a little weird to me, but Blair assured us it was common practice.

"Just like Coca-Cola," she explained, "at some point authors become a brand. And it's simply good business sense to manage that brand to its full potential. And if that means working with a ghostwriter, then so be it."

"But don't the ghostwriters feel slighted?" asked Odelia.

"These people are professionals, Mrs. Kingsley. Ghostwriting is what they do. They decided long ago that they wanted the paycheck but none of the circus that goes with writing a bestselling series—the press tours, the signings, the endless interviews, and the whole rigmarole, and that's how they accomplish it." She extended her hands, palms up. "In other words, a win-win for both parties."

CHAPTER 37

We met the Extons on the patio, which offered a stunning view of the garden. Lucas Exton was obviously a very skilled gardener. And since I had yet to detect a single dust bunny, and the floors I'd seen had been so clean I could have eaten my kibble off them, I could tell that Lucy Exton was an excellent cleaner. Lucas looked a little weather-beaten, but then I guess that's what you get when you're out in the open air all the time. He was a tall man who walked with a slight stoop and had carrot-colored hair, just like his son. Mrs. Exton was a full head smaller than her husband, and judging from the dark rings under her eyes, hadn't slept much since her son had been arrested. She was a diminutive and petite woman with a perpetual look of concern on her face.

"I wouldn't know," said Lucy when Chase had asked her if she could confirm that the Beacocks had been home the night of Vernon's death. "I don't work nights. Why, you think they've got something to do with the murder?"

"Just trying to form a picture of where everyone was on the night, Mrs. Exton."

"You have to let my Jerald go," she said now. "He didn't do it. He couldn't have. He's such a sweet boy. He would never lay a finger on Vernon, even if Vernon wasn't all that fond of him."

"Once he got to know him, he would have changed his tune," said Lucas, nodding fervently. "And it would have happened. Jerald had told Gwen to wait until she turned eighteen. Then he was going to introduce himself to her father and officially ask if he could date the man's daughter. Vernon would have seen for himself what a well-raised young man our Jerald is. And what a catch for his daughter."

"My husband is right. Vernon never gave Jerald a chance. Took one look at him and told Gwen she couldn't see him anymore. But Jerald was prepared to wait. They love each other, you see. Even though they're both still so young, they love each other." She had threaded her arm through her husband's. "Just like we did, isn't that right, Lucas?"

"Yeah, we met when we were fifteen and haven't looked back. When you know, you know," said the man. "And Jerald and Gwen know."

"Too bad her father didn't realize it," said Lucy. "But then I guess we can't blame him. What with his marriage failing so badly, he probably turned into a cynic."

"Cynics are the worst," her husband agreed. "Incapable of recognizing a good thing when they see it. And then trying to destroy other people's happiness because they can't have it." He shook his head. "I'm not saying Vernon was that kind of person, but he came very close to being a cynic."

"That's what you get with those intellectuals," his wife added.

"Isn't your employer an intellectual?" asked Odelia.

For a moment, Lucy looked confused, then she recovered. "She is not. She didn't go to college. Started working when she was sixteen. Salesgirl in a boutique. Had to because her family needed the money. She worked her ass off, Mrs. Beacock did, and so did Mr. Beacock."

"Hard workers, all of them," Lucas said. "Their success is well-deserved."

"There's a lot that goes into being a successful writer, you know," said Lucy. "People don't realize how much work it takes and how many sacrifices a person has to make. But we know, don't we? We can see how hard they all work. Blair and Teddy, but also Dylan and Carey. Such great kids. How blessed Blair and Teddy are. And how blessed the kids are with such wonderful devoted parents." She sighed. "Now if only Jerald would come home." She directed another pleading glance at Chase. "Can't you please let him go, detective? He's done nothing wrong, I promise you. Nothing at all."

Unfortunately, it didn't work like that. Parents may believe that their kids are innocent like the driven snow, but that isn't always the case. And with the evidence in place, Chase simply couldn't release Jerald. Not until he could prove that someone else had committed that murder.

BLAIR WATCHED through the window as the detective and his wife talked to her staff. She felt bad for the Extons. Poor Jerald languishing in prison like that. She could tell that it was wreaking havoc on Lucy and Lucas and hoped that the police would be able to resolve the matter quickly and painlessly.

Her husband joined her. "How the hell did they know about the ghostwriting?"

"We better schedule a meeting with Michael," she said, referring to her literary agent. "Either it's someone at the agency or the publisher. Either way, the cat is out of the bag now, Teddy. If the cops know, and that reporter woman, it won't be long before the truth is out there."

"We had a good run, didn't we?" said Teddy as he placed his arm around her shoulder. "And besides, so many writers use ghosts these days that it's become the done thing."

"Yeah, I guess you're right." She watched as Lucy held out her hands in an imploring gesture, and she felt for the poor wretch. "What do you think will happen to Jerald?"

"No doubt he'll be charged. And then it's up to the courts to decide." He shook his head. "The kid's always been too impetuous for his own good. And with this whole drug business hanging over his head..."

"He should never have gotten involved with Gwen. She's too young—they're both too young. I personally blame Vernon and Diana. They should have nipped this romance in the bud."

"Hard to present a united front when you're divorced."

She smiled as she hugged her husband close. "I'm so lucky to have you, Teddy," she murmured, and pressed a kiss to his cheek.

They formed a tight little unit, she and Teddy and the kids. Teddy was the money man in the family, who made sure the accounts were always balanced. Dylan was her right-hand man and a creative genius in his own right. And Carey was their marketing maven who ran the website, the newsletter, and their social media pages. Which left Blair, who was the creative force behind the Blair Beacock brand and the person their family revolved around. She might not be as active now, but she had been. Without her, there never would have been a Chanel Birdsey, and those millions of readers worldwide would never have been entertained by Miss Birdsey's madcap adventures.

The Kingsleys were done putting Lucy and Lucas through the wringer, and so she stepped out onto the patio to see them off. Even though she was fond of Odelia Kingsley and had always thought of her as an enthusiastic and intelligent interviewer every time she had sat down with her, she hoped she and her husband wouldn't be back. This whole murder business had greatly perturbed her. And as she waved them off, she said a quick prayer for Vernon. He really had been a valued member of Team Birdsey and would be greatly missed.

CHAPTER 38

Once again, we found ourselves holed up in Chase's office at the police station. Uncle Alec had a wedding to get ready for, so he was still out of the office at the present time, but at least Chase and Odelia were still on the case, and so was the rest of the detective's team. Most of them would all be leaving soon, so they could attend the Chief's wedding, but at least for now, the focus was on the investigation, with Chase giving a brief summary of the state of affairs.

"We got the ballistics report," he said as he read from his computer. "Turns out the gun that was used to kill Vernon was also used in a robbery six months ago—a family-owned jewelry store in Brooklyn. The robbers got away with half a million worth of gems, which puts a completely different spin on things."

"So you think the same people who hit that jewelry store killed Vernon?"

"It's not inconceivable," the detective said. "Think about it. Some of these first-edition books are worth a small fortune, so it wouldn't surprise me if the same gang who hit that Brooklyn jewelry store was also responsible for the hit on The Mighty Pen. They were interrupted by Vernon, so they shot him and left without taking the rest of the loot, only removing the single book from his inventory. I guess they hadn't reckoned on Vernon being present at the scene."

"It's possible," Odelia allowed. "But what about that page from his manuscript stuffed into his mouth?"

"A flourish," said Chase with a shrug. "They were probably angry that the robbery didn't go off without a hitch, so they decided to express their annoyance this way. Or maybe we're dealing with a bunch of psychopaths. The main thing is that at least now we have a solid lead, especially since that Brooklyn jewelry store had CCTV, and one of the robbers was caught on film." He turned his computer screen and treated us to an image of a man with a particularly hideous aspect. We all winced. "Luigi Buoni," said Chase. "Also known as the Tweaker."

"The Tweaker?"

"He enjoys tweaking his victims' noses—in other words, breaking them. Though he has also been known to tweak other parts of their anatomy."

"But Vernon's nose was fine," I pointed out. "As was the rest of him."

But the detective ignored me. "Does that mean Jerald Exton is in the clear?" asked Odelia.

"On the contrary, I think it puts him squarely in the frame as part of that same gang. I think we should lean on him to give us the names of the other gang members. That way, we can round them all up and hopefully solve two robberies in one go. Though it wouldn't surprise me if they had made other victims."

"More jewelry stores."

Chase nodded. "I was hoping to wrap this up before the

wedding, but looks like we'll be going into overtime on this one, babe."

"Yeah, I was also hoping to deliver the culprit to my uncle as a wedding present."

"Oh, well," said Chase as he got up from behind his desk. "Tomorrow is another day. And Exton isn't going anywhere."

They walked out of the office, clearly eager to get ready for the big wedding. The odd thing about weddings is that it's not just the bride and groom who are supposed to dress up but also the wedding guests. And so Chase had rented a tux while Odelia had gone shopping with her mom to buy themselves new dresses for the occasion. The only ones who didn't need to get dressed up were us.

Dooley looked a little crestfallen. "Max? I think they forgot about us."

"Yeah, I got that same impression," I said.

That's what you get with these big events: people get a little distracted.

Lucky for us, they hadn't closed the door, and so after a moment's hesitation, wondering if they wouldn't come back for us, we walked out under our own steam. "So do you think that a gang killed Vernon, Max?" asked Dooley.

"I'm not sure," I said. "The letter writer known as the well-wisher doesn't seem to think so. Though of course, he could simply be some extremely spiteful person wishing harm on other people."

"Poor Gwen," said Dooley as we traversed the station vestibule, nodded our greeting to Dolores Peltz, and exited through the main doors like any visitor—or detective. This place was starting to feel like home, and Dooley and I like a pair of police cats. Minus the snazzy outfit, of course, though we did have the badges to prove we were in the unofficial employ of the HCPD.

"Yeah, poor Gwen. First, she lost her dad, and now her boyfriend will be tried for his murder."

"His parents seemed convinced he didn't do it."

"No parent would ever admit that their son is a vicious killer," I said.

"No, I guess not." We contemplated these recent events for a moment, then Dooley said, "Just to humor me, Max, could you go over the other suspects in the case? I know Chase and Odelia think it was this gang of robbers, but what about the other people we talked to? Do you think they're all in the clear now?"

"Well, let's see," I said as I gathered my thoughts. "There's Diana Ludick, Vernon's ex-wife, who wants to marry Cesar Roughsedge, the man with the ambition to become our new governor. Vernon refused to grant her a divorce, which was going to hamper Cesar's election campaign to some extent, so now that the man is dead, that's one obstacle removed. But both Diana and Cesar claim they were home at the time of the murder."

"Which they could be lying about."

"Then there's Gwen, who was unhappy that her father didn't allow her to see her boyfriend, and Jerald, who felt the same way. Her alibi is that she was asleep in bed, and Jerald was in his van."

"Not much of an alibi if you ask me."

"Then we have the members of Vernon's writers' group. Kenton Clarey, the thriller writer, had recently lost his book deal and was jealous of Vernon, who was trumpeting to all and sundry how he was about to sign a very lucrative deal."

"Which wasn't true."

"But Kenton didn't know that. He admits he felt jealous about Vernon's success, and also, he has a sick wife at home and a lot of bills coming in that he was finding it difficult to pay now that his publisher has dropped him. His alibi is that he was walking Mickey at the time, which Mickey has confirmed to us."

"But which he could be lying about, since all pets lie."

"Not just pets, Dooley. Everybody lies."

"Except us, Max. We never lie."

"Well..."

We had reached Town Square and decided to take a load off our paws in the shade of one of the big trees planted there. Kids were playing in the fountain, with their mothers looking on. Those same mothers were chatting with other mothers, and generally the atmosphere was relaxed, not to mention pleasant. It isn't every day that the Mayor and the Chief of Police get married, and the ripples of the event were spreading throughout our small town.

"Okay, so who's next?" asked Dooley as we relaxed for a moment.

"Well, there's Marina Steele," I said. "Our young romance writer who was desperately in love with Vernon—a sentiment that wasn't reciprocated since Vernon was still in love with his ex-wife. She felt sad about this state of affairs, and possibly it made her so upset she could have gone down to the store that night and shot the man she professed to love so much."

"If she couldn't have him, no one could."

"Exactly. Her alibi is that she was home alone. With her dog Meena."

"Who has confirmed this."

"Who has confirmed this.

"But who could by lying."

"Just so. Then we also have Tarsha Kettles, the elderly cozy mystery writer. Real name Kay Parker. As a young girl, she set her own house on fire, killing her parents in the process. So when Vernon criticized her work in progress, humiliating her in front of the other members of the writers' group, it's possible she snapped and decided to punish the man for his impudence."

"Sounds plausible," Dooley said. "Though according to Min, she couldn't have done it, since the two of them were home together at the time, curled up with a book. Unless of course Min is lying."

"And finally, we have the Beacocks. Blair Beacock gave up writing years ago, and Vernon took over, in secret. He was the man who actually wrote her bestselling Chanel Birdsey books."

"But what could her motive be?" asked Dooley.

"Well, he was trying to venture out on his own. Launch his own series of books about an antique-dealing amateur detective. So maybe he had decided to stop writing the Birdsey books entirely?"

"And so Blair decided to punish him?"

I shrugged. "It's possible. Far-fetched but possible."

"But Blair was home with her family, eating homemade pot roast."

"Yeah, so I guess that rules her out as well."

"Which only leaves... the jewelry thieves."

"Unless one of the pets we spoke to was lying."

"That would be either Meena, Min, or Mickey."

"Or all three could have been lying, of course."

It was a tough proposition. How do you determine who's telling the truth and who's lying? It's not as if you can hook up a dog or a cat to a lie detector and determine the veracity of their statements. And even then, humans have been known to beat a lie detector test.

"I think it's either Mickey or Meena," said Dooley. "Cats would never lie to a pair of fellow cats, so that leaves out Min."

"Cats do lie, Dooley," I said. "Even to their fellow cats."

He thought about this and had to admit there was a

certain truth to it. After all, we had been lied to before by other members of the feline species.

"But then we have no way of knowing who the guilty party is, Max!"

And that was the sad state of affairs as we got up and started wending our way home.

We had a wedding to attend, after all, and we didn't want to be late.

CHAPTER 39

I think you'll be gratified to know that the wedding between Alec Lip and Charlene Butterwick went off without a hitch. Father Reilly was in his element and gave a rousing sermon—well, maybe not exactly rousing, but definitely a moving sermon. The bride looked gorgeous in white, and the groom didn't look too shabby either. No one got up to protest the wedding, not even us, and at the end of the ceremony the groom kissed the bride and the couple looked deeply relieved.

When exiting the church, to the cheerful peal of church bells ringing out overhead, the couple beamed at all those present and were treated to a nice helping of rice.

"Why are they throwing rice, Max?" asked Dooley.

"I have no idea, Dooley," I admitted.

"Maybe they think Uncle Alec and Charlene are hungry?" Harriet suggested.

"I think rice is a symbol of fertility," Brutus said.

This had us all look up in surprise.

"So... are they going to have kids?" asked Dooley.

Charlene had mentioned something about having kids on

our last cruise together as a family, though I'd figured she had been joking.

"How old is Charlene?" asked Harriet.

"Um... forty-eight, I think. Same age as Marge."

"And Uncle Alec is fifty-four." She thought for a moment. "Well, I guess it's possible. There's probably a lot they can do nowadays, medically speaking, so maybe it will happen."

"Imagine that," said Dooley. "Charlene pregnant. That means that Grace will have a cousin to play with."

"Not... really," I said. Somehow I had the impression it was a little more complicated than that. But even though I have a big head, as Brutus never fails to point out, even for me this was too hard to fathom. And anyway, I thought that the chances of it happening were probably slim to none.

All of Hampton Cove seemed to have come out to see their mayor and chief of police get married, and loud cheers now rang out from the mass of people wishing the new couple all the happiness in the world. The church had been full to capacity, and that mass of people now moved in groups to Town Hall, where the wedding reception was being organized. There would also be a picnic in Town Square, and then later that evening an actual feast, though that was by invitation only.

At the wedding reception, suddenly Gran asked to address the gathering by getting up and tapping her glass with a knife. "I have a pleasant surprise for you all," she said, "but especially for my dear Alec and his beautiful new wife."

She gestured for one of the servers to approach with a large carton box, causing all those present to murmur in excited anticipation.

"From me to you," she said the moment the first box had been opened.

"This is so great," said Harriet next to me. "This is the moment you've all been waiting for, you guys!"

The box turned out to contain books, and as Gran now gratefully accepted one, she held it up. "My autobiography!" she cried with justified pride. Only something must have gone wrong with the printing process, for instead of her picture on the cover, it featured Harriet's picture instead.

Amused noises now rose up among the crowd, and when Gran handed the first copy to a confused-looking Uncle Alec, he stared at it for a moment, then asked, "Why is there a cat on the cover, Ma?"

Gran's face, so happy before, now sagged. "What do you mean?"

He turned the book. "It's a cat. On the cover. And it says, 'My Life, by Harriet.'"

"Oh, it's Harriet," said Charlene. "Isn't that cute?"

"But... but that's impossible," said Gran. She grabbed the book from her son's hands and stared at it with utter confusion. "I don't understand. This is supposed to be my autobiography. I worked very hard on it."

"How Gran ever thought that her autobiography would make a great wedding gift I'll never know," Brutus whispered into my ear.

"Me neither," I whispered back.

Gran had unearthed more books from the box, and when she discovered all of them featured Harriet's visage, she became more and more agitated. The servers, who had begun to distribute the books amongst the guests on Gran's orders, didn't seem to mind. Eager hands practically grabbed them from their hands, and soon the merriment was complete, with people laughing out loud as they leafed through the book and started quoting from it to each other.

"Do you see that? My book is a great success," Harriet said with pride.

I had the impression it was more a source of amusement than instruction, but that didn't stop Harriet from going around the room and welcoming the attention her autobiography was garnering. People were over the moon to see the star of the book live in the audience, and her star turn was well received.

Not so much by Gran, though, who was darting vicious looks at the white Persian. If I didn't know any better, I got the impression she wouldn't have minded grabbing Harriet by the scruff of the neck and giving her a good thrashing. Or even wringing that very same neck!

"I don't understand," the old lady kept repeating. "I really don't."

"It's all right, Ma," said Uncle Alec. "It's the thought that counts."

"It was a very thoughtful gift," said Charlene. "And definitely unique."

"What do you think happened, Max?" asked Dooley.

"Well, as far as I can tell, this autobiography is an online service from some website. You enter your information and answer a bunch of multiple-choice questions, upload your picture, and the computer turns it into a book, prints it, and sends it off. Only when Harriet came upon that website on Gran's tablet, she must have accidentally deleted Gran's original answers and replaced them with her own. So even though Gran paid for her autobiography, what she got instead was Harriet's."

"Oh, that's too bad," said Dooley. "Poor Gran."

The old lady looked thoroughly crestfallen, and it took the concerted efforts of her daughter and granddaughter to cheer her up. But it was only when Scarlett finally walked in and joined her friend that Gran rounded the corner and decided to put this whole thing behind her.

Scarlett had arrived at the church dressed in her usual attire, which consisted of a rather provocative and revealing décolletage and a hemline so short I thought I could see her underwear. Father Reilly, who almost had a heart attack when he caught sight of Scarlett, had hurried to her side and beseeched her to return home and change into something more appropriate. But since she didn't want to miss the service, instead Gran had loaned her a coat that she could use to cover up. The moment the wedding ceremony was over, Scarlett had hurried home and had now returned, dressed a little more conservatively.

"My mistake, of course," she proclaimed. "First rule of a wedding: never upstage the bride. And even though Charlene is twenty years younger than me, I should have realized that simply by being myself I was stealing her thunder." She grabbed Harriet's autobiography from one of the high-top tables carrying flutes of champagne and smoked-salmon canapés. "What's this?" she asked.

"My autobiography," Gran said morosely. "Only something must have gone wrong with the works because this isn't my life story at all."

"'My mother's name was Fiona and she was a lovely feline,'" Scarlett read from the book. "'My dad was George, and both of them loved me from the moment they laid eyes on me and said I was the most gorgeous creature in the whole wide world. Which is understandable, since I am the most gorgeous creature in the whole wide world. My name is Harriet, and I'm an *artiste* in every sense of the word. I sing, I dance, I entertain with my enormous talent and leave the audience breathless from the moment I hit the first note. Yes, I'm a star. Probably the biggest star that has ever lived, and this is the story of my enchanted life.'" She glanced up at her friend. "This is great stuff. Who wrote it?"

Gran pointed to Harriet, who was still busy running victory laps around the room and being petted and feted by all.

Scarlett grinned. "I love it, don't you?"

Gran rolled her eyes. "I guess."

"Oh, cheer up, honey. This is one of those stories that will go down in history. We'll be laughing about this for years to come. How Harriet stole the limelight." She gave her friend a gentle nudge. "That's what you get when you adopt a Persian. So don't go crying over spilled milk now, you hear?"

"Cry over spilled milk," scoffed Gran. "How very apt." But finally, she cracked a smile and soon saw the joke in the whole episode.

"The good thing is that no one is trying to kill us today," Dooley said and gestured to Corinne and Horace Butterwick, who were as docile as a pair of lambs. They just sat there looking completely out of it. Almost as if they'd been sedated, which quite possibly was the case.

And so, all in all, the wedding feast went off without a hitch—or at least not too many hitches.

* * *

ODELIA THOUGHT that the bride looked absolutely radiant, and the groom looked so happy he could cry, and he did, even though he tried to hide it. It was a great moment for all of them, and when Odelia's mom got up and raised a glass to her big brother and wished him every happiness, there wasn't a dry eye in the room. Before long, food was served, and conversations turned to the stunt Gran had pulled, though it was probably safer to say that Harriet had pulled her own stunt. Every person present had received their copy of the Persian's autobiography, and Harriet looked like the queen of the ball.

Charlene didn't mind sharing the stage with her. She was too busy marveling at the good fortune of having finally pulled off this wedding.

At one moment, Dan came over to have a chat with

Odelia and announced that another letter had arrived from the 'well-wisher.' This time he—or she—accused Jerald Exton of the crime of murdering Vernon Langridge. The detail the letter writer added was that Jerald was in cahoots with Diana Ludick, Vernon's ex-wife, in plotting and perpetrating the heinous crime. Even though Jerald held the gun, the evil genius behind the crime was, in actual fact, Diana herself.

Odelia told her editor that they were now convinced that a gang of robbers had committed the murder, the same gang that held up a jewelry store a couple of months ago.

Dan's hand massaged his long white beard while he considered this angle. "I hope you will turn this into an article," he admonished her.

"Oh, don't worry, I will," she assured him.

"I'm not sure if I should put the wedding on the front page or the Langridge murder," he said, wavering. "Though I'm leaning towards the wedding. I have a hunch people are more interested in their burgomaster's marriage than the murder of a bookstore owner."

"Fine by me," she said.

"And please add a little piece on this," he said, holding up Harriet's book. He grinned, causing his beard to waggle with delight. "I thought it was a real hoot."

"They are a handful," she admitted.

"Who wrote it?" asked Dan.

"Well... my grandmother, I suppose," she said. She couldn't very well admit that Harriet herself had written the book. Though as far as she could tell, she had a lot of assistance from the artificial intelligence system powering the website she and Gran had used. Answer a couple of questions and out pops an autobiography. The things they could do with a computer these days.

"Maybe I should write my autobiography," said Dan. "I've

led quite a long and interesting life, and so my life story should be of interest to everyone."

"Of course, Dan," she said. She didn't mention that most autobiographies are excruciatingly boring and only of interest to the subject of the biography.

She watched as her editor made his way over to Gran, no doubt to glean some tips about how to write his own life story. Gran still didn't seem fully recovered from the shock of seeing her precious book being hijacked by Harriet, and Odelia could hear her say something along the lines of, "It's my reputation, Dan. All you have is your reputation, and my reputation is well and truly ruined now!"

Odelia smiled, but then she happened to glance over to where her cats were sitting, in their own corner of the room. Not exactly the kids' table, but their own little spot where they wouldn't be disturbed and didn't get in anyone's way. With a frown, she saw that her cat's face had suddenly adopted a sort of blank look that she knew all too well.

It was the face Max pulled when he just had an idea.

And something told her he had just solved the murder.

CHAPTER 40

Two days had passed since the wedding, but before the couple could leave on their honeymoon, Uncle Alec had briefly returned to work, and so had Charlene. Out of necessity, their honeymoon was going to be a short one—just a couple of days in the Maldives. That was the advantage of being an older couple, or perhaps one could also say it was a disadvantage. But as things stood, they had already planned a longer vacation later in the year when things were a little quieter, and they could get away without being nervous about things falling apart on the home front.

Odelia, Chase, and Uncle Alec had gathered all the suspects in the Vernon Langridge case in the little room at the back of the man's bookstore, and so we now found ourselves in the company of Diana Ludick, Cesar Roughsedge, Gwen Langridge, Jerald Exton, Kenton Clarey, Marina Steele, Tarsha Kettles, and the Beacock family. One of these people had murdered the late bookstore owner, and both Chase and Uncle Alec had asked Odelia to take the reins of the meeting and reveal all.

"This has been a most baffling case," Odelia began, "with a

lot of misdirection and a confusing array of facts and clues. Vernon Langridge was killed with a gun that was also used in the robbery of a jewelry store six months ago in Brooklyn, which I will admit threw us off the track for a while. As it turns out, the gang that held up that jeweler's wasn't involved in the murder. As often happens, the gun used in the hold-up was sold on the black market and acquired by the real killer in this case.

"Another thing that led us astray was a string of anonymous letters from a person who calls themselves 'well-wisher,' though they didn't exactly wish anybody well. Accusing all the different people present here one by one and pointing out certain incriminating facts was ultimately designed to throw us off the scent of the real culprit. The letter writer accused Diana of the murder because she wanted to marry the new man in her life and couldn't get her ex-husband to sign the divorce papers. They also accused Jerald because Vernon wouldn't allow him to date Gwen. Kenton was accused because he needed money to pay for his wife's medical treatment and because he was jealous of Vernon's success. Marina was in love with Vernon and couldn't stomach it when he spurned her advances. And Tarsha wasn't happy when Vernon criticized her work in progress."

"I would never murder the man over that," the elderly mystery writer stressed. "Such a terrible thing to accuse me of."

"The only person the so-called 'well-wisher' didn't accuse was Blair Beacock," Odelia continued. "Though, of course, it's possible the letter was written but hasn't been posted yet. Blair, as we now know, availed herself of Vernon's services as a ghostwriter to pen her Chanel Birdsey books."

A gasp of shock echoed through the room as Blair pressed her lips together and gave Odelia a look that could kill. "I thought I told you to keep that information to yourself!" she said in measured tones.

"Her motive for murdering Vernon could be that he wanted to carve out a career of his own, and possibly end his work on the Birdsey novels."

"I had nothing to do with this sad affair," Blair stressed. "And to claim otherwise is libelous."

"So who killed Vernon Langridge?" asked Odelia. "Who pulled the trigger on that fateful night, robbed a valuable first-edition copy of *The Adventures of Huckleberry Finn*, the contents of Vernon's safe and cash register, two laptops, and his phone? The most likely suspect was Jerald. We found his lighter not six feet from the body. It had slid underneath one of the bookcases and had his fingerprints on it. We also found that same book in his van when we searched it later. So did he do it?"

"I didn't," Jerald stressed. He and Gwen were holding hands, and he seemed determined to defend his innocence.

"You're correct, Jerald," said Odelia. "You didn't kill your girlfriend's father."

This time, a cry of outrage rang through the room as those present let this sink in. "But that's not possible!" said Teddy Beacock. "What about the lighter?"

"Planted," said Odelia curtly. "As was the Mark Twain book. To incriminate Jerald and deflect attention away from the real killer." She smiled a fine smile. "As you well know, Mr. Beacock." She let that sink in for a moment, and when all attention turned to Blair's husband, a flush mantled his cheeks.

"But... You're crazy!" the man cried. "I never came anywhere near the man!"

"That's true," said Odelia. "But your son did. Isn't that right, Dylan?"

Now it was Dylan's turn to turn crimson. "This is bullshit," he growled.

"It was you who pulled the trigger," said Odelia as she squarely faced the young man. "The trigger of this gun, in fact." And like an experienced conjurer, she spirited a gun from behind her back, as handed to her by Chase. "This is the gun that killed Vernon Langridge," she said as she held it up. "We found it in the canal that runs behind your house, Dylan, alongside these items."

In short order, Chase produced two laptops, one phone, and one dark gray fleece hoodie.

"You dropped them in the canal on your way back from the murder," said Odelia. "Which wasn't a very clever thing to do, Mr. Beacock, you have to admit. We dredged them all up yesterday, along with a couple of old bicycles, car tires, and assorted paraphernalia, but the most interesting item, apart from the gun, is this very peculiar laptop." She pointed to the sleekest of the two laptops. "This is the dedicated and encrypted laptop Vernon used to write the Chanel Birdsey books. It was supplied to him by the publisher and was only to be used for that specific purpose.

"We spoke with your publisher, Mrs. Beacock, and they confirmed that all communication about the novels was to be conducted via an encrypted app on Vernon's phone to make sure that absolute secrecy was guaranteed at all times. Vernon met with his agent, Oliver Levy, once a month in New York, at which time the agent downloaded the latest chapters to his own laptop and delivered them to Mrs. Beacock's agent, Michael Holden. All to make sure there were no leaks. Because if word got out that Mrs. Beacock had stopped writing her own books fifteen years ago, it would no doubt damage the reputation that she had carefully built up and break the bond of trust between author and reader to such an extent it might very well torpedo the entire multi-million-dollar Chanel Birdsey brand."

"I don't believe this," said Kenton Clarey. "You actually used a ghostwriter?"

"I'd like to see you write the same book thirty times over," Blair snapped.

"At least I'm not cheating my readers!" Kenton yelled back.

"Okay, settle down, people," Uncle Alec implored.

"So on the night of the murder, Dylan snuck out of the house shortly before eleven, using the rowboat moored at the pier behind the house. He couldn't go out the front door since the whole street is covered by CCTV cameras. But the canal isn't. Dressed in a hoodie, you rowed the length of the canal until you reached Canal Street, looked around to make sure you weren't seen, then snuck along as far as Barnaby Street, where you entered The Mighty Pen. We all assumed that the purpose of the break-in was to steal the rare and valuable first-edition books Vernon had collected, and that when he surprised the burglar he was shot as a consequence. But that wasn't the case. The real purpose was to murder Vernon, and the theft of the book was simply a smokescreen to make it look as if the killer was after the books. But you weren't, were you, Dylan? Vernon had to die, and you needed a patsy. So you planted Jerald's lighter where you knew we would find it, and after the murder, you hurried back to the canal and your rowboat, dumped the laptops, the phone, the hoodie, and the murder weapon in the canal and returned home, where your co-conspirators anxiously awaited your return."

"Nonsense," said Blair hoarsely. "Why would we want Vernon dead?"

"Because he was about to make things very difficult for you. Vernon was sick and tired of working for a pittance while you raked in millions, so he instructed his agent to renegotiate his contract. He wanted more. A lot more. He wanted a bigger advance and a cut of the royalties instead of the lump sum for each book he agreed to fifteen years ago. Back then he was happy to accept any terms, hoping to use his new position as a writer for the Birdsey books to launch his own series. But try as he might, the publisher wouldn't have it. And that's because you sabotaged him, didn't you, Blair?"

"I have no idea what you're talking about," Blair said stubbornly.

"You were afraid that if Vernon's own career took off he wouldn't be able to keep writing the Birdsey books, so you instructed your publisher to keep stringing Vernon along with promises of a contract for his own series. But when his book was rejected, he realized it was never going to happen, and so he decided to play hardball. And the worst part was that he wanted his name on the cover. He wanted official recognition as a co-writer, not a ghostwriter. And you couldn't have that. Especially when he threatened to break the NDA he signed and reveal to the world that he was the real writer of the Birdsey books and had been for the past fifteen years. You stood to lose millions, and your perfectly curated reputation in the process, if Vernon made good on his threat. And so he had to die."

"We spoke with your publisher, your agent, and Vernon's agent," Chase clarified. "And they've all agreed to cooperate. So the jig is up, Blair."

"He would have ruined us," Blair now hissed. "That horrible little man was about to destroy me. Destroy the empire I've built for the past thirty years!"

"And so you arranged for Dylan to kill him, for Teddy to plant the Mark Twain book in Jerald's camper, and the rest of you to provide Dylan with an alibi."

Blair nodded. "Vernon wanted his name on the covers—retroactively. All the books he had written. Plus a cut of the royalties for all of those books. And an advance on royalties for the books he was yet to write. And a contract for his own Mark Barker series with the same marketing budget put behind them as the Birdsey novels. And if he didn't get what he wanted, he would organize a press conference and reveal the truth: that I haven't written a single word for the past fifteen years. That stupid man was going to ruin everything. The whole Birdsey brand is built on the idea that I'm Chanel Birdsey. That she's based on me—on my life. To reveal the truth would destroy that illusion and turn me into a laughingstock. What reader would buy another Birdsey book once it became known that some unknown bookseller was writing them? It would have destroyed the illusion."

"So for the first time in fifteen years, you wrote a plot," said Odelia. "Only this time not for one of your books but for a real-life murder."

"It felt good to write again," said Blair with a smile. "And even better to get rid of that traitor."

"Hey, that's my dad you're talking about!" said Gwen.

"I'm sorry, honey," said Blair. "But your father had lost his mind."

"More like his patience with your nonsense," Tarsha said.

"Where did you get the gun?" asked Chase.

"Just some ex-con we used for the Birdsey books," said Dylan. "Vernon may have written the books, but I helped him plot them out. And when you're writing mysteries, it's always handy to have a contact with some knowledge of the underworld. He sold me the gun, no questions asked."

"But why pick Jerald as the fall guy?" asked Uncle Alec.

"We knew all about Jerald's criminal past from his mom," Teddy explained.

"She couldn't stop talking about it," Blair murmured.

"Always going on and on about what Jerald had been up to now. So when it was time to figure out who to blame, it wasn't hard to choose. Also because Teddy regularly dropped by the Extons to discuss gardening stuff with Lucas."

"I knew about the van," said Teddy. "So it wasn't difficult to sneak out of the house when Lucas took a phone call and plant that book."

"Man," said Jerald. "And to think that my mom and dad always spoke so highly of you. And that you once told me that you considered me your second son!"

Blair's lips twitched into a cruel smile. "Never believe a writer, son. We lie for a living."

"And what was your part in all of this?" asked Marina, addressing Carey.

"Carey is our well-wisher, aren't you, Carey?" said Odelia.

Carey nodded. "Someone had to write those letters."

"Where did you get all that information on us?" asked Tarsha.

Carey smiled. "Vernon liked to blab. Didn't he, Dylan?"

Dylan nodded. "Every time we started work on a new book we would get together at my place, Vernon and I, to spitball ideas and try to work out a plot. He liked to have a few drinks while he worked, to get the creative juices flowing, as he called it. And invariably he'd start telling me what was going on in his life and also the lives of all the people he knew."

"The traitor," Tarsha growled unhappily.

"The letters were designed to further confuse us," said Odelia. "And to throw us off the scent of the real killer. And I have to admit it worked. For a while at least."

"But how did you figure it out?" asked Blair.

"Several things," said Odelia, darting a quick look in my direction. "First, the piece of paper in Vernon's mouth. According to Gwen, it was part of his manuscript, the one that the publisher had rejected. It seemed odd to us that a burglar would do such a thing. Unnecessary."

"I told you that was a mistake!" said Blair. "It wasn't in my script!"

"I know, Mom," said Dylan. "So you keep telling me."

"So why did you do it?" asked Chase.

Dylan shrugged. "It seemed like a nice touch, you know. After all, the man had betrayed our trust. So it felt appropriate to make him eat his own words."

"And then there was the fact that the letter writer never mentioned you, Blair. The letters ran the gamut of all possible suspects, but not a word about you."

"I was going to," said Carey, "but Mom rejected every single draft."

"You said some pretty nasty things about me in that letter," said Blair.

"It was necessary, Mom! Don't you know anything about crime fiction?"

"Oh, dear Lord. See what I have to deal with here?" Blair lamented.

"And then there was the fact that only one book was stolen, with the others left untouched," Odelia continued. "Which struck us as odd for a supposed robbery. And finally, why didn't we find the laptops and the phone in Jerald's van? Or the murder weapon? Because the real killer needed those items to disappear. The laptop and the phone contained clues as to the actual motive for the crime." She held up the phone. "Our tech team managed to decipher the messages you and Vernon exchanged these past couple of months, Blair. And they provide very interesting reading. Extremely salty language on your part."

She shrugged. "I'm a straight shooter. So I told him he would be sorry if he continued down this road. I just wish I'd seen the look on his face when Dylan shot him. He tells me it was priceless."

Expressions of disgust were uttered by several of the people present, except the Beacocks, who stood firm as a family, as they had always done. Even when they had plotted to murder the man who was threatening their livelihood.

But as Chase had said so eloquently, the jig was up. And so the Beacocks were all placed under arrest and carted off. The thirtieth Chanel Birdsey book would also be the last one, as both her creator and her writer were out of commission. Unless, of course, the publisher found a new ghostwriter for the books. After all, as the man said, all publicity is good publicity, and there would definitely be a lot of publicity now.

CHAPTER 41

The time had finally come for all of us to get together as a family and celebrate the bonds that make us who we are. Not murderers like the Beacocks, but connoisseurs of good food cooked on the barbie, as our Australian friends like to call it. Tex was giving of his best, as he always does, happy to be providing for his family as only a family man can. With the assistance of Chase and Alec, he watched that grill like a hawk, lest it misbehave.

The rest of us were in happy anticipation, as is often the way at these family gatherings, spread out across the backyard. The newlyweds were present at the scene, even happier than the rest of us since they were looking forward to a nice week spent in the Maldives and would leave the following morning. Uncle Alec also looked happy because the murder had been solved just in time so he could enjoy his honeymoon without a single worry.

Gran had been in touch with the autobiography people, and they had assured her they would look into the technical glitch that had caused her life story to have been transmuted into that of a cat. They were apparently laboring under the misapprehension that Gran's real name was Minerva McGonagall, the Harry Potter character who could turn herself into a cat. Gran might be a lot of things, but she certainly wasn't a professor of wizardry. But since the mood was mellow and food was in the offing, even she was relaxed and had decided to let bygones be bygones and make peace with Harriet.

The latter was still basking in the afterglow of her great stunt, and since by now all of Hampton Cove had read her book, she was quite the local celebrity. People greeted her in the street and were dying to take a selfie with her in lieu of an autograph. Especially among the younger crowd, she was a big hit, and there was even an idea being floated to set up her own TikTok and Instagram.

"I don't know about that," she now confessed. "I mean, I always dreamed of being a singer, you know, or an actress. But an influencer? What do influencers even do?"

"I'm not sure, but they're very popular," I said.

"Mh. As popular as Celine or Beyonce?"

"More," I said. "Some of these influencers make millions with their posts."

"Okay, so maybe it's not a bad idea," she admitted.

"It could be a springboard for other things," Brutus suggested.

"I like that, stud muffin. A springboard to greater things. Sounds like the story of my life." She tapped the book next to her on the porch swing. "And in fact, it is the story of my life —as available from all good bookstores."

The vanity press Gran had employed definitely hadn't stinted on making sure that Harriet's book was available everywhere. But then for the platinum package Gran had paid for—two thousand smackeroos according to certain well-informed sources—that was the least they could do.

"Didn't you say that you were going to write all of our

autobiographies, Harriet?" asked Dooley. "So where is our autobiography?"

"Patience, my dear," said Harriet with a smile. "Patience is a virtue."

Uh-oh. That did not bode well!

"So what are you going to do with the Birdsey books?" asked Scarlett.

"I'm not sure," said Marge. "We're already removing them from the shelves, and other libraries are considering the same thing."

"You're not going to... burn them!" said Scarlett.

"Oh, no, of course not. We're going to reclassify them. Put them under the 'L' of Langridge. It only seems fair, as he was the one who actually wrote them."

"What about your signed copy?" asked Gran.

"I'm going to keep it," said Marge. She had thought long and hard about what to do with the book that Blair had signed, and so had Odelia. But at the end of the day, they were both going to keep them for now. Prices of signed copies of the Birdsey books had gone through the roof on second-hand book sites, and it wouldn't be long before they could sell it at a hefty profit.

"We're going to give the money to charity," Odelia explained when Scarlett questioned the ethics of this move.

"You should give it to Gwen," Gran suggested.

"Gwen doesn't need it," said Marge. "Now that she's moving in with her mom and stepdad, she has all the money she needs."

"Or you could give it to Kenton Carey so he can keep taking care of his wife," Scarlett said.

"Kenton just signed a new contract for his Marvin Amis series," said Odelia. "The publicity surrounding the Vernon Langridge case has really put him on the map. He's getting a pretty hefty advance that should be enough to take care of his wife's medical care for a long time to come."

The other members of Vernon's old writers' group had also benefited from the notoriety the affair had garnered, with Tarsha getting a book deal and Marina writing her autobiography—a real one this time—detailing her relationship with the victim. Oddly enough, even the sales of the Birdsey books had shot through the roof, though it remained to be seen how much the Beacock family would actually benefit. In hindsight, the publisher had decided to posthumously make Vernon a co-writer on the books he had written, so the money would have to be split between the Beacocks and Vernon's estate.

Meanwhile the Extons had quit their jobs and had been hired by Cesar Roughsedge, who was still charging ahead with his bid for governor.

And Jerald and Gwen? The latter was turning eighteen soon, and already the lovebirds had declared that they were officially going to be a couple. And Gwen's mom hadn't even lodged a single word in protest this time. Jerald had suffered enough and had proven his mettle throughout his lengthy ordeal.

"So what do you think, Max?" asked Dooley.

"About what?" I asked as I happily snacked on a delicious morsel of meat.

"Well, about the fact that Harriet is a star now."

"It's odd," I said, after ascertaining that Harriet and Brutus were well out of earshot. They had retreated to their favorite rose bushes to celebrate Harriet's newfound fame. "Usually, a person becomes famous first and then writes their autobiography. But in Harriet's case, it's the other way around. First she wrote the book, and now she's becoming famous—though only in Hampton Cove."

"Maybe it's a sign of the times," Dooley declared as he, too, dug in.

"A sign of what?"

"The times. Nowadays, people become famous for no discernible reason at all, so why not Harriet being famous for writing an autobiography?"

"You're absolutely right, Dooley," I said. "It is a sign of the times. And it couldn't have happened to a greater cat."

The doorbell rang, and all those present looked up in surprise. Then Marge went to open the door, and moments later we could hear her bellowing, "Anyone? A hand, please?"

Chase and Odelia hurried to give her a hand, and moments later the trio returned carrying boxes. They placed them on the porch, and as they opened them, our faces appeared! I could see my face, and Dooley's face, and also Brutus, Gran, Marge, Tex, Odelia, Chase, Charlene, Uncle Alec, Scarlett... Even Grace's face graced one of the covers.

"But... What's this?" asked Gran as she joined the others, all gathered around the boxes with books.

Scarlett picked up one of the books with her face on it. "It says it's my autobiography," she said, much surprised. "But I didn't write it."

"That's normal," said Dooley. "Everybody uses a ghost-writer these days."

She opened the book as the others all picked out books with their pictures on the covers. Some of the pictures weren't very nice, almost as if they had been taken from their social media and blown up.

"'I was born and then I went to school and then I went to work,'" Scarlett read from her autobiography. "'My main accomplishment in life is that I have the honor of babysitting Harriet, the most amazing cat in existence. I adore her, and that's only natural, for she is absolutely adorable.'"

"'I'm a police chief and I catch crooks for a living,'" Uncle Alec read. "'I also catch the eye of Harriet from time to time, a gorgeous Persian who lives with my sister. She is beauty, she is grace.'"

"'I was with the NYPD and now I'm with the HCPD,'" read Chase. "'I'm a police detective and I'm married to Odelia, who is a fine reporter, and I have one daughter, Grace, and some of the most amazing cats. The most beautiful one is Harriet. She's so beautiful it takes my breath away just to look at her. I love my wife and my daughter but sometimes I think I love Harriet even more.'"

"'I'm old but not dead yet,'" Gran read with a frown. "'My cat is named Harriet, and there's simply no one like her. I tear up every time I see her. Her sheer beauty makes me happy to be alive.'" She gritted her teeth and bellowed, "Harriet! Where are you?! Harriet!"

"'I'm a reporter for the *Hampton Cove Gazette*, and I like to write about my cats,'" Odelia read with an amused smile. "'My favorite, of course, is Harriet, not just because she's so pretty, but also because she is clever and sweet and kind and lovely and cute and wonderful and amazing and generous and—'"

"Harriet!" Gran screamed. "Come here! Now!"

Harriet came traipsing up from the location behind the rose bushes, looking a little flustered. "What is it? Ooh, my books have arrived. Goodie!" She beamed at all of us. "Aren't they amazing? I worked very hard on them. So now you all have your own autobiographies. You can thank me later."

"But they're all about you, Harriet," I said. I had opened a copy of my own autobiography and read, "'I'm a big cat with a big head who sometimes solves big mysteries. But I couldn't do it without the invaluable assistance of the lovely and gorgeous Harriet. I don't know what I would do without her. Just to be able to call her my friend is the greatest honor in my life. To bask in her presence—simply to be near her—is my life's greatest ambition fulfilled.'"

"Pretty neat, huh?" said Harriet. "And to think I only had a couple of days to write all of these. A lot of work, you guys!"

"'I'm a small gray cat and I simply adore Harriet, who will always be my role model and the cat that I most aspire to be like,'" Dooley read. He seemed a little disappointed that his autobiography turned out to be so very thin.

Gran had discovered the bill that accompanied the boxes of books and almost had a heart attack. Tex had to hurry over to support her, or she would have collapsed. And when Marge glanced at the bill, she also had to swallow a couple of times. Vanity presses aren't cheap, and to produce boxes full of these books clearly cost a pretty penny.

"We're sending them all back," Charlene declared now. "All of them!"

Harriet didn't agree. "But you can't," she said.

"Harriet, you can't go and charge Gran's credit card with a bunch of useless junk," Marge said sternly. "So all of these are going back, and we're demanding our money back."

"But..."

"No buts!" said Marge.

"But there's a no-refund policy," Harriet pointed out.

"She's right," said Odelia, who had been checking the itemized bill. "All sales are final."

"We'll see about that," said Uncle Alec. He grabbed the bill and immediately got on the phone with the vanity press's customer service department. And while he waited until the music stopped, we all leafed through our respective autobiographies. I had to admit it wasn't all bad. There was a lot of fun stuff about my adventures and the mysteries I had solved, and Dooley told me that it even described how much he liked to watch the Discovery Channel.

"We should keep them," Brutus now said. "Listen to this. 'I'm a handsome hunk. The handsomest hunkiest tootsie roll in all of Hampton Cove. Possibly all of the country. No wonder Harriet loves me. A princess needs a prince, after all.'" He grinned. "Now if that ain't literature, I don't know what is!"

Harriet, who had been slightly disappointed by the statement that all her books were to be returned to sender, perked up at these words. "I think I have it in me to be a great writer. Don't you think?"

"And even if you don't, you can always hire a ghostwriter," I pointed out.

"I could be your ghostwriter," Brutus said. "I got a feeling I'm pretty good at this stuff." He jutted out his chest. "To be or not to be, that is the question."

"I have a feeling that has been done before," I said.

"Everything has been done before, Max," said our friend. "But that doesn't mean you can't do it again. Just look at Hollywood. They keep making the same movies over and over again. So why not books, huh? Same principle."

"You write your books, chocolate drop," said Harriet. "And together we'll become famous. Now all we need is a killer idea!"

And as they went off to brainstorm their 'killer idea,' Dooley and I relaxed on the swing. We had plenty of food, some nice reading material, and for the moment, no cases to solve. How much sweeter could life get?

All around us, people were reading their own autobiographies and giggling all the while. Clearly, Harriet had done something right. Uncle Alec now returned. His attempts to reach the customer service department having failed, he said, "I'll try again after our honeymoon." Charlene handed him her autobiography while she read from his. After all, love is… reading each other's autobiographies.

"Are you going to be a writer, Max?" asked Dooley.

"I don't think so," I said. "I prefer to live my mysteries instead of just writing about them."

"Very deep, Max," he said appreciatively.

"Thanks, buddy."

And since no more food seemed forthcoming, we decided to go foraging. And after we had polished off all the plates of all the humans present, who were too busy reading about themselves, we decided to take a nice long nap.

And I'd just closed my eyes when Dooley asked, "Max?"

"Mh?"

"Can I be your ghostwriter?"

"Sure, buddy."

"I'll only write good things about you."

"That's very kind of you, Dooley."

"I'll write how you're the greatest cat detective that ever lived. And how you're so smart and clever that you can solve any mystery in no time. And I'll write about all of the adventures we have lived through and all the mysteries we have solved together and how you're my best friend and—"

I guess I nodded off around that time. Harriet may thrive on praise, but on me it seems to have more of a soporific effect. Then again, I had been on my paws for days, what with the wedding and the murder and the stake-out. I woke up just in time to see that our small band had been expanded with two more additions. Reading from left to right, they were Roosevelt and Taft Toal. Roosevelt to let us know that his friend had found a match between his DNA and the DNA of a rhinoceros, and Taft to allow us to partake in his pancake-making skills. But since I'm not a big fan of pancakes, I decided to forgo this rare treat, and soon was firmly resting in the arms of Morpheus once more.

I may be a decent detective, but my skills as a napper are what really sets me apart from the rest of the herd.

It wouldn't surprise me if my dad was actually a sloth.

THE END

Thanks for reading! If you want to know when a new Nic Saint book comes out, sign up for Nic's mailing list: nicsaint.com/news

EXCERPT FROM PURRFECT PRINCE (MAX 74)

Chapter One

The sun shone through the window of Vaasu Castle, eager as always to spread some sweetness and light amongst the inhabitants of that ancient pile, located in the heart of Vaasu, the capital of Liechtenburg, a pleasant little country wedged in between Liechtenstein and its bigger neighbor Switzerland. For centuries Liechtenburgers, as they were affectionately called, had been ruled by the noble House of Skingle, and even to this day, King Thad, the most recent spawn of his family's infamously fertile loins, inhabited the family's royal dwelling and reigned not with an iron fist but with a benevolent hand. Supported by his consort of thirty-five years, Queen Serena, King Thad was a much-beloved sovereign, and if some thought it anachronistic that a monarch would still be as invested in the day-to-day running of his country, at least his subjects didn't seem to mind. Then again, Liechtenburg was a prosperous country, and so no one had much to cavil at and much preferred things to stay the way they were.

EXCERPT FROM PURRFECT PRINCE (MAX 74)

Unbeknownst to many, the king had recently been struck by a mysterious illness that had left him bedridden, his royal duties mostly having been taken up by his two sons: Crown Prince Dane and Prince Urpo. The fact that King Thad's illness hadn't been officially communicated didn't preclude it from being widely commented on throughout his realm, since a thing like that is very hard to keep a secret. And so, gossip had been circulating, with some speculating that the king's final hour had struck and that very soon now an announcement would be made that Prince Dane had been induced to step up to the plate and was to be crowned the new king and head of state.

But as sunrays fluttered across the noble visage of King Thad, laid up in bed as he had been for the past three weeks, they found the subject of all these rumors and gossip in a most foul mood indeed. Now the king had never been accused of being a ray of sunshine himself, but even for him, his mood today was beyond the pale. His wife, Queen Serena, had entered the royal bedroom with an eye to ascertaining whether the monarch felt up to offering his views on the upcoming Christmas ball, but instead of being enlightened by her spouse's ideas on the matter, she was subjected to the kind of verbal abuse she had come to expect in recent weeks.

"Oh, get lost with your nonsense about the Christmas ball," the king grumbled annoyedly. "Who cares about some stupid ball when I'm about to die, you silly woman!"

"You shouldn't say such things, darling," said the queen, shaken but determined not be browbeaten by her husband. "You're not going to die."

"You're not a doctor, so what would you know?"

Serena had taken a seat next to her husband's bed and now studied the man she had said yes to in an unguarded moment thirty-five years ago. Back then, he had been as handsome and charming as could be, and the whole prospect

EXCERPT FROM PURRFECT PRINCE (MAX 74)

of being married to an actual future king had momentarily blinded her to the fact that her betrothed possessed a certain meanness of character that she had only caught glimpses of. But as the years passed, she had come to appreciate the real measure of the man, and the results unfortunately weren't much to write home about.

Back then, her mother had warned her that Prince Thad was easily the nastiest of the two princes, but she had thrown caution to the wind, having been swept off her feet by the dashing nobleman who was first in line for the throne. To one day become queen was such an enchanting prospect that it had momentarily made her blind to the man's faults, of which she would soon find out there were many.

"A letter arrived," she now announced primly.

"What letter? What are you talking about?" Thad grunted as he idly played with his phone. He might have been struck down with illness, but that hadn't made him put down tools for a single second. Even though the prime minister had suggested he momentarily place Dane in charge of things, Thad wouldn't hear of it. He might be down, but he wasn't out—not by a long shot.

"A letter from Buffy Kurikka," said Serena. She had positioned her hands in her lap, and it took every ounce of self-control to maintain eye contact with her husband, even as his eyes had suddenly gone a little wary.

"Never heard of her," he blustered.

"She wants to pay us a visit," Serena continued, undeterred. "To introduce her son."

"What son? What are you babbling on about!"

"I probably should have said: your son." Or she could have said: 'Your bastard son.'

For a moment, neither of them spoke, then Thad impatiently motioned with his hand. "Tell her to get lost. Her and that son of hers."

EXCERPT FROM PURRFECT PRINCE (MAX 74)

"You better tell her yourself. After all, he is your son, and she was your mistress."

Thad grumbled something under his breath, and for his doing he appeared unusually abashed. This reminder of his infidelity, at a time when Serena was pregnant with their first child, clearly didn't sit well with him.

It was, of course, an open secret that King Thad, who prided himself on being a man's man, had never taken the marital vows he had spoken too seriously. In his view, those vows were more a guideline than a set of rules set in stone. A gentle hint or vague suggestion, in other words. And since he was the king, the man who ruled all and sundry, he felt that he was perfectly entitled to sow his oats wherever he damn well pleased, whether in the nuptial bed or without.

The many affairs Thad had engaged in over the years had driven a wedge between himself and Serena, but that had never stopped him from continuing the much-maligned practice until he was of an age when women started to look at him askance when he made advances. Also, with his sons coming of age, Dane and Urpo had started asking difficult questions, mostly concerned with the impact their father's philandering had on their mother, whom they both loved very much. And so, the affairs had ended, but not the resentment Serena still felt.

It was no big secret that the king and queen occupied separate wings of the castle, and only when in the public eye displayed some token form of affection. Keeping up appearances was important to both of them, if only for the sake of their two sons, who wouldn't have taken kindly to an official separation or, God forbid, an actual divorce.

Only one of Thad's affairs had ever led to actual offspring, and even though he had never officially recognized the boy, his existence was no big secret, even though

EXCERPT FROM PURRFECT PRINCE (MAX 74)

everyone knew well not to bring it up in conversation with either King Thad or Serena.

She threw the letter down on the bed. "Here. You answer it. I don't want to have anything more to do with that woman or her son." She got up and prepared to take her leave when a cough from her husband arrested her departure.

"They're trying to kill me, you know," he said.

She glanced down at him with a cold look. "Who is trying to kill you?"

"Well, our boys, of course. They want me dead."

"Oh, nonsense," she said with some vehemence.

"They hate me," he insisted. "I can see it in their eyes. Especially Dane. He can't wait for me to die so he can become king. But I won't let him, you hear."

"Nobody is trying to kill you, Thad," she said emphatically. "You just haven't been taking good care of yourself, that's all. Or did you really think you could eat and drink with abandon and not suffer the consequences?"

In no way did Thad even remotely resemble the man she had married more than three decades before. For one thing, he had tripled in size due to his intemperance, and with the amounts of alcohol he liked to imbibe, his liver had probably gone down the same road. According to the Physician to the King, the only way he might be able to save himself was by going on a very strict diet. That and a prolonged period of complete rest. But of course, Thad would have none of that. He wasn't merely the supreme ruler of the realm but also of his own body, and no silly doctor was going to tell him what he could and could not eat or drink.

He made an impatient gesture. "They're poisoning me!" he insisted. Then he frowned as he regarded her strangely. "My God!" he suddenly cried. "It's you, isn't it? *You are* trying to kill me!"

"Oh, Thad," she said with a shake of the head, causing her

platinum tresses to envelop her well-preserved features. Contrary to her husband, even at sixty, she still cut quite a handsome figure and was admired by all for her timeless sense of style, her grace, and her patience and kindness.

"You're out of your mind."

"No, but it's true!" he insisted, sitting up straighter. "I thought it was the boys, but it's you, isn't it? You are trying to get rid of me." He picked up the letter and waved it angrily in her face. "And it's all because of this. Revenge!"

"I don't have to listen to this nonsense," she announced, head held high in a regal fashion.

But as she made her way to the door, he yelled after her, "I'm on to you, Serena! And I'm going to beat you at your own game. You hear me? You can't kill me! Not if I get you first!"

Chapter Two

Having returned to her own suite of rooms in a private wing of the castle, Serena lost some of her regal fervor. It wasn't that she was about to break down into tears over her husband's latest delusional rant, but the fact of the matter was that they had suffered another security breach last night, this time resulting in the theft of a very precious brooch, one that used to belong to her grandmother.

She entered the sitting room and as she did, her good friend Tiia Pohjanheimo immediately rose from the settee where she had been enjoying a cup of jasmine tea, her favorite.

"And?" asked Tiia anxiously. "How did he react?"

"Badly," said Serena. "As was to be expected."

"He's not going to invite the woman, is he?"

Serena shrugged. "He actually accused me of trying to poison him, can you believe it? I'm telling you, Tiia, the man is becoming more and more delusional with each passing day."

"What do the doctors say?"

Serena had taken a seat next to her friend on the settee, but found she was too wound up to sit still, so immediately she rose again and paced the room, wringing her hands as she did. "They've advised him to go on a very strict low-fat diet. Cut out all alcohol, for one thing, which is exactly what he doesn't want. Oh, Tiia, maybe we should postpone the Christmas ball? With Thad in the state he's in, I don't feel up to it. He seems to be getting more belligerent with each passing day."

"Nonsense," said Tiia, who might look like the sweetest woman in existence but could be quite forceful if she wanted to be. "As far as I can tell Thad only has himself to blame for the condition he is in right now. You can't expect to spend all your life eating and drinking and… to put it bluntly, whoring, and not have your body break down at some point. It's a miracle he's made it this far, considering he's put on about a hundred pounds in the last five years alone. The man looks like a whale, honey. And a very unhealthy whale at that."

In spite of her anxious state, Serena had to laugh at these words. "Thanks for that," she told her friend. "If there's anyone who can cheer me up, it's you."

She had known Tiia longer than she had known Thad, having met in kindergarten. The two had become firm friends from the first day, and even after fifty-five years, that hadn't changed. Throughout it all, they had shared joy and pain, heartache and personal triumphs, and frankly, Tiia was in many respects the best thing in Serena's life, apart from Dane and Urpo and Serena's grandkids.

"It's that brooch, isn't it?" said Tiia, who had an uncanny knack of reading her friend's mind. "Why don't you get the police to investigate?"

EXCERPT FROM PURRFECT PRINCE (MAX 74)

"Oh, you know what the police are like. Before you know it, the story will be in all the papers, and that's the last thing I need right now. More scandal and gossip."

Tiia nodded. "I see. Well, then there's only one thing for you to do."

She looked up in surprise. "There is?"

"Do you remember Opal telling us last year how she was being threatened?"

"Of course. Such a terrible business." Their good friend Opal, who was a big thing in the States, having had her television show for many years and now her own television network, had been plagued by someone sending her threatening letters and messages and even going so far as to try and kill her.

"Then you'll also remember how Opal enlisted the help of a woman named Odelia Kingsley and her husband, who is a police detective. Together Odelia and her husband managed to expose the culprit and bring them to justice. They did what the police couldn't do, and in all discretion. So what I would advise is to get in touch with Opal and ask her to arrange for the Kingsleys to come here and catch this jewel thief for you. That way at least one problem will be dealt with, leaving you to handle Thad without the Tiffany Thief adding to your worries."

Tiia was right. She had enough on her plate right now without the added anxiety over this thief making their lives miserable. So far only a few items had gone missing, oddly enough all of them pieces at one time or another acquired from Tiffany's, one of the jewelry houses the family favored. Which is why Dane's wife Impi had decided to christen the thief the Tiffany Thief. She also had one of her favorite pieces of her collection stolen only a couple of nights ago. In her case, it was her engagement ring that had disappeared.

EXCERPT FROM PURRFECT PRINCE (MAX 74)

Dane had been on the verge of calling the police when Serena had intervened and told him to wait.

"Maybe you're right," she now told her friend. "If these Kingsleys are as good as Opal believes they are, maybe we should ask them to look into this for us."

"The only problem will be that it's such short notice," said Tiia. "And of course… it's Christmas."

Serena glanced out of the window of her sitting room at the snow carpet covering the ground outside. It had been snowing steadily for the past ten days, and the whole world had suddenly been magically transformed into a winter wonderland. With the castle as its backdrop, the scene now closely resembled a fairy tale. She could see a group of tourists being led through the grounds, eagerly taking selfies with Vaasu Castle as a backdrop. The sleigh that took the tourists around the gardens shimmered brightly, and as the sun hit a patch of snow, it glittered like diamonds. Serena even thought she could hear Christmas music drifting in from down below. One of the tourists must be playing it on their phone.

If only they knew what the actual situation was behind the fairy-tale walls of the castle, they would probably be shocked, she thought with a touch of bitterness. Then she abruptly turned. "Let's do it," she said, displaying her usual knack for making snap decisions. "Call Opal and ask to get in touch with the Kingsleys. If they're available over the holidays, I'll cordially invite them to join us here."

Tiia smiled as she took out her phone. Then she frowned. "What time is it in LA?"

"Better wait until they wake up over there," Serena agreed. The Tiffany Thief might be something of an emergency, but the last thing she wanted was to wake Opal up in the middle of the night. Or the Kingsleys. She just hoped they hadn't planned anything for Christmas. Most people

EXCERPT FROM PURRFECT PRINCE (MAX 74)

did. And they might not take kindly to having to suddenly change those plans just because some queen on the other side of the world was faced with a problem.

Then again, no doubt Opal would give it her best shot. And knowing the former talk show queen, she could be very persuasive indeed.

Chapter Three

The living room was abuzz with activity as Dooley and I rested peacefully on the couch. Our humans were enjoying one of their oft-organized family dinners, and for the occasion had also invited Uncle Alec and his wife Charlene. As it was, it was one of the last times we'd see the new couple for a while, since they were leaving to go on their honeymoon soon.

"Honeymooning in the sun!" Uncle Alec caroled loudly as he raised a glass to his new bride. "Finally!"

It had been a little while since the couple had been married, and except for a brief vacation, they hadn't actually had time to go honeymooning. But now, with a lot of businesses closing down over the holidays, and hopefully criminals deciding to spend time with their families instead of relieving hard-working families of their possessions, they had decided it was now or never.

"So where are you going again?" asked Scarlett Canyon.

"The Maldives," said Charlene with a smile. She looked more relaxed than I'd seen her in a long time. Being mayor of a small town may sound like a great proposition, but Hampton Cove can hardly be called a typical small town, in that we do get our fair share of trouble and mayhem visiting these shores, causing both Charlene and her new husband to be on their toes. But now it sounded as if they were about to

EXCERPT FROM PURRFECT PRINCE (MAX 74)

dig those same toes into the warm white sands of a sunny tropical beach.

"God, I'm so jealous," said Marge as she pronged a piece of lettuce with her fork and started eating it with small nibbles. For some reason, she reminded me of a rabbit. "I wish I could join you guys. I could really use a vacation."

"Well, why don't you?" said Charlene.

"Take a vacation, she means," Uncle Alec hastened to add. Clearly, the last thing he wanted was for his family to gatecrash his honeymoon. "Plenty of last-minute destinations to book," he added for good measure.

"As long as they're far away from the Maldives," said Gran with a wink. "Isn't that right, son?"

Alec grimaced. "Oh, you can come if you like," he said reluctantly, making it sound as if the prospect of traveling with his sister was about as enjoyable as having his teeth pulled.

"That's all right," said Marge with a smile. "The last thing I want is to disturb you and Charlene on your honeymoon."

Uncle Alec looked relieved. "I hear San Diego is very nice this time of year. Or what about Puerto Rico?"

"What I would like most of all," said Odelia, "is a nice vacation in the snow. We haven't had snow in Hampton Cove for a while, and I think it would be great if we could build a snowman with Grace and get our sleds out."

"I would love that," her husband grunted. "Christmas isn't really Christmas without a nice thick carpet of white."

"That's the spirit!" said Uncle Alec. There definitely was no snow in the Maldives. Not even a single flake anywhere to be found. "Go up to Canada if you want snow. Plenty to be found there. Or how about Alaska?"

"Or Europe," Scarlett suggested. "Though you'd have to go to the north, of course. I doubt they get a lot of snow in Spain or Italy."

EXCERPT FROM PURRFECT PRINCE (MAX 74)

"Oh, but they do," Tex assured her. "They've got some great ski resorts in the Italian Alps if that's your bag."

Judging from the dreamy faces all around the dinner table, it was obvious that a nice Christmas vacation was on everyone's mind. Except mine, of course, or that of my three friends.

"Imagine having to wade through a couple of inches of snow," said Brutus with a shiver. "Yuck!"

"And the slush and the muck it leaves behind," Harriet added.

"Oh, I don't mind snow," said Dooley, offering the contrarian view. "As long as it's still fresh, it's a lot of fun to traipse through it. Though it is a little chilly on the paws."

"It *is* chilly on the paws," I agreed. The moment those snowflakes started to flutter down was the moment I'd hunker down next to the heating and not move an inch until springtime. I don't know about you, but there's something very disagreeable about the cold. I much prefer to stay indoors while all those foolish humans rush to be outside at such a time. But then I guess humans are a little weird. At the first sign of snow, they can't wait to race one another to the door and head out into that world of white. Brrr!

"I hope they won't go anywhere for the holidays," Brutus confessed.

"Same here," I said, adding my voice to the choir.

Unfortunately for us, our most fervent wish wouldn't be answered, for even at that moment, and unbeknownst to us, dark forces were already conspiring to get us out of the safety and comfort of our own homes and into the wild open spaces of the European heartland, where snow and freezing temperatures would await us. Okay, so maybe it wasn't as dramatic as all that. But suffice it to say that the moment Odelia picked up that phone—yes, the phone that you can hear ringing if you pay close attention—our dreams of staying would be rudely interrupted.

"Oh, hi, Opal," we heard Odelia speak into the device.

We shared a look of apprehension. Twice before, this woman had entered our lives, and each time a period of some turmoil had preceded. Once to induce us to pay her a visit in a place called Los Angeles, where we had been instrumental in catching a wannabe murderer, and once when a friend of hers had more or less invaded our home and caused us no small measure of grief.

So it was with a sense of impending doom that we now paid close attention as Odelia exchanged pleasantries with the former daytime talk show host. Before long, she was listening intently, a frown on her face, as no doubt Opal poured yet another story of heartache and sorrow into her ear, requesting her assistance in a matter of the gravest importance and the greatest urgency.

Finally, she nodded and said, "I'll have to discuss it with my family. But I'll let you know as soon as possible—I promise."

That same family was also looking on with a distinct sense of expectancy, and when Odelia hung up, Marge was the first to speak. "And? What did she want?"

Odelia smiled. "You guys, we have all been formally invited by Queen Serena of Liechtenburg to spend Christmas with her and her family at Vaasu Castle! That's in Europe!" she added for good measure.

The four of us closed our eyes in abject dismay.

"I knew it," Brutus grunted. "I just knew it."

ABOUT NIC

Nic has a background in political science and before being struck by the writing bug worked odd jobs around the world (including but not limited to massage therapist in Mexico, gardener in Italy, restaurant manager in India, and Berlitz teacher in Belgium).

When he's not writing he enjoys curling up with a good (comic) book, watching British crime dramas, French comedies or Nancy Meyers movies, sampling pastry (apple cake!), pasta and chocolate (preferably the dark variety), twisting himself into a pretzel doing morning yoga, going for a run, and spoiling his big red tomcat Tommy.

He lives with his wife (and aforementioned cat) in a small village smack dab in the middle of absolutely nowhere and is probably writing his next 'Mysteries of Max' book right now.

www.nicsaint.com